Oblivion

The Rise of the Sphinx, Volume 1

J. Kearston

Published by J. Kearston, 2020.

© 2019 J. Kearston

All rights reserved

No part of this work may be duplicated, reproduced, or transferred by any means, without the written approval of the author.

This is a work of fiction. Any resemblance of characters to actual people (living or dead), places, or events is purely coincidental. While part of the story may take place in the United States, specific locations such as street names have been altered for this story.

While there is no graphic detail on the subjects, there are mentions of self-harm and sexual assault in this series. Depression also plays a key theme. If you find any of these subjects triggering, you may want to avoid this series. While I'd love for you

to read my novels, your own mental health is always the first priority.
*Cover by Simply Defined Art

Oblivion
(Rise of the Sphinx Book 1)
By: J. Kearston

This is a work of fiction. Similarities to real people, places, or events are entirely coincidental.

OBLIVION

First edition. January 17, 2020.

Copyright © 2020 J. Kearston.

Written by J. Kearston.

Chapter 1
Raina

"Sonofaflyingbitchwhore!" I can't help but shout as coffee spills down my front, staining my shirt and splattering on my hair. The inky black strands can't get much darker, but they certainly can get wetter. I had just enough time to stop on my way to pick up Skye from preschool, so sadly, no time to replace it now. I'll just have to settle for smelling the delicious caffeine instead today.

The man that shouldered past me on his way out of the gas station actually has the nerve to shoot me a glare. If it wasn't for the venom in his gaze he might even be considered attractive, but it takes more than just a pretty face to redeem an asshole.

Well excuse the heck out of me then, I suppose. I internally scoff, glaring right back at him. Just over four years in this town and it's just as welcoming as it was on day one. The scenery may be gorgeous, but it hardly makes up for the company.

Sighing, I make my way to my SUV and manage to bang my head on the door frame getting in. What better to accompany first degree burns than a massive bruise? I proceed to do my best to clean myself up with some crumpled napkins before I simply give up. This just isn't my day. Hell, it hasn't been my day for a while now. I should be used to it by now, it's the same old, same old. The only variations are in the form of misery the fates deem fit to screw with my day. At least I have Skye to keep me going, that little girl really is the best thing to ever happen to me.

Checking my watch, I'm pleased to find out that I actually made it to Denver Elementary with fifteen minutes to spare after all. Flipping open my book to the last page I was working on, I figure I can most likely finish up the last few crossword puzzles before needing to walk up to the school doors. I could stand outside the doors like everyone else, but I truly hate making small talk with the other parents. Either the moms are constantly bragging about how their child is better than another or I have to deal with the lecherous single dad that always manages to corner me for a conversation I can't escape quickly enough. No thanks, the peace and quiet is much preferred.

The time flies by as I get caught up in my word games, the much enjoyed solitude quickly coming to an end. As much as I adore my daughter, keeping a smile constantly plastered on my face for her sake gets exhausting. Working at a bookstore you would imagine I would have plenty of alone time, right? Wrong. I'm constantly being bombarded to help customers find the most obvious of things. You would think people in a bookstore would know how to read a sign or know what alphabetical order meant, but no, unfortunately that would be too much to ask. Then, when I *should* have a bit of blissful silence while restocking, one of my coworkers always manages to trap me with their company.

Elijah, though sweet, really does nothing for me. With his light brown hair, shy smile, glasses and lean build, he's cute enough I suppose, but nothing about him really draws me in. It's nice to have a friendly face around sometimes, but when nearly every conversation steers back to him wanting to take me out on a date, it gets a bit tedious. I've always been polite in my denials, not wanting to hurt the feelings of someone who has only ever been kind to me, but I just can't be one of those people that leads someone on and gets their hopes up if they aren't actually interested. It wouldn't be fair; he deserves a nice girl without all the baggage I bring to the arena.

Callie on the other hand brings out my bitchier side. Constantly prattling on about anything and everything, nearly every conversation leaves me with a headache. Always going on about who did what with whom, or what's-her-face went to this place or some other like I actually know any of her gossip victims. I spend the majority of the one sided conversations tuned out, lost in my own head, not even nodding occasionally to show interest in the hopes she'll get the hint and leave. I'm never that lucky.

But Callie, not one to be deterred, always invites me to tag along to whatever after work plans she has with her friends. Honestly, I know I should be grateful that she tries so hard to include me, but really it sounds just awful. I've never been one for all the drama her lifestyle tends to include. Clubs, parties, hookups, or whatever spur of the moment idea that she and her friends cook up. Being a twenty-five year old widowed, single mother just doesn't give me much to relate to that sort of crowd. I *have* contemplated dating again- after all, it was more of a marriage of necessity anyway before my husband was killed about five years ago. Even though I've made my peace with it by now, no one has really interested me enough; certainly none of Callie's entourage. No, after work I would much rather just go home to spend time with my daughter. Maybe *really* jazz things up and have a hot bath and a drink before bed. Exciting, I know.

Though honestly, I long for the peaceful moments where I don't have to pretend. I don't need to fake a smile or say that everything's fine. I don't need to worry about anyone else's feelings or being a burden. I can just be me. I can grieve the life I expected, but had stolen from me. I can allow myself to be overwhelmed at trying to do everything- raise my daughter alone, work, find time to take care of the house, and keep track of appointments. We may have everything that's necessary, but that doesn't leave a lot of wiggle room for extras.

Sometimes I hate myself for never feeling like I am enough for her, pulled too many directions at once until I am being torn apart. I can lament the shell of a person I have become over the years; leaving me to somehow feel hollow and numb, yet at the same time like I'm endlessly drowning. At night after Skye has gone to bed, I allow myself to fall apart in silence, only to glue myself together again in the morning, somehow finding the strength to go through the day to day motions.

I'm not always like this, but some days it hits me harder than others. Weeks can go by as I truly laugh, smile and hope, only to find myself once again trapped inside my mind. The shadows threaten to pull me under and never let me go; some days the temptation is strong enough that they nearly succeed. But I always manage to fight off the feeling, refusing to allow myself to be sucked in so far that I can't find my way out again. I could never leave Skye alone like that. I've already been abandoned; I don't need my daughter following in my footsteps.

Mentally I may struggle, but physically I've been lucky enough to rarely need to see a doctor throughout my life, not that I could have afforded one anyway. No illnesses that I can recall and any scrapes or bruises I collect heal insanely fast. A blessing, seeing as the huge welt on my forehead is already starting to shrink.

Once, when my depression was bad enough, I did go see a shrink as a last ditch effort, but no magic cure there either. It's just a feeling that I've had for as long as I can remember, like I'm in the wrong place in life. Always feeling like a part of me is missing. I don't need to pay a psychiatrist an obscene amount of money to tell me that I'm lonely and blame it on my husband's death or the cross country move. I can't even describe it properly, it's just an itch that I can't seem to scratch that makes me restless. So without any close friends to talk to I just internalize everything, probably making things worse.

A small scream pierces the air and my head snaps up, dropping my pen in my haste. I know that voice, but have never heard it laced with such fear. I'm out of the car faster than I have ever moved before, just in time to see my daughter being thrown over the shoulder of a man taking off at a run down the sidewalk as the other children continue to pour out of the school doors. The sound of my shoes slapping against the pavement and my racing heart are all I can hear as I sprint after them, my heart sinking into my stomach with every thunderous beat.

Seeing Skye's eyes filled with such terror will forever be burned into my soul, torturing my dreams for years to come. Her mouth is open as she tries to scream, but her voice catches in her throat as the terror holds her vocal chords in a vice grip. The tears openly stream down her face, pleading with me to help as she struggles to comprehend what is happening.

How can no-one be helping? It's as though everyone else is either screaming or simply staring, but not a soul races to help, probably assuming somebody else must've called the police by now. How can you see someone in need and not try to help? Here we are in a sea of people, yet we may as well be alone.

Heart pounding out of my chest, I continue to shove people out of the way as I try to reach them. When some idiot actually steps *into* my path instead, my numb terror is finally replaced with the rage I need to push myself harder.

"Fucking MOVE!"

I place both hands on his chest and shove him to the ground out of my way, leaping over his scrambling limbs so that I don't trip and finally get to where I need to be.

Time seems to slow down as I'm finally near enough to launch myself at the stranger, tackling him to the ground. Thank god they landed in the grass so that Skye didn't crack her head. What was I thinking, I could've hurt her! I guess that's just it, all sense of rational thinking is gone at this point except stopping the man threatening to tear away the only person I've ever loved from me.

Skye wiggles and squirms in the grass, her palms skidding over the ground as she tries to break free while I attempt to pry the man pinning her legs with his shoulder off of her.

"Get off of her you bastard!" I grunt as I struggle to budge his heavy weight, but before I can blink he quickly rolls onto his back and a fist comes flying at my face.

His knuckles catch my cheek, knocking me to the side with the impact. A burst of pain lances through my head as I hit the cement; one side of my face screaming in pain from the hit, and the other from getting scraped along the concrete.

Dazed and disoriented for only a moment, I scramble back to my feet as the adrenaline coursing through my veins helps to keep the worst of the pain at bay for now.

"Skye run! Get back inside!"

I'm no fool; I may have been in more than my fair share of scrapes before, but this guy is built like a brick house. It's only a matter of time before he knocks me out, so the best I can hope for is to hold him off long enough for help to arrive or my daughter to get behind the locked doors of the school into relative safety.

Being not quite five years old, I really should have anticipated it, but Skye doesn't move. She can only sit there paralyzed by fear; helpless to do anything more than watch us in stunned silence and confusion. I thought I would have more time to prepare her to face the horrors of the world, wanted to keep her far away from anything resembling my childhood, but any hope of preserving her innocence is gone now. Every pounding beat of my heart feels like another nail being hammered into my coffin. The longer she sits there as I struggle, the more it really hits me...*fuck, we're screwed.*

I launch myself at the bastard, ramming my shoulder into his stomach in an attempt to tackle him to the ground again to try and buy more time. He doesn't budge, so I just manage to fuck up my shoulder. That pain is quickly forgotten as a fist buries itself in my stomach, knocking the breath from my lungs as I fall to my knees, scraping my palms on the pavement.

I fight the urge to vomit as I struggle upright to shaky legs, wiping away some of the blood from my face, but only making it worse as my hands are scraped up as well.

"What the hell do you want!?" I scream at him, but my question echoes in the breeze without any answer.

He sneers down at me in disgust as he moves to shoulder past me, dismissing me. I let my hate flow through me like molten courage, jumping onto his back and wrapping an arm around his neck to steady myself. He stumbles half of a step before grappling at my arm, no doubt about to toss me off.

Fumbling my way through the scuffle, I continue my futile efforts at subduing the man who obviously has the upper hand here. He may have size and experience, but I have something worth protecting to fuel me. I manage to rake my nails across his face as I go for his eye, ready to throw every low blow and cheap shot his way. Far better my daughter and I to walk away from this alive than with pride.

He barely even flinches, the blood dripping down his cheek a mirror image to half of my face right now. His hand fists in my hair and he lets a frustrated sound slip out in his agitation.

Heaven forbid the kidnapper's day is mildly inconvenienced.

Pain lances through my skull as he yanks me upwards and tosses me to the side like I am nothing more than a ragdoll, dislodging me from my perch with ease. For all of my panic induced attacks, I'm still a bumbling mess compared to him. As he turns away from me without a second glance, his eyes seeking out my daughter once again, I kick my leg out as hard as I can and connect with the back of his knee. With a startled "Fuck!" he falls back to the ground. I would find it insulting he didn't even register me enough of a threat to worry about turning his back to me if it wasn't for the fact it worked to my advantage.

I can't keep this struggle up much longer. The adrenaline is beginning to fade and the pain is starting to settle in next to the hopelessness of the situation. I'm battered, bruised and bleeding, yet I have done nothing more than land a few scratches and delay him. I look around and see everyone watching us, some even recording on their phones, but no one moves, the useless bastards.

When the man starts to get up and reach for my daughter yet again, something inside of me snaps. It's like those moments where a person suddenly has the strength to lift a car off of a baby, or however the stories go. A red haze clouds my vision and it feels as though someone else is controlling my movements as I roll to my feet with more grace than I thought I was capable of.

Faster than should be possible, I launch myself at the man with renewed vigor. Blood pours from him as my nails sink into the side of his neck, tearing back hard enough to leave deep punctures coated in blood. He howls in pain as a knee to the groin brings the asshole down to a hunched over position, which is all the leverage I need to grab his head in a firm grip and twist, using my weight as leverage and effectively snapping his neck as I land in a crouch. His blood still on my hands, it smears across his face as I jerk my hands away from him. His broken body falls face first in a crumpled heap to the ground, hitting with a sickening thump.

Silence, so quiet you can hear the drops of blood falling from my hands as they pool onto the sidewalk beneath my feet. Time appears to be at a standstill as shock sets in and the last fifteen minutes of hell replay in my mind on a loop, trying to allow things to really sink in. My daughter was almost kidnapped. I fought a man. No, I *killed* a man. How could I have killed someone? But the worst realization is that…I don't feel bad about it. Shouldn't I be feeling some sort of remorse? Some sort of grief over taking a life? But no, I feel nothing except for relief that the threat against my daughter is gone.

My eyes snap up to meet my daughter's stormy grey ones looking back at me, so much like my own, though hers are filled with silent tears that are freely flowing, threatening to wrench my heart from my chest. With every teardrop that hits the ground, a small piece of her innocence is lost. The world she knew doesn't exist anymore and the one she is left facing is dark and full of nightmares that she doesn't know how to handle.

I don't even realize I'm holding my breath until it shakily falls from my lips. Reality finally crashes back into me like a freight train as I break the spell we were under and it feels like waking up in more ways than one. It isn't as quiet as I thought; people are shouting and running, dragging their children away from the scene and to the safety of their cars.

Now they move, the useless sons of bitches.

Police sirens meet my ears as four cars race up, haphazardly parking in the street or on the grass not far from us. Officers start pouring out of their cars to assess the situation, their guns drawn. It takes less than two minutes before Skye and I are surrounded, my view of the dead body lying so close to us obstructed by the blue uniform clad men and women. I wipe my bloody palms on my jeans before I pull my daughter closer, glaring daggers at everyone that showed up late to the party.

Gee, the thought escapes me, *nice of you to finally show up.* As eight pairs of eyes snap down to me I realize I must have thought that last part out loud.

Oops.

Chapter 2
Raina

The following chaos was a blur, Skye and I being loaded into the back of a car to be taken in for questioning. Somewhere along the line, new clothes were brought for me since mine had ended up drenched in blood.

It's strange, killing a man and not having a name to attach to the face. He was just here and then he wasn't; his family might never know what happened to him. The thought should make me sad, logically I know that, but the fucker tried to kidnap my daughter. Hard to pity the family that raised a man like that.

The navy blue clothes were too big for me, but they were better than nothing. The baggy sweatshirt hung past my ass and I had to tie the drawstring of the borrowed sweatpants tight to keep them from falling off, but I have more pressing concerns. Seeing as my shirt had already been covered in coffee stains, I told the guy that brought me the new clothing to just burn my old ones if they didn't need them for evidence. I sure have no desire to keep them. I don't need any mementos to remember today by; it's seared into my brain permanently.

Skye stayed in her black long-sleeved shirt and light grey pants since they had nothing small enough to fit her anyway. They were covered in grass stains and dirt, but thankfully she was out of the splash zone when the blood started flying. Black covers a lot though, so I could be wrong. You'd think it was Halloween year round from this girl's wardrobe. Most girls go for unicorns and sparkles, but not Skye. '*I like simple and easy, what's wrong with that? Just because other girls like silly pink dresses, doesn't mean I have to,*' she explained to me once when I tried to push the issue. It's hard to argue with her logic when she makes valid points, so I lost that battle quickly. I'll be royally screwed when she hits the teenage years.

Her usually long, straight black hair is tangled and windswept and my fingers itch to comb through the knots on reflex. Her face is even paler than usual, her lips the only source of color left. She is a hauntingly beautiful sight sitting there, looking older than her short years as her grey eyes swirl with an inner storm as she struggles to process.

The worst part? She simply stopped talking. Nothing I said got so much as a reaction out of her and it terrifies me. I'm fumbling my way through raising her already and have no idea how to help her. No one can get her to talk about it, she simply just shut down. After the initial panic, she didn't cry, she didn't talk; she just sat there, vacant eyes staring through everything and seeing nothing. A few times I thought I caught her mumbling to herself, but I'm chalking it up to wishful thinking at this point. We've been here for hours upon hours; me repeating the story on autopilot and Skye ignoring the social worker and officers as she became lost in her head.

"Well it's a pretty open and shut case as far as self-defense goes Ms. Adams, so you won't need to worry about that part," the officer in front of me starts in, pulling my worried thoughts away from my little girl and back to him. "We got a copy of the video which makes everything even easier on our end. The real question here is figuring out who that man was and if he was working alone. Can you think of anyone who would want to kidnap your daughter? Someone who might want to use her to get to you? Anything odd happening lately that you might have noticed? Even the smallest detail that you think might be insignificant could matter, so I really need you to try to focus."

Thinking back, I try to replay the last few days for anything out of the ordinary, but my mind kept pulling me back to hearing my daughter's scream, her eyes locked onto mine as who knows what raced through her mind. "I can't really think of anything out of place, I'm sorry." Gods, but I'm useless. I can't even think straight long enough to try and help.

"What about the father, is he in the picture?"

"No, he passed away before Skye was born."

It may have been nearly five years since I lost Marcus, but that still doesn't mean I like to talk about it. It took nearly a year before I gave up hoping they were wrong, for my heart to stop racing every time the phone rang or my heart to stop pounding whenever there was a knock at the door.

"Ms. Adams? Raina?"

I jerk back to reality like someone has slapped me, startling and jumping a bit in my seat. I didn't even realize I had fallen down the rabbit hole of painful memories until the officer's voice yanked me back to the present. Right, I killed somebody. Someone tried to kidnap my daughter. On second thought, I guess it really is just pulling me from one painful memory into newer ones. Sighing, I face the man across the desk.

"Sorry, I got lost in thought there. What were you saying Mr...... what was your name again?"

"Officer Samael ma'am. I was just saying that if you think of anything that may help, please do not hesitate to call, day or night," he states while handing me his card.

"Samuel?"

"No, Samael. Yes, like the stories unfortunately."

"Oh that's-."

"You're not the first, nor will you be the last. Just call me Officer S., everyone else does. Unfortunate names aside, here is the number for someone you can take your daughter to if you can't get her to talk to you." He slowly hands me a second business card, frowning down at it as he does so before continuing on.

"And please...take my advice. This was an incredibly traumatic thing for a child to go through and I can't tell you how often parents just disregard their children's feelings, assuming they will get over it. Don't be that sort of parent. Maybe you can get her back to her normal self without help." He looks oddly...hopeful? I'm shit at reading people, probably why I'm always the odd man out.

"What kind of parent would just write off their child like that?" His words catch me off guard. Of course I would get her some help; any idiot can see she isn't ok.

His eyes harden as he tries and fails to keep the venom out of his voice when he responds with, "In all my years one thing holds true; the monsters of this world may do some terrible things, but it is a child's parents that truly hold the power to gut and destroy them. All a child wants is to be loved and accepted and will keep coming back even as their parents hurt, neglect, and abuse them; thinking that if they try just a little harder, then Mommy will love me again. If I was better behaved, than maybe Dad wouldn't beat me."

He pauses to take a deep breath to try and get himself under control and pinches the bridge of his nose, shaking his head as if he can physically remove the thoughts. "And I watch as time and time again parents don't listen to their children's cries for help as they are struggling. The world is a cruel place Ms. Adams, and your daughter found out about it far too soon. Help her learn to fight the demons before they consume her- darkness needs only a small seed to grow. In her case, especially." He shoots me a loaded look and I'm the first to break away from the intense staring contest, my social skills failing me miserably. I scrub a hand down my exhausted face, sick of reading too much into innocuous gestures and ready to take my daughter home.

With that last ominous statement apparently dismissing me, I take his offered cards and scoot my chair back as I stand to go get Skye and leave. I find her in the same position I left her in, sitting in a room with a nice female officer prattling away with idle chitchat while my daughter just sits stoically, knees at her chest with her arms wrapped around them, staring at the wall. My heart breaks just a bit more as I scoop her up, hug her tight and we make our way outside where we are given a ride back to my SUV that is still parked outside of the school. The school is eerie this time of night, devoid of life. With all of the windows shrouded in darkness, it feels as if there are eyes on me without me being able to assure myself there's no one there. The police officer waits until I start the engine and pull away from the curb before falling into line behind me.

We pull up to the dark, hopefully empty house and I unlock the door before stepping back, clutching Skye to my chest as the officer brushes past me. He inspects the house carefully and I'm thankful, not that they have been any help up until this point. But when it's creepy and you're alone, you'll accept the devil's hand just to know where he is in the darkness.

The house feels too empty and too quiet as we make our way inside after the officer departs with a nod. I take Skye upstairs and tuck her into my bed, knowing I won't get a wink of sleep if she isn't within arm's reach.

"I'll be right back sweetheart," I whisper as I place a gentle kiss on her forehead.

Jogging downstairs, I triple check that the doors are locked, close the couple of windows I had left cracked to let in the fresh spring air, and lock the house up tight. I go to search out her favorite stuffed animal, a little tiger she has dragged around by the tail since she could walk, thinking she could use any extra comfort available. It's battered and dirty at this point, but she loves the thing. I rush around her room trying to find it, but come up short. She must've left it lying around somewhere again.

"Why is it so hard for kids to pick up their toys?" I sigh to no one in particular.

A quick run to the bathroom to brush my teeth and relieve myself and I am back to Skye in a matter of minutes. I crawl in next to her and pull her tight to my side as once again today's events replay in my head. Why my daughter? Of everyone, why her?

Eventually, I feel her even breathing beside me signaling she fell asleep and let go of a breath I didn't even realize I had been holding. Tomorrow will be better. It *has* to be better. After all, it can't really get that much worse.

Chapter 3
Cain

It has been months since my brothers and I started this mission and we have nothing to show for it. Nothing! My team doesn't fail. I. Don't. Fail.

"Gods be damned!" Punching the wall next to me, I hear a satisfying crack as I pull my bloody knuckles away from the new hole in the plaster, the wounds already stitching together as though nothing happened. It's a good thing we have such rapid healing, we certainly do enough damage to appreciate the gift. Between our bloody knuckles and their bloody faces, we put the ability to good use. But what can you expect when you put the three of us together?

I make my way further into the house, not bothering to kick off my boots. Let Ryker get pissed about it, I could use the fight to burn some of the anger from my system. I pass by the pristine, white walls- minus the one in the entryway- and search out my brothers. I find Seros lounging on the black leather couch in the living room, a glass of whiskey in one hand as the fingers on the other fidget restlessly against his leg, tapping out a steady rhythm on his thigh.

"Cain, chill the fuck out. We don't need to waste more time having to patch the walls too," Seros bites out before taking another drink.

It doesn't matter that we have no blood relation, truth be told we actually look nothing alike. Seros; with his dark hair, green eyes, and lean build is without a shadow of a doubt the stealthiest of us. A snake in the dark, striking before you are even aware of his presence.

He is my complete opposite. Taller and broader than either of my brothers with untamed, pale hair so light it is practically white, golden eyes and tanned skin; I stand out like a sore thumb beside my brothers.

These men have been by my side for centuries; we've bled for each other and nearly died for one another more times than I can count. They are closer to me than my own family once was and I'll be damned if I think of them as anything less.

"What do you expect me to do then? It isn't as if I can shift and go for a run to burn off some of this energy. We've been here too long and I've spent far too long confined to one skin."

I pace back and forth across the room, wearing a path in the carpet. Seros bites his tongue, knowing nothing he says can help. We're all feeling the stress. The frustration at our lack of progress is even eating away at him this time, the most lighthearted one of us all, leaving him subdued and quiet. Who could blame him though? Every trail we have picked up on has led us to nothing more than a dead end and time wasted.

After King Strom summoned us to his castle to offer us the job of hunting down rogue shifters, we began our bets on how many each of us could find before the others. We scattered across the mortal realm's North America; Ryker in Arizona, Seros in the Dakotas, and myself throughout Canada. I'm not sure what it was, but after weeks of none of us getting anywhere, we decided to reconvene and try a new approach as a team. We ended up gathering in Colorado; Ryker, the stubborn ass, didn't want to travel as far, so that left Seros and I to drive the majority of the way so we could regroup.

Each of us alone is a force to be reckoned with- typically-, but put us together and not a soul stands a chance. Until now, it seems. As some of the rarest breeds in our land, it took little time for us to rise through the ranks as our strength became noticed. Even in our human forms we are tough opponents, but when we let our beasts free? Not a chance. So how is it then, that months could pass by and *nothing*? We are the ones called upon when the king can't trust his regular soldiers to handle something, the ones he entrusts with the most discreet matters. I'll be damned if I return home empty handed.

"Did you feel that?" Seros asks, not seconds before a wave of unexpected power slams into me. "Finally!"

Seros, looking like he won the lottery, jumps off the couch and begins bouncing up and down on the balls of his feet. His drink sloshes over the rim of the cup in his excitement and leaves a dark, wet stain on the carpet.

Ryker is going to have a fit.

His enthusiasm is contagious and I can't seem to contain the grin that takes over my face. Seros slams down the rest of his drink and sets down his glass quickly.

"Come brother, it's time to hunt." The grin stays plastered on my face as we move towards the door, not waiting around for Ryker for fear of losing this gift.

Chapter 4
Raina

"Come on baby, please eat something," I plead with the shadow of a girl in front of me. Silence is all I receive in response, just like the last two days of trying. The school completely understood why I had to pull Skye out for a while; it was to be expected after everything that happened. Work on the other hand won't put up with my absence for much longer and I still haven't figured out what I'm going to do. I need to find someone to take care of Skye while I work if she's not in school, but in the four years we have been here I haven't truly gotten close to many people and my savings are getting dangerously low.

"Honey, if you don't start eating, you're going to waste away. Please? For me?"

My heart flutters with renewed hope when she leans forward to nibble on the toast I have held out for her. It isn't much, but a glass of water and a few bites of breakfast do wonders to ease the tension building up inside me.

"That's my girl, you did a great job. How about we go look for Rory together, hmm? I really wish you would tell me where you left him, I know how much he would love to snuggle up with you."

After two days I still can't find that dang tiger and I've looked everywhere, except of course, where he actually is hiding. Worse still, even after two days of trying, I can't get Skye to talk to me. No matter what I try she just stares past me, trapped in her own thoughts. She mumbles a bit to herself, but so quietly I can barely discern it and I know she's not talking to me, just processing in her own way. Her eyes are either constantly flitting around the room, or focused on a sole point for extended periods of time. I can stand right in front of her and talk, but it's like she can't even see me or register that I'm there.

As is my luck, when I move away from the kitchen table to begin our search anew, I slip. Seconds before my head would crack against the countertop, time seems to slow, giving me the opportunity to snake out my hands to catch myself. As my heart starts beating again, I straighten myself, confused. I've really never had good reflexes. Or luck. I can't tell you how many bruises I'm usually sporting on my shins from some stupid accident, tripping over seemingly nothing half the time. I waste no time adding more to my collection, a glutton for punishment. Maybe all of this newfound adrenaline from the last few days finally taught my stupid limbs they are supposed to try to keep me alive.

Continuing through the house, we still come up with no sign of her favorite toy. Normally I wouldn't be too heartbroken, assuming a young girl will have a new favorite in no time, but Rory is special. The day after Marcus and I found out I was pregnant, he came home with the little stuffed tiger, orange and black with a bright, metallic blue colored collar, for the baby. "A child should always have a friend to look after them," he had said.

Shaking my head to clear away the memories before they can pull me under, I start to give up hope. When we head upstairs to check her room again though, there it is, right smack dab in the middle of her bed. The little stuffed animal seems to pull Skye a bit out of her shell as she walks over to snatch him off the bed and choke the life out of the thing. She crushes him to her chest as though he were her anchor to a reality she no longer believes in, clutching him in a way that has me grateful I never caved in for that kitten she wanted a few months ago.

Making my way over to her, I lean down to pick her up and notice a soft breeze blow past her curtains. Like a bucket of ice water was poured on me, I freeze. The cold settles into my bones as if it plans to stay, leaving me with a perpetual sense of dread. I'm sure that I locked all of the windows the first night we came home.

I held onto Skye and walked over to the window, carefully peeking outside. The neighbor's dog is sleeping peacefully in the morning sun. *He would have stirred if someone ran through our yard, right? That dog is always barking over something.*

Slamming down the window, I turn the lock and proceed to check the entire house. Closets, behind doors, the basement, not a stone is left unturned. All the locks are still engaged. Nothing seems out of place. I was so focused on securing the downstairs that night, that maybe I didn't worry about upstairs?

It's the second floor after all, so it isn't like someone was going to climb in through the window unless they brought a ladder to a break in, right? No, that's just stupid, I'm being ridiculous.

Nothing is missing that I can tell and no one has tried to take Skye away from me again. Nobody is *going* to take her away from me. It really just must have been a sick dose of luck that had her being the targeted child that day. That's what predators do, they find children they think they can snatch and then they steal them away for horrible things I don't even want to imagine. And won't. Oh god, I'm going to make myself sick. I can't keep thinking like this. Staying cooped up in this house is giving me an awful case of paranoia.

I go find my purse and rummage through for the card Officer Samael had given me in search of the therapist's number. I had really hoped Skye would bounce back once we were safe at home and I wanted to give her the chance before dragging her to a therapist, but I'm not going to wait any longer. Like Officer S. pointed out, too many people disregard their children and I refuse to be one of them.

The phone rings only once before it is picked up by a chipper sounding receptionist.

"Dr. Jane Turner's office, how may I help you?"

"Umm yes, I need to make an appointment for my daughter. She went through something terrible and hasn't spoken since." I feel like such a shitty parent.

"Do you have a referral?"

"Well, Officer Samael from the downtown Denver PD gave me your card, does that count?"

Well shit, the cop never said anything about a referral! So now I need to take her to the doctor first, just so another one will see us? What a waste of co-pays. Our health system is garbage and so is my insurance. I doubt they'll even cover a therapist and I'll have to sell a kidney to pay for it. If my daughter needs it though, I'll go climb in that back alley ice bath. Maybe I can even fix up my car if there's anything left.

"Oh really!? That man is such a gem. In that case, we actually have a last minute opening in an hour if you would like?" she chirps, far too chipper for someone dealing with head cases all day.

"Yes please! I appreciate it."

I quickly scribble the address on a stray scrap of paper and get us ready to rush out the door. We climb into my SUV and proceed into town, hoping traffic isn't that bad today so we won't be late.

"I spy with my little eye, something that is blue."

I glance back at Skye in the rearview mirror, hoping I can coax her into playing one of her favorite games. Besides my features, she also inherited my love for riddles. Where other children her age would play with blocks or color in books, Skye loved to spend her time engaged in guessing games. Nothing could beat her prideful smile as she solved any little challenge, working hard to try and best me with her own. They aren't always the best, but she certainly is well versed for someone her age. I have seen several of the children in her class just beginning to learn their letters, so I know she is pretty far ahead of the curve for her age already. Not only can she read, but she can hold her own and carry on our conversations better than several of my coworkers.

One look at this broken girl sitting in the back of my truck has my heart skipping a beat in pity with the stolen glance. I drive just a bit faster than is wise, anxious to have my sweet girl back again.

We pull up to a tall building that resembles more of a two story mansion than an office. I triple check the address the receptionist gave me, but it matches. I step out with restless tension and proceed to unbuckle Skye. She grips Rory a bit tighter and it draws my eye to the toy. He looks…cleaner than I remember. With having a child dragging him around by the tail all day, the poor thing is usually pretty grungy by bedtime. I guess he's had more in the way of snuggles and less of getting dragged around like an old blanket lately. Skye must finally be learning to take better care of her things.

Walking up the imposing marble steps has my nerves at a new high. It just feels….off. This place doesn't feel right. I attempt to shake off my paranoia and keep going though since this is for Skye. She needs help and I'm going to make sure she gets it. Heck, maybe they'll have a two for one special going on and someone can talk me out of being a paranoid cynic.

The heavy wooden doors creak as I shove them open, echoing across the lobby and drawing far too much attention to our arrival. We proceed inside, spotting a massive desk farther in, just beyond the open space of the lobby. A few men mill about the waiting area just off to the side of the entryway, some seated in plush chairs that match the opulence of the room and others languidly walking as they make their way across the vast space towards the hallways that branch off of it. They all pause and turn to gawk at us when we enter. The door shuts behind us with a jarring thud, reverberating around the massive space and echoing off of the high ceiling, further drawing attention to how out of place I feel in such an upper-class sort of place. Someone should have told me there was a dress code.

A woman sits at the desk that I can only assume is the bubbly receptionist I spoke to, clad in pink from head to toe. Her platinum hair is pulled back into a severe bun, nails neatly manicured and the fakest smile I have ever seen plastered on her face.

I hate her instantly.

"Ahh, this must be our last minute appointment?" she purrs, managing to look down her nose at us even from her seated position. A talent, really.

Swallowing back my tumultuous emotions, I simply respond with, "Yep." Nailed it. No one is any the wiser to my disdain or discomfort.

"Right this way please."

She rises to a stand with effortless grace as she proceeds to saunter down the hallway behind her, practically gliding along the gleaming floor. We pass dozens of doors on our way deeper into the building. A sensation of what I can only describe as strutting straight into the lion's den washes over me. I grip Skye's hand tighter as a few businessmen pop their heads out of their cracked office doors to investigate the loud staccato rhythm that the heels of the bubblegum-clad receptionist make as they echo off of the marble with every step.

Once they see the source of the disturbance, they retreat without even so much as a 'hello', firmly resealing their doors with a click. They must like her about as much as I do it seems.

Gods I don't like this place, I stick out worse than I usually do. But a quick glance at the girl clutching my hand is all it takes to steel my resolve. We will come, Dr. Turner will help her or tell me what I can do to get through to her and we will get back to the way things used to be. I refuse to believe that the Skye I know is gone forever, along with the relatively decent life we've managed to build. As her eyes flicker to mine briefly, I send her a small, reassuring smile and give her hand a gentle squeeze. She scrunches her brow and tilts her head slightly, mumbling to herself under her breath.

After a small eternity, we finally stop in front of the last door in the hall. It's taller than the others lining the hallway and the wood is nearly as grey as ash, making it further stand out from the dark chestnut of the others. Our escort raps her knuckles in quick succession and opens the door without waiting for a response, perfectly comfortable in her position to barge in on the therapists, apparently.

A beautiful, yet severe looking woman sits primly behind her desk across the room from the door. Her black hair is pulled back into an even tighter bun than the receptionist, with a pair of silver hair sticks crossing through it. She is very slim and appears to be of Asian descent, but her body is longer and lankier than looks natural, the only thing taking away from her good looks. She seems awkward and stretched out, like one of those walking stick bugs. What are they actually called? Eh, who keeps track of all the technical names anyways, stick bugs- enough said. Not exactly what a lady wants to hear though, so I keep my mouth shut.

The window behind her takes up the majority of the wall, starting as high as my waist and extending up to the high ceiling. With the sun directly behind her, it makes it hard to focus with the shadows it casts and the glare. Curtains would certainly help; you would think someone as intelligent as a psychiatrist would think of that. It leaves me partially blinded and unable to focus on her for more than a few brief seconds without having to blink and look away.

I glance down at Skye and see a look of brave determination on her face. *That's my girl.* Following suit, we take a few steps inside and the receptionist shuts the door behind us, sealing us in with a click. I can't say I'm sorry to see her go.

"Skye Adams, correct?" she asks in a clipped tone.

"Yes, that's us. Well, her."

I ramble when I'm nervous and it obviously doesn't impress the sharp woman in front of me very much. She shoots me a withering look without deigning to acknowledge I spoke, refocusing solely on Skye.

"Come child, sit." She gestures to a chair in front of her, so Skye pointedly sits in a different one, eyeing Ms. Turner with challenge and a hint of fear she quickly tries to cover up. Her bedside manner is severely lacking for anyone who works with children.

It seems to amuse the stern woman and her eyes light up at the stubborn display. "Little Adams, whatever seems to be the matter? No need to look so grim, you're right where you should be."

"I know, but I don't have to like it," Skye pipes up, her stubborn streak giving her courage. I'm elated to hear her voice again and barely breathe for fear of breaking the spell the two have fallen into. I was expecting the whole 'lie on the couch and tell me your woes', or 'tell me what picture you see in this ink blob', not this. But I'm not a doctor so who am I to criticize?

Ms. Turner grips the edge of the desk as she leans closer to look at Skye, never once breaking eye contact. "Do you now? And what is it, pray tell, that you think you know?"

Skye's bottom lip quivers for a moment before she bites it. She releases her hold to answer, "Nothing can end before it begins."

I furrow my brow and look at her, trying to understand what the heck the two of them are talking about. I keep my questions to myself for now, figuring either things will make sense as the session goes on or that I can ask her once we get home, so long as she continues to speak once we leave the hypnotic spell Ms. Turner is weaving.

Ms. Turner rises to a stand, slowly coming around the desk in front of Skye and leaning her hip against the front of it. "Ms. Adams, you can leave us for a bit. I wish to speak to the child alone."

"Umm thanks, but no. I'll be staying."

"Children tend to be more reluctant to open up if their parents are in the room. You *do* wish for me to help your child, correct?"

"Well yes, but-"

"Perfect! You can come back in an hour then."

"I don't think you're hearing me, Ms. Turner. I am *not* leaving my daughter alone." I huff, getting annoyed.

"Always so insolent, the lot of you. Always making things more difficult than they must be," she sighs. "Have it your way then, the hard way it is..."

Wait, what?

The therapist's body begins to stretch even further gradually, her already awkward limbs extending. I reach out to snatch Skye from the chair and pull her back, eyes trained on the monstrosity before me as best as I can with the sunlight still distorting my vision.

A pulse of force knocks me back another step and I watch with rapt horror as something from my nightmares forms in front of me. From her rib cage and sides, four more limbs break through the skin, protruding out awkwardly as they continue to gain length. Her lower half morphs into the black, bulbous body of an enormous spider and not long after, her top half follows. The sounds are sickening; the snapping, crunching, and squelching sounds of flesh being rearranged into something unholy.

Forget walking into a lion's den, I would much rather face a lion than what stands before us in the spider's lair.

Her body has stretched to the size of a seven foot spider and the monster's purple face is...dripping? *Oh gods, why is it dripping!?* As a drop lands on the desk and it starts to dissolve, the horrifying realization slams into me- it's venom, one more akin to acid than anything I've ever heard of in spiders.

She opens her mouth wide to display a whole array of venom covered fangs. What in the ever-loving-Hell did I do in a past life to deserve coming face to face with this thing?

I back us up the way we came and reach behind me to firmly tug on the door. Yep, I should have figured as much- locked. My anxiety flares up another notch as finding myself locked in this room threatens to send me spiraling back into my nightmares. Skye's tightening grip keeps me grounded though, forcing my mind to stay in the present horror instead of past ones. *Deep breaths Raina, deep breaths.*

She is clutching onto my hand for dear life and whispering to herself as I rush to try and think of a way out of this. With the way behind us not an option, my eyes quickly dart to the left and right, finding only solid walls lined with bookcases, a few chairs, and cobwebs I had assumed were from neglected use, but now I have to wonder.

Facing straight ahead, a rush of relief slams into me as I focus on the window behind the desk. The one that is, you guessed it, behind the obscenely huge arachnid. How the hell am I going to get us out of this? The window is at least twenty feet away and behind a monster, all of its eyes trained on our position. Even if I try to distract it, I can hardly expect a four year old to jump through a window and escape on her own. *Fuck. Fuck fuck fuckity fuck!*

I release Skye's hand long enough to pick up a wooden chair from nearby and smash it on the ground. It doesn't work like they show you in the movies, it just kind of flops down on the floor with a few hairline cracks. I grab the bottom of the leg and stomp higher up, thankfully managing to snap it off. I snatch up the splintered leg, prepared to fight our way out. What other choice do I have? When push came to shove, I managed to kill a man after all, so squishing a spider should be a piece of cake, right? *Right!?*

As if on cue, the window shatters as a body busts through the glass into the room. Glass shards assault me as I yank Skye behind me to shield her from the shrapnel. I swear to the Gods, if it's another spider, I'm burning this whole damn place to the ground and spitting on the ashes.

Chapter 5
Seros

As soon as I felt that wave of power hit, I couldn't contain my excitement. All these months of hunting and we finally found one. When Caspian tasked my brothers and I with finding any rogue shifters and either bringing them home or eliminating them, I will admit I was a little disappointed. How much fun could it be to be a glorified babysitter playing hide and seek with some unruly shifters? There aren't that many of us that choose to live outside of our society these days, what with the human's first thought of killing anything they don't take the time to understand. So anyone choosing to confine themselves to their human form in an effort to blend into this depressing world is likely either a criminal fleeing like a coward, or a half-breed offspring so weak their parents abandoned it. Why waste my talents on cowards and weaklings? But where my brothers go, I follow. Always.

Chasing the direction the power originated from left us shit out of luck. By the time we got to a small field next to a dull looking brick building, all that was left was some dried blood on the sidewalk and some empty parked cars. Licking my finger, I crouch down to dip it in our only bloody clue- literally- and l bring it up to my mouth.

Even in this form my abilities are still prevalent, something Cain's beast is obviously jealous of with the way he's glaring down at me. Flicking out my tongue, I gag a little.

"Human."

Cain grunts and stalks off, looking for something we might have missed.

Whatever happened here, it looks like our rogue only drew blood, not lost any. A weary sigh escapes me before the dawning awareness that this must be some type of actual worthy opponent. To walk away from a fight without losing a drop of blood must mean he's good- a criminal then. Which means that when we catch him he may just give us a bit of a run for our money. Not like we can't crush him easily, but I haven't had a good fight in far too long. It's no fun when they just roll over and beg for mercy. I say as much to Cain, but he crushes my brief hopes.

"Humans are weak, Ser. It wouldn't take much to kill one, you know that. They're only dangerous in mobs. Get one on their own and they're pathetic."

We wait around for a while, hoping another burst of power will be released and give us a direction. Cain tries to keep his composure as he stomps around the field looking for more clues, but as the day wears on so does his patience. That little surge of hope we felt, as short lived as it was, only helped to fuel the fire in our bellies and exacerbate our frustrations. I grind my teeth in anger. If you had asked me how many rogue shifters we would have caught by now, I would have said all of them. Cocky? Maybe. Confident? Definitely. After spending centuries as the best team in the King's court, we earned every accolade that's been bestowed upon us and more. Even if those insufferable cocksuckers refuse to acknowledge us anymore.

"Come on, let's get out of here," I sigh, feeling more dejected than ever.

"We're not going to be able to show our faces at home," Cain mumbles as we start walking back to the house.

"So it'll be like any other Tuesday then," I snap back, regretting it instantly.

Cain falls quiet, falling into a pit of self-loathing once more.

The next two days pass by uneventfully and we are all becoming more and more irritable, to the point we can hardly be in the same room as one another. I can't even bring myself to find a human girl for the night, though it'd be a good way to work out some of my energy. Cain insisted though, no rewards without results.

The failure grates on our nerves and our pride. So when a small pulse of power jolts me awake from my nap, I am out the door without bothering to explain or find either of them. Really, where else would I be going in a hurry? My brothers follow immediately; after all of these centuries together, we hardly need to speak to know what the others are thinking. Since I am more sensitive to the power that shifters give off when using their gifts, I usually notice it a split second before Cain and Ryker do and I don't want to lose a second this time in our pursuit. We can't lose him again.

"Ser," Cain warns, knowing I am seconds away from letting my wings come out to get there in time.

"Like any humans are going to believe it if they saw anyway!"

"Humans *are* impressively stupid," Ryker adds, eyes gleaming.

"We do this right, we don't need to add the shitstorm that follows being seen on top of everything else," Cain barks, shutting down the conversation.

As we approach the back of a colossal building, we quickly scan the rooms through the windows when I pull to a hard stop, Ryker crashing into my back at the abruptness. Before we can fully formulate a plan of attack, I burst in like a Wraith out of hell, too anxious to wait another minute and risk losing him again, especially now that I see who we're dealing with. These bastards always take things too far.

Glass shards go flying as I tuck and roll into my landing, the scrapes and cuts across my arms already beginning to stitch together before I fully stand to take in the scene. Before me is the underbelly of something I haven't come across in decades. A Jorōgumo. In human form it appears as a beautiful man or woman to lure its prey close before it shifts into its demonic spider form to devour them.

Gods, I hate these things. They're creepy bastards that find way too much joy in toying with their prey and don't give two shits about exposure.

Across the room, something catches my eye that chills me to the bone. A woman with long black hair and eyes that shine with fierce determination stands in front of a small child. The beauty of the mother is reflected in what no doubt is her child, a small carbon copy of the warrior shielding her.

Just because we don't care to live in the human world doesn't mean we are foolish enough to think that all humans are terrible. The same goes for any person of any race-magically inclined or otherwise. There are always good ones and bad ones. And in the very fiber of my being I can tell that they are a couple of the good ones, lured somewhere they shouldn't be. Something inside of me rises up, demanding to protect the females in front of us.

With that last coherent thought, I attack. My scales rise to the surface of my skin as a barrier, just as the Jorōgumo spins to face me and latches its fangs onto my arm. If I had been a split-second slower, that venom could have really inflicted some damage. We may be able to heal, but regrowing bones and flesh still hurts like a motherfucker.

The rest of my body stretches out, elongating and changing to take up far too much of the room for my comfort. It doesn't leave me with enough room to fight like I'd prefer, especially if I want to avoid the females becoming collateral damage.

A burning sensation takes over between my shoulder blades as my wings burst free, Cain be damned. Their pastel blue, green, and purple feathers tipped in silver a pale complement to the darker matching tones of my scales. My shirt shreds from the force, falling in tatters around me. Luckily for me, morphing into a serpentine body means my jeans are saved and fall to the ground to be salvaged later.

Once I feel the fangs in my mouth and my shift completes, I launch myself at the beast, giving in to the primal side of my nature, allowing instinct and centuries of training to take over, fueled by a rage that I hardly understand. I live for these battles, for the give and take, for the moment I see the realization of imminent defeat in my opponents eyes. Victory in a well fought battle fills me with pride, but even now, knowing that I will win leaves me feeling hollow. Instead, I am filled with fury that this beast would attack a human woman and her child. I enjoy these battles. I enjoy my victories and I have defeated these beasts before. So why do I feel so furious?

My distraction costs me, the beast's leg catching on my wing and knocking me to the ground. *Gods, I am better than this!* I need to get my head back in the game. I whip my long serpentine tail around two of my enemy's legs and jerk, causing the disgusting creature to crumple to the ground in a tangle of limbs. The screech it lets loose has the humans in the room covering their ears and shrinking back. Fortunately for me, in this form I am more attuned to vibrations than actual sound, so I am spared that pain.

Wrapping myself around the Jorōgumo is unpleasant, but necessary. As I trap its legs against its body in a murderous embrace, the fine hairs jab against my scales. It doesn't hurt me, but it feels like nails raking across my body and I fight a shudder. I continue my assault though, knowing it's a necessary part of defeating this wretched overgrown insect. I coil myself tighter and tighter until I feel the snapping of legs beneath me. A loud cry shakes the room as the Jorōgumo continues to fight for survival, bucking and spasming as it tries to gain purchase on my body with fangs and fury. But it's no use; once I wind myself firmly around the beast, I rear back and strike out, fangs sinking through the beast's exoskeleton with an audible crunch, and releasing my own brand of venom. I hold on until I feel the last spasms of life leave the creature's body, the occasional jerking dying down to a few shallow twitches and then finally…nothing.

I release the lifeless husk and let it fall to the floor, broken and defeated. We'll have to dispose of the carcass before the humans stumble across it, though I'm surprised no one has burst into the room already to investigate the racket. Normally at a time like this I would relish my victory, savoring in the adrenaline high that battle brings on, but the second the threat has been neutralized my eyes search out the females.

On instinct, my tongue shoots out to taste the air for more threats, but what it senses is an abundance of fear. As my eyes zero in on the source, I see the woman and her daughter surrounded by my brothers, their rough hands holding them back from me. My beast registers them as threats and reacts without hesitation, spurred on by the waves of terror billowing in the air so thickly I could choke.

Fast as lightning, my wings carry me across the brief distance separating us in this confined space, my body cutting through the air easily. Hissing at the men I call family, I knock them aside to gently coil around the humans. Not to harm, but to protect. From what, I don't know, but there is an undeniable force pulling me to these females with no thought other than to shield at all costs. I can't seem to fight the all-encompassing feeling, nor do I really try to.

To give them credit, my brothers recover quickly. The initial shock left Cain and Ryker gaping at me with comically surprised faces as they sat sprawled out on the floor they were thrown onto. Moments later they are both up assessing the room for missed threats, coming up short just to stare at me once again.

"Seros, rein yourself in. We aren't your enemy," Cain cautiously says, his voice laced with confusion.

When I don't respond the way he wants, Ryker starts verbally berating me.

"Get your addled thoughts together, Ser. We have no intention of harming the females; you and your beast should know better than that. Now shift back, or we'll be forced to handle this another way," he warns, his tone unamused by my volatile reaction.

"I know you can smell their fear, but tell me, do you think they are more frightened of the men," Cain gestures between himself and Ryker, "or the monster imprisoning them?"

I register the truth in his words, but my beast, the stubborn bastard, refuses to budge. It wants nothing more than to rub his scent all over them to warn others away. When Ryker makes an attempt to get closer, I hiss in warning.

"You have three minutes to get your beast in check, Seros," he threatens, stepping closer to look me in the eye without a trace of fear. "You may be strong, but you are not strong enough to beat a Griffin and a Manticore, especially without moving away from the humans."

My beast huffs, knowing they are right, yet still hellbent on taking the full three minutes down to the very last second before ceding control.

I had just started to wrestle back control when a soft touch on my body has me whipping my head around to come face to face with the most perfect little girl I have ever laid eyes on. Her body is small, so fragile even for a human, so she must be quite young. Dark hair sets a stark contrast for her pale skin and lips so red you would think they were painted in blood. But it's her eyes that truly undo me. For one so young, it isn't innocence reflected back to me as I would have expected. No, wisdom far beyond her years lies in her eyes. Eyes so turbulent and swirling grey it's as though a storm rages inside.

What could have happened that has caused one so young to seem so haunted? Something ferocious builds inside me, a need to protect this child from any horrors cast her way. A protective fire I have not felt since the days our kingdom was torn in war, innocents slaughtered out of spite, stokes to life, blazing in a way that refuses to be ignored. Just as the memories of burning flesh and dying screams starts to pull me under, the small angel before me whispers words so soft I feel them more than hear them.

"……..you're late."

Chapter 6
Ryker

Seros launches himself through the window before we can even formulate a plan. The fool! He is always doing reckless things that put us all in danger. And does he even care? No, this is the way he has always been and probably always will be. Cain and I exchange a glance and I can tell he feels similar frustration at our trigger happy teammate. Nonetheless, we rush to follow the idiot.

Come death or dismay, we look out for each other, so we charge in guns blazing. As we land amongst the broken glass and debris, my eyes widen. Seros is making quick work disposing of the Jorōgumo, but that is of little surprise. Our strength and powers are unparalleled, the three of us the last known in our lines of our respective breeds.

No, what has my eyes widening are the two humans in the room; females none the less. Women are rare amongst shifter kind for whatever reason. I don't think anyone truly remembers what happened after this many centuries, but for nearly every fifty male births one female is born. Because of this, females are highly coveted and cherished. It's not uncommon for a woman to be claimed by a pack or group, other units similar to what my brothers and I have created. Men bonded together through trial and tribulation, forged from fire to create a bond worth far more than blood.

Actually, I would be surprised if a woman chose to be paired with a single mate in the current times. Female children are strongly guarded until mates can be chosen once they come of age, the boys taught to fight nearly as soon as they can walk. The more men in the unit, the better the female can be protected from the Raiders- groups of criminals that have made it their life's mission to steal females for themselves and force the mating bond upon them or sell them to the highest bidder. Using and abusing the woman they get their hands on, they are the bane of the realm. Bunch of sick bastards. They don't deserve to live on our world, much less have a female they've no idea how to properly appreciate.

Cain must have noticed at the same time as I did, already crossing the room in quick strides towards them. They shrink back, the mother tucking what I presume is her daughter firmly behind her.

Like that would do any good against us. The thought makes me smirk.

As the creature lets out an awful shriek, Cain and I close the distance to the females as they cover their ears and shrink back from the noise. Keeping them behind us and away from the threat in the room, I watch my brother make quick work of the vile creature. That's what he gets for charging in first and I'll gladly let him claim the kill. I hate those things.

It isn't long before Seros strikes the killing blow to the hideous beast. While a Jorōgumo may be beautiful in human form, their shifted spider body is quite the grotesque sight to behold.

The next thing I know I'm knocked back flat on my ass with a hissing Seros in front of me. *Damn it!* I must have been so caught up with the females that I stopped watching for additional threats. How could I be so stupid? This is a prime example of why I don't care for human women, they're nothing more than temporary distractions. I'm better than this, and the human realm is rubbing off on me in the worst of ways.

After a thorough scan of the room turns up nothing, I turn back to my brother wrapped around the females in a protective embrace. If there are no other beasts in the room, that would mean he is shielding them from...us? What in the world?

Before I can let loose the string of curses on the tip of my tongue, Cain slowly makes his way closer to our brother with his hands out in a placating gesture. It takes a bit of arguing between us, but eventually Seros regains his wits and transforms back.

What was that about anyway? Could he have been bitten? Of everything I know about the Jorōgumo, nothing has ever come up about their venom having a hallucinogenic effect, but it would be foolish to dismiss the possibility until I'm certain. If so, we'll be going on a spider hunt to harness some of their venom. That would be a delightful weapon to have on hand.

Once the little girl mumbles something I can't seem to hear towards him, Seros finally calms enough to shift back, alleviating my concerns that this will have to escalate in a battle of dominance.

Slowly, even more so than normal, I watch on as his wings are pulled into his back once more. Next, his long snake-like body shrinks back to his human size, legs forming beneath him just before he would tip over. He shakes his head, the face so similar to a raging dragon distorting to become human once more. The scales are always the last to go, a final form of protection. The scales shimmer across his body in hues of blue, purple, and green;

catching the light in a truly magical sight to behold. I may be a bit jealous, not that I would ever let the cocky bastard know.

Without tearing his eyes from the females, he holds onto the last bit of his armor until he can yank back on his jeans, covering himself up. His shirt is destroyed, nothing more than tattered rags at his feet, so he remains shirtless as he lets his scales finally recede.

Himself once more, my brother still cannot tear his eyes from the humans he fought to protect. It would appear the older of the two has had enough scrutiny of her daughter and breaks the tension.

"Sooooooooo……..that was pretty fucking weird." Her voice resonates deep within me, awakening something I cannot name, nor do I truly wish to, so I stuff it back down.

"Are you hurt?" Cain asks, his eyes focused solely on the face of the enchantress speaking.

"No, we're fine, but thank you. Really. This has all been a bit…surreal though, but really, thanks again for all of your help fighting the spider…monster…lady. We're just going to head out while I can still pretend this was all just a weird nightmare."

She turns to leave, but finds the door locked. Picking up the child, she slowly inches around the room, always keeping her back to the wall and her eyes trained on the three of us. With her gaze set firmly upon us, she bumps into three separate chairs and the corner of the desk. That's going to leave a few marks. Humans truly are a careless lot.

She makes it to the window, bending over to set the child outside first and giving us a fine view all the while. She slides out after her, glass shards tumbling off the window sill onto the floor.

I can't stop the nagging feeling that I have seen her somewhere before, but for the life of me, I can't seem to place her.

Once out of sight, my brothers race to the window as though their feet have minds of their own. I follow at a more languid pace, not nearly as enthralled by a mere human as my brothers seem to be. If you went by the look on their faces, you would think she was sent to be their ruin; one they would happily allow.

Sure, she is pretty as far as humans go, but what use have I for a pretty face for more than a night? There will be others, there are always others. We may never get another chance to claim a true mate after what happened, but I am not fool enough to fall for a mortal. Our fate is sealed and no amount of bitching will change it. Better to just accept it rather than suffer twice.

"You know we're going to have to handle this," I warn them, but they both pointedly ignore me.

We just catch a glimpse of her racing off around the back corner of the building before we hear an engine roar to life shortly after. Tires skidding, she floors it as she heads away from the horrors they had just witnessed. I can't say that I blame her one bit either. Humans…they're weak.

Chapter 7
Raina

What. The. Flying. Fuck.

I barely pay attention to speed limits as I haul ass home. Just have to get home, then everything will be fine. It's all just a dream. Or that crazy ass therapist drugged me with something. Yeah, that has to be it. Drugs. It's the only thing that makes sense. They pump something into the air of their office to get you to relax and spill all of your dirty little secrets. That must be why it's so expensive, those kinds of drugs must be pricey. At least we left before I could pay. Oh Gods, I'm spiraling.

Glancing in my rearview mirror I see the last thing I expect. There sits Skye, smiling serenely out the window with a sense of peace I haven't seen on her before. I mean ever. Sure, she has been happy or content, these last few days aside, but never before have I seen my daughter have such a sense of comfort and peace. It's as though she knows something that I don't as she sits there like the cat that ate the canary.

Obviously she got better drugs than I did.

Pulling up to the house, I hurry out of my seat, grab my daughter out of her carseat and race inside. Once I triple check the house is locked tight-upstairs too for sure this time- I finally allow myself to breathe. Ok, I just need to process.

The therapist was really a giant spider. The pink bitch locked us inside- I knew I hated her. A flying snake dragon killed it. Then he turned human like the other two men that showed up.

I got a pretty nice look as I left the room and I must say, they were much nicer to look at than the spider carcass. Ok, so three attractive men were at the therapist's office just killing a spider. I can live with that. Yep, that's totally what happened, just three hot guys killing a spider.

As I calm myself down, Skye comes up to me, her previously serene face twisted into a frown. "Mommy we forgot Rory."

Of course that's what she takes away from the day; let's just forget about the unimportant, huge-ass spider getting crushed by a flying snake. But really, I should probably be fine with that seeing as she is at least speaking again and actually looks better now than she did this morning. I guess something good came out of this fucked up day after all.

"Well sweetheart, I'm not sure we can go back there. We might have to get you a new tiger instead."

Tears immediately fill her eyes and I feel like I just kicked a puppy.

"I'll try my best, ok?"

It's the only thing I can think of to placate her, but I can't very well take her back there can I? Sighing, I scoop her up and decide it is time for a bath and bed. I just can't handle anything else today.

I make quick work washing away the memories of today between the two of us and get us changed into fresh clothes. I offer to make Skye something to eat, but she refuses and I certainly won't be able to choke anything down quite yet.

Tucking her in beside me as I have done the last few days, my eyes begin to close with the hope that tomorrow everything will make sense again. Just before I drift off I hear the sweet, small voice beside me.

"You."

"What was that love?" I ask, groggy and confused.

"The I spy riddle, something that is blue. It's you mommy."

And with that, silent tears stream down my face as I softly cry myself to sleep, trying to hide my grief from my much too perceptive daughter.

Chapter 8
Cain

I feel hollow. Ever since I laid eyes upon the humans, just to see them flee from me in fear, I have felt this aching pit that seems to stretch deep into my bones. My job is to protect, to save those not strong enough to save themselves. Yet here we are; a female running from me as fast as her feet can carry her, all the while eyeing my brothers and I as though we mean to strike her down the second her back is turned.

I run my hand through my pale hair, fighting the urge to tear it out in frustration. I glance over at my brothers. Ryker just stands at the window, saying nothing as he looks out on the human world with his lip curled in disdain. Ryker carries himself every bit the prince he once was; brown hair neatly trimmed, hazel eyes searching for a weakness, and his face practically elven in nature with slightly pointed ears to match. A regal air follows in his wake, an upbringing ingrained into his very being. Even though hundreds of years have passed since his title was revoked, his demeanor has not changed much. The only time that mask falls away is when the adrenaline takes over, turning him into a force to be reckoned with. A bloodthirsty beast, more animal than man.

Seros is bending down to pick up... a stuffed animal? He lifts it to his face, inhaling deep. Eyes flashing bright silver, he struts to the window with confidence and determination the likes of which I rarely see on the cocky bastard.

He braces one hand on the window sill and hops through the window with ease, making it a few feet before turning around to shout, "Well? Are you two coming or what?"

He doesn't wait for our response before continuing to walk. I follow, quickly eating up the distance and falling into step beside him. He's going to need someone to pull him back if he goes too far and if there's one thing you can always count on, it's Seros going too far.

Ryker snaps out of his trance, but seems much more reluctant to fall into line, obviously coming to the same assumptions that I am. I have a feeling I know just what Seros has planned and I haven't the faintest idea of how I'm going to make him see sense.

Ryker turns to me asking, "You know what has to be done, right?"

"We're not killing them Ryker," I snap back, trying to convince myself that there's another way out of this just as fiercely as I'm trying to convince Ryker. There has to be another way.

"They're going to talk, look how panicked they were," he emphatically points out.

"You want to be the one to update Seros on your plan?" I bite out, wanting him to just drop it for a few minutes so I can think.

Pompous bastard that he is, he increases his pace to go fight with Seros, but a sharp look from our brother has Ryker biting his tongue. Seros is too on edge, it isn't the time to push him just yet and even Ryker can sense that.

The time will come though, it always does. Nothing can be ignored forever.

Chapter 9
Seros

It isn't hard to pick up their scent. Now that I have the child's toy as a reference, their trail is clear. With flying not being a wise option in this realm, we are stuck walking. *Again.* It sucks ass, and I make a mental note to shake Ryker down for enough to get us our own car for when we're here. Whose bright idea was it to have the Griffin hold the purse strings anyway? *Stingy bastard.*

Nearly an hour passes before we make it to what is no doubt their home. Two stories, a small fenced in backyard and an open front porch gives off the impression of a picture perfect small home. It feels...like it's all for show. There is no sense of home to this place, just a house to live in. It's as though someone wanted to project to the world that everything was fine so that no one would delve any deeper. Not someone, *her.* The woman that stood fierce in the face of a demonic creature that no doubt terrified her. Who held strong in spite of that fear for the sake of her young. A Mother.

My heart skips a beat as I realize...that means there must be a father as well. I hadn't considered that crucial fact yet. The beast inside of me writhes and hisses in outrage. How could anyone call himself a man if he allowed his mate and child to face such danger alone?

Taking a deep breath, I scent the air. The woman, the child...another deep breath....nothing else prominent. There is the faint trace of an occasional visitor or two and a dog, but it's so minute it's hardly noteworthy. How could two females be allowed to live alone? Humans are just asking for trouble; no wonder the Jorōgumo was able to prey on them.

With a few easy maneuvers, I settle down on the rooftop across the street from them, content with merely watching for now as I try to sort through the intense spikes of emotions I rarely feel. If I really focus, I can hear the soft breathing of slumber from inside. Good, after such a trying day they deserve peace. They would always have peace if I had anything to say about it.

Silence reigns as neither my brothers nor myself speak a word, each lost in our own world of thought. The gentle calm of night wraps the neighborhood in a peaceful blanket, letting all who look on be momentarily lost in the simple beauty as the stars start to fade from view with the rising sun. It's just beginning to crest the horizon when Cain shatters the temporary serenity.

"It's a bad idea, Ser."

"I don't know what you're talking about."

"Don't play dumb. You can't keep her and you know it," Cain warns.

"I know that. I just...I can't leave yet. I don't know what the fuck it is about her, but my instincts are going haywire. I need to make sure they're ok."

"You sound like a sap," Ryker interjects. "The humans saw you. We can't very well leave them to spread the truth and cause us trouble. Caspian will have our heads."

"We're not killing the mortals, Ryker and that's final. They're females," Cain commands.

"Humans waste no time killing us," Ryker presses.

"Let me keep an eye on her for a few days, make sure she doesn't get the torches and pitchforks ready. Who's going to believe her anyway? She has no proof and the humans will think she's crazy. It's a different time now than it used to be; they've even stopped the witch hunts. You'd know these things if either of you paid any attention when we were sent here over the years. The child isn't an issue either way though, no one ever pays much mind to the imaginative ramblings of children."

"Two days, then we need to move on, no matter the outcome," Cain relents, though he settles right in at my side to wait. He can bolster all he wants, the females have him acting all squirrely too, it's not just me.

The next couple of days they never come out of the house, I never even get so much as a glimpse of them. Ryker comes and goes, scoffing at us when he does. At one point he brought me a new shirt, so he can't be as annoyed with me as he appears. The last few hours he's even been perched on the ledge of the rooftop across the street with us, probably trying to burn a hole in their house with the way he is glaring.

"There, by the fence, do you see it?" Cain suddenly asks.

My eyes scan the scene before me in earnest, but Ryker is already in motion before I can spot what Cain spoke of. Fierce, proud, and regal; Ryker carries himself the same in both forms. One of the abilities that his Griffin offers him is his keen eye; useful for the pilfering he thinks we don't notice, the kleptomaniac. It's what Ryker does best...watch.

He jumps down from the rooftop, gracefully landing without a sound. On silent footsteps he darts up the steps onto the front porch of the females' house, braces one hand on the railing and swings his body over onto the back of the crouched figure by the window. With a blade pressed to the man's throat, he tugs him upright and hauls him towards us in the front yard.

His dagger digs into the neck of the whimpering male, drawing blood. I can tell the exact moment Ryker notices the red bead trickling down the stranger's collar, his pupils dilating as his hand almost imperceptibly shakes.

One of Ryker's personal favorites is to fly his enemies high into the sky before releasing them, letting their panicked screams fill his ears before they meet a painful death. Being surrounded by humans though, his typical tactics are limited. In his eyes, I can see the war he fights with himself for restraint as he merely holds the man before us, not allowing himself to succumb to the temptation to finish slitting the human's throat. Ryker would gladly dance in the man's blood in a bout of madness and I doubt any of us want to draw that much attention to ourselves here, so I appreciate his struggle with restraint.

"What are your intentions here?" Cain's authoritative voice leaves no doubt that he expects an immediate answer and complete compliance. As silence fills the air around us, it is soon joined by my rage.

"Speak! Or I will cut the tongue from your mouth."

"Alright, alright!" the man cries out. "Sheesh, I was only coming to check on them. The kid hasn't been to school since her mom killed the guy that tried to make off with her, and I was just seeing if she needed a shoulder to cry on, if you know what I mean. Bitch seems lonely."

The scumbag actually has the nerve to wink, as though we are all in on his filthy scheme. While I battle the disgust at this human, the rest of what he claims sinks in. Attempted kidnapping. Someone tried to steal away the sweet, innocent little girl for only Gods know what reason. An all-consuming fury quickly replaces the disgust I was feeling until I'm seeing red, but then the rest of the statement filters through the haze. Her mom killed him. Pride begins to swell in my chest at the strength of this champion. I'm struggling not to get whiplash from these sudden mood shifts.

"Let's see if your story checks out, shall we?" Ryker states as he begins the walk to the front door, removing his blade and clutching the man roughly by his upper arm. "We need to put an end to this nonsense regardless."

Cain flanks his other side, his arm reaching out to grab the back of the bastard's shirt in his fist. Ryker swiftly knocks on the front door and with our enhanced hearing, we all hear the soft shriek and what sounds like someone falling out of bed.

A few minutes later the door opens and I allow my gaze to roam over the sensual female that stands before me in appreciation. Her hair is still mussed from sleep and she is wearing nothing but a baggy button up shirt that falls to mid-thigh, leaving her long legs on display. But the best part? The baseball bat that she has pressed to the throat of the man in our clutches.

"You? How the hell do you know where I live? Did you follow me here?" Her voice betrays no signs of just having awoken as she faces off with the man before her, her defensive stance so natural it seems ingrained.

"You know him?" Ryker asks.

It's as though she didn't realize the three of us stood there until that moment. She jumps slightly, but to her credit she keeps her weapon trained on her perceived threat.

"So it wasn't drugs..." she mutters softly.

"Drugs?" Cain this time, the fury evident in his voice at the thought of someone drugging a woman.

"Nothing, nevermind." She shakes her head as if to clear her thoughts. "What are *any* of you doing at my house? Why are you following me?" Her eyes flick back to Ryker, confusion in their depths rivaling with her wariness.

I choose this moment to step in, seeing how out of hand it could get and quickly. Ryker and Cain are clearly caught off guard to see her aggressive. The females back home are coddled to the point of uselessness, so submissive and spoiled that I doubt many of them have even the faintest idea how to defend themselves from a splinter, much less an actual threat. My brothers don't pay much attention to the humans while we are on this side of the veil, but I do. Things are far different here and in my opinion? Not everything fails in comparison to home like Ryker seems to think.

"She dropped this. I thought she might like it back." I hold up the little stuffed animal in offering.

"Rory!" a small voice exclaims just before rushing to the door.

"Skye, I told you to stay upstairs where it's safe. Head back upstairs now, love." Her mother's eyes widen to show that she is starting to panic now that her child is steps away from intruders.

She makes to stop her, but the little girl slips beneath her mother's outstretched arm to run to my side. Her small hands making 'gimme' motions as she silently demands her toy back. I crouch down to her eye level, hoping it makes me appear less of a threat. Handing over the tiger, Skye clutches it to her chest as if she'll never let it go again. Now reunited with her lost friend, the small waif of a child peers straight at me unblinkingly.

In all honesty, it's pretty fuckin' creepy.

But then she reaches out and places her hand on my cheek, the stubble evident from staying watch for several days and looks at me with unwavering determination.

"You're the snake man from the other day, right? You stay. We're gonna need you, Rory always gets lost." With that, she turns and heads back into the house, throwing over her shoulder, "By the way, you're late again. You're gonna' have to work on that," leaving us adults in awkward silence to consider her nonsense.

Skye's mother is the first to snap out of it.

"To answer your question, I sort of know him. Honestly, I try to avoid him when I pick up Skye from school. Well, used to. I don't know how he found my house. Or you three either, for that matter. Why are you stalking me?"

That's all Ryker and Cain need to hear. They turn, dragging the pleading man away. This leaves me standing at the door with an angry looking woman with a bat, lucky me.

Now that it's just me she seems to relax a bit. A small bit. Like a *really* tiny bit, but I'll take it.

"Who are you? Or *what* are you, I should ask?"

She sees me as a threat and I don't much care for the feeling. I'm used to human women feeling something far different around me, not suspicious disdain. Though to be fair, if someone had tried to kidnap my child, I wouldn't trust anyone either. I also revealed myself to her, so that can't be working in my favor either. I have to fight the urge to slap myself so I can stop rambling in my head and actually have a conversation with the catty female.

"Are you sure you really want to know? Once you do, there's no going back. For now you can still pretend that everything is fine; it seems like you're more comfortable like that anyway. Sticking your head in the sand and waiting for the desert poppies to bloom." I can't seem to stop my cheeky reply from falling from my mouth, flirting with her as I inch closer. I don't really know how else to put women at ease, my experiences limited and fleeting. Thankfully, instead of putting that bat to good use, she rises to the challenge.

"Maybe I stick my head in the sand so the seeds can have my company. When in a dark place, you think you've been buried, not planted. All they know is they're being baked alive, with no idea of what they're about to become."

"But you couldn't see them as they bloom if you're burning beside them."

"No, but I would be content knowing I gave a part of myself, no matter how small and insignificant; to allow them my tears to slake their thirst so that they could know the sun, however brief and blinding."

It takes every bit of my self restraint to keep my hands to myself. The sorrow in her speech speaks of a weary loneliness that calls to my own and I wish to wash it away. Fuck, Ryker's right; I sound like a sap.

My eyes flick down to her lips in time to see the tip of her tongue dart out to wet them, as if she's as drawn to me as I am to her. My jeans begin to feel awfully constricting as I imagine what else that tongue of hers could do.

The spell is broken as Cain returns, sans one sniveling human. Our eyes meet, promising all will be discussed in private. Later. For now, my attention returns to the beauty in front of me.

"Do you plan to invite us in, or do you leave all of your guests leaning against the threshold?"

"You're not my guests, you're three stalkers that showed up on my doorstep," she replies without missing a beat, glaring back at me with distaste. I absolutely detest it and swear then and there that I will do everything in my power to never have her look at me like that again. Not that that'll be long.

Fuck.

"I see human hospitality hasn't changed since our last visit," Cain grumbles as we remain huddled on the porch.

"Human? You know what, never mind." She shakes her head, sighing. "I'll make you a deal," she decides, "answer a riddle and I'll let you three-two?- in so you can answer all of my questions."

"That seems to have you as the winner regardless. What's our prize?" Cain's interest is piqued though, his eyes flashing with guarded intrigue.

"Your prize is to be allowed into my home without busted kneecaps." A smirk plays across her lips.

Ah the things I want those lips to do...

Shaking my head a bit to regain focus, I ask instead, "Why a riddle? How does that help you decide whether to let us in or not?"

"I don't allow idiots into my home, especially ones I don't know. Personal rule," she states dryly.

I'm just about to ask what that's all about when Cain interrupts me.

"Challenge accepted."

Chapter 10
Cain

Now far enough away as to not be overheard, Ryker and I turn to the sniveling male between us.

"Why did you stalk her to her home?" I demand of him, shaking him by the collar to gain his attention.

"I...well...you see...I mean did you *see* her? She's always alone when I see her, so I figured I had a shot. I don't mind putting up with another sniveling brat running around for a while if it means I get a piece of that—"

The rest of his statement is cut off as my fist sinks into his face. Blood coats my knuckles as his nose breaks with a satisfying crunch. His ensuing howl of pain is a balm to my raging soul. How dare this pathetic fool speak of them in such a manner! I release him and he falls to the ground in a bloody heap. Pathetic. Ryker's nostrils flare, his only reaction as he watches in silence.

"Ryker, make sure he finds his way to his car. I'd hate to find out what happens if he were to take a detour."

With that final threat I wait for him to depart, gazing on with distaste as he scurries his way up and towards his vehicle, Ryker in tow. As the human opens the door to his car that is parked down the street, Ryker grabs him by the front of his shirt and tosses him inside the car. He stands there for a few moments before returning to my side, the car never starting.

"We might have a slight problem," Ryker informs me with a neutral expression.

Instead of answering, I raise an eyebrow and wait for him to continue.

"Apparently humans are more fragile than I remembered. He snapped his neck while getting settled into his vehicle," Ryker informs without the slightest hint of remorse, his voice deadpan. "It was tragic really, but there was nothing that could have been done to prevent it."

"Damn it, Ry! Could you at least *try* to blend in? Like we don't have enough on our plate already?" I grind my teeth as I try not to throttle the man in front of me.

"Seems to me our other problem could be handled just as easily," he challenges, face devoid of emotion.

Pinching the bridge of my nose as I try to gather my scattered thoughts, I take a few deep breaths and pray for patience.

"Go dump the body in the nearest river and come straight back, alright? And for the love of the Gods, be discreet about it."

I turn my back on the infuriating man and return to deal with our first problem. Amazing how quickly they seem to be piling up.

Upon my arrival, I hear the tail end of my brother's conversation, the air charged with tension. I meet Seros' inquisitive gaze, conveying the promise we will get each other up to date as soon as we are alone. My gaze returns to the vision before me. Eyes full of fire as she offers us a challenge, her pale blue sleep shirt only reaching halfway down her thighs. All it would take is the slightest effort to slide it up a few inches and discover what was beneath. Would her underwear match her shirt? Was she bare? My fingers twitch in response to my thoughts, wishing I could reach out and assuage my curiosity. As she shifts slightly, moving the hem just ever slightly higher up her leg, I wrench my sight upwards in an attempt to ease my torment. The top few buttons are undone beneath her collar, giving me a glimpse of the soft flesh beneath. It's incredibly distracting.

Her taunt pulls me from my torturous thoughts. I may have missed the majority of the conversation, distracted as I was, but I have every intention of rising to whatever challenge this beauty presents us with.

"Challenge accepted."

With a quirk of her brow at my excitement, she pauses for only a few moments before beginning.

"It brings back the lost as though never gone,
Shines laughter and tears
With light long since shone.
A moment to make, a lifetime to shed.
Valued then, but lost when you're dead.
What is it?"

This causes me to pause. I really should have paid better attention before accepting her challenge. Riddles....I'm terrible at riddles. I glance at Seros to the side of me and see him already lost in thought. Not one to back down from a challenge, I attempt to truly focus, but I still come up with no answer. As the minutes tick by, her dry look is replaced by a smug grin, sure that she has bested us.

Just as I begin to add this failure to our ever growing list as of late, Seros' fingers snap as the answer comes to him. "A memory."

Her smug grin is washed away in favor of a disgruntled scowl. "At least it wasn't the smug bastard," she mumbles, likely thinking she's too quiet for us to hear. I grin, silently laughing at Ryker's expense.

"You're right," she continues, "I'm surprised though, nobody has managed to guess that one until now." With a shrug, she opens the door the rest of the way, inviting us inside.

"That's seriously how you vet who you let into your house? How have you not been murdered yet?" Seros asks in disbelief.

"Of course not, I was just hoping to wipe the smug look off of the pompous bastard over there for a little while at least," she gestures to Ryker's scowling face as he climbs the steps on the porch, "but he missed all the fun. You turned into a goddamn snake, obviously I have some questions here. I was going to let you in regardless; his face just annoys me for some reason." She turns her back on us and heads inside without a backward glance to see if we're going to follow.

I shoot a glare at Ryker before we go in. There's no way he made it all the way to the river and back with a dead body in so short of time. Either he shifted, or he dumped the body elsewhere. This mission is going to Hell.

I head into the house before she can change her mind and take in the room, a basic and practical setup with no personal touches in sight. A black leather couch, a matching recliner, wooden coffee table, television and a handful of toys in a corner are all that fill the space. There are no pictures on the walls and no unique touches that one usually finds in someone's home.

She waves us in and sits on the arm of the couch, crossing her legs, eyebrow raised expectantly. The action causes her shirt to rise up far enough that I catch a glimpse of purple fabric and I have to clench my fist until my nails cut into my skin to keep myself from reaching out. The damn woman is getting under my skin far too quickly. *Fuck me, Ryker is the voice of reason around here.*

As Ryker moves to take the chair-as close to a throne as he will ever have- I grip his arm and haul him closer to furiously whisper, "What did you do with the body?"

"Body?" the girl squeaks out, tensing up as if prepared to bolt.

"There is no body," I quickly recant, the lie escaping on impulse to try and set her at ease.

"You lost it?!" she whisper-shouts instead, not at ease at all.

Seros snickers as he chimes in, filling in the gaps of what he missed with all the ease missing from the human. "You know, for someone suddenly so hung up on discretion, I would think you would be the last to be so careless."

Ryker's face actually tints slightly red, either from anger or embarrassment I'm not sure, as he snaps back at us. "You think I was going to leave you two idiots alone with the girl after the way you've been acting?" He turns his back on us as he settles into the chair as if he owns it, looking down his nose at us. "I'll move him when we leave, that way I won't need to make two trips," he threatens as if it's second nature, the color gone from his face once more.

"You're not touching her," Seros growls, eyes flashing silver as he wrestles to remain in control of his baser instincts.

"ENOUGH!" I bellow, blessed silence finally meeting my ears. "Shut the Hell up for five seconds and stop acting like children. Seros, find a seat."

Seros shoots one last glare at Ryker before he rushes over to sit as close as possible to our host, leaving me the other side of the couch. Turned slightly to face her, my new position does not make my predicament any easier as I get a good glimpse beneath the hem of her shirt that has ridden up much too far to be decent. I try to subtly adjust myself, refocusing on the fact that she's now aware of the creatures that walk amongst her in different skins and try to figure out a way to keep her from sparking a manhunt. Caspian will be pissed if we get sent back to the dark ages due to a slip-up we should have prevented.

She eyes us with caution, but with far less fear than before, her eyes lingering on Ryker's face a bit longer than ours with extra suspicion. She stays perched next to Seros without retreating, obviously choosing to stay near what she assumes is her ally and refusing to look away from her perceived threat for long.

So what category does that leave me in?

Clearing her throat of nerves, she begins the impromptu meeting now that everyone has calmed down.

"I guess we should start at the beginning. Who are you three? *What* are you? What was that...thing...from the other day? Why did you follow me home and what do you want?" she fires at us in rapid succession.

My brothers and I share a glance, trying to decide how much to reveal. Shifter society lives separate from the humans for a reason after all. But the more I think on it, the more my better judgment ebbs away, turning me into as reckless of a fool as Seros. This woman has already witnessed Ser transform and here she sits beside him, not shrinking back. Actually the closer I look, I notice she's sitting close enough for her leg to brush against his.

With a soft growl reverberating in my chest, I yank my brother away from her, a warning flashing in my eyes. We're already getting in too deep with her. As the female meets my eyes, I know the illuminated red rings in my irises will scare her away, but perhaps that will be for the best. We could frighten her into submission. We just need to make sure she stays quiet about what she saw and get back to the mission, though I'm not sure what we'll do if she doesn't agree or starts getting hysterical. They always get hysterical. Usually, that's when Ryker steps in, but I just can't bring myself to accept that's a possible outcome this time.

Bracing myself for the oncoming rejection I stiffen, but she refuses to look away. The display of dominance has my beast purring its approval in my chest, longing to break free and lay claim to the woman before me. Not that it could, but it's a tempting, albeit dangerous, thought.

Ryker's condescending voice has the both of us turning to face him as he speaks. "How about we start with who *you* are and why you were foolish enough to be caught in the Jorōgumo's lair?" He all but demands answers from her. The sudden interrogation makes the woman bristle with contained fury, but as she replies her voice is deadly calm.

"That wasn't the deal. The deal was I would let you in to answer *my* questions. And what the hell is a jorgamomo?" her voice leaves no room for argument as Ryker grinds his teeth. Seros, the fool, decides to continue to push her though.

"Can we at least know your name first? It's awfully awkward to have to keep referring to you as 'female' or 'woman.'"

"Refer to me? You've been talking about me?"

"What else have we had to talk about the last few days?"

Of all things that could have happened, I did not expect my smooth talker of a brother to blush. He turns his head away quickly and coughs into his fist. I choose this moment to come to his rescue, perplexed and amused.

"My name is Cain, Cain Areli. These are my brothers, Ryker Haytham and Seros Doryu." Gesturing while I continue, "We need to make sure you—"

But I am cut off as the female jumps up, jabbing her finger in accusation at Ryker "You! You're the asshole that ran into me at the gas station the other day! I knew I recognized you from somewhere. You ruined a perfectly good cup of coffee, dickface."

She sits back down slowly, shooting daggers at the man across the room, but for now content to have at least remembered where she had seen Ryker before. Now all those odd, frequent glances make sense. Note to self, never mess with a woman's coffee.

Ryker just sits back with his trademark smirk upon his face, not even missing a beat at the chastisement in her tone. When it's clear he has no intention of apologizing, I choose to carry on.

"Need to make sure you understand the severity of your situation. We remain in the shadows for a reason; to keep the peace between the veils. The humans can't handle the knowledge of our existence without it leading to war, something all of us would prefer to avoid. You need to keep what you saw to yourself, otherwise more drastic measures will need to be taken to ensure your silence that I would prefer it not have to come to.

"We were assigned the task of locating stray shifters and either bringing them home or eliminating them if they present a threat." Ryker shoots me a glare from across the room that I choose to ignore. "Though we are expected to handle any fall out from our actions swiftly. I don't want it to come to that."

"Shifters?" she asks, her focus swiveling to me in rapt curiosity.

"Others like us. As you witnessed yesterday with Seros, we have the ability to switch between two forms." She nods in reply so I take that as encouragement to continue.

"The *Jorōgumo*," I correct, "is a beast that lures its prey under the guise of a human male or female. Unlike us, who are two equal halves for lack of a better term, the *Jorōgumo* are barely more than rabid beasts. The only time they wear their human form is to hunt. Once back at its lair, the creature shifts back into the spider-like beast you saw the other day, devouring the victim. They are a rare nuisance to our society, not one of us." This causes her to shudder slightly in revulsion.

"So don't tell anyone about the monsters under the bed or humans will get stabby and you'll feed me to a spider. Check." She actually gives us a thumbs-up, the strange little human.

"You're handling all of this…remarkably well."

She looks at me as if I'm an oddity on display as she says, "Television and books have pretty much prepared me for something like this happening and made it all seem relatively plausible. Is that where all the inspiration and stories come from? Humans you threaten into silence that you forgot to go back and murder? It's either believe you, or I'm hallucinating. I'd like to lean towards the option that doesn't get me committed. Or stabbed."

My hand runs through my hair, messing it up further as my nervous tension shows and I scratch my head. "I can only speak for myself, but I don't think we can leave until we monitor you for a while longer. I've never met a mortal that took this news so well and I'm honestly concerned you're going to panic as soon as we leave and Ryker will have to kill you. I don't want that to happen. Besides, you could use the added protection anyway if the last few days are any indication."

I can't help the small smile that tugs at the corner of my mouth. Yes, even if our first meeting had this female wary of me, being here to dispose of the slinking male outside of her home has left pride and purpose settled upon my shoulders. It's a welcome change from the consistent failures as of late, though an admitted distraction from our mission.

I was bluffing when I said I'd be able to allow Ryker to kill them to ensure their silence, something I sincerely hope she doesn't call me out on. Never again will I fail at protecting a female, even a couple of humans. The sharp stab of grief pulls me away from the moment and launches me back into my recurring nightmare.

Smoke fills the air, hiding the horrors that surround me, but not the screams. My senses overloaded as death fills my nose with its putrid stench. Every breath I take threatens to make me vomit, but I can't help the heaving gasps my weariness forces me to take. Bodies lay at my feet, men I called friends and their executioners that I killed in vengeance.

A soft shout stands out above the din of battle, a voice I would recognize anywhere. Charging forward, my heart plummets at the sight before me. Through the haze of smoke I can just make out the canine figure poised above a small slip of a woman. Not just any woman, but Amara. Our Amara. The female that chose to accept us as mates.

With so few females, matches were often arranged to produce heirs for lines of shifters dying out. As the last known Manticore, Quetzalcoatl, and Griffin, my group was able to move up on the list of potentials to be considered; but ultimately the female still held the power to reject the suggested match or not. We were weeks away from the ceremony that would seal our bond.

With a roar, I rushed forward to tackle the beast away, my rage letting my beast burst free with ease mid-leap. I towered over the ca-

nine, the strength my manticore offered me filling me with a high. Not only was my lion half ferocious on its own, but the venom from my scorpion coursed through my veins, melding with the adrenaline already pumping.

Hackles raised and fangs bared, the wolf spun, its speed rivaling my own. As we battled in a flurry of swiping claws and snarling mouths, I lost track of the world around me. Teeth sunk into my front leg and I roared with frustration more than pain. He used my distraction to tackle me to the ground, attempting to pin me and tear out my throat.

Flinging the beast off, I rolled to my paws, my tawny fur stained in a mixture of our blood. It was splattered across my face, dripping into my eyes and burning. The coppery scent blended with the smoke around us, making it nearly impossible to see or breathe as it blinded and suffocated me.

As we stalked before one another, circling in the hunt of an opening, I raised my barbed tail in preparation to strike the killing blow with no further preamble. Quick as a flash I struck, ready to end him before the loss of my senses led to my defeat.

Feeling the barb sink into flesh I momentarily rejoice, with as swiftly as my poison acts, the battle is nearly won. But beneath me is not the lupine form I aimed for, but Amara. I underestimated the beast's agility. In the heat of battle I had lost track of her, my focus solely on protecting her from the snarling creature beside her, it never occurred to me that the beast she truly needed protection from...was me.

The ravaged wolf used the opportunity to flee, off to lick his wounds and live another day while Amara lay dying before me. I shifted back to my human form, the beast curling up within me to wallow in shame. As I reached a hand out to her she flinched back, *causing everything inside of me to shatter in the face of her fear. I did this. It's my fault. A tear rolled down my cheek as I watched the life fade from her eyes all too quickly.*

That's how my brothers found me. No, I don't deserve brothers. I don't deserve anyone. Seros left and came back with the wolf's severed head some time later, but it was a pitiful token to be had.

I recoiled from Ryker's hand placed on my shoulder, attempting to steer me away from the scene. I deserve to see, to suffer.

"What's wrong with him?" a feminine voice faintly asks, though I can't convince my voice to function.

"None of your concern, *female*," Ryker sneers and I can practically picture his face.

My breath is tight in my chest, my lungs forgetting how to function as I struggle to breathe. The heavy weight of failure crushes my chest, locking me in a vice grip that I struggle to remove.

"It's alright, leave him be. This...it happens sometimes. Life has left scars on all of us," I hear Seros cajole in an attempt to get her back to her seat.

There's a loud rushing sound in my ears, making it near impossible to hear anything else. The room begins spinning, everything blurring out of focus.

"Hey, breathe with me, alright?" The feminine voice snaps me from my internal downward spiral.

Her hand is inches away from my cheek when I catch her wrist on instinct, the world rushing back into focus as blessed air fills my lungs once more. I release it just as quickly. I don't lay my hands on a woman, ever. If I hadn't been so distracted, I wouldn't even have flinched at her approach.

"My apologies," I rush out.

"Are you alright?" she asks.

"Of course I am, why wouldn't I be?" I reply a bit too quickly, too defensively to be believable even to my own ears.

"You just looked.... " she seems to wrestle for the words, not finding the ones she needs. "I get it. I've been there."

She moves to sit between Seros and myself on the couch. I breathe in her scent, a heady combination of spring rainstorms and citrus. It's intoxicating. I see Seros adjust himself subtly, the female obviously affecting him just as strongly.

"Raina," she whispers.

"Excuse you?" Ryker retorts.

"My name," she snaps at him. "Someone asked it earlier and since *he,*" she gestures towards me, "at least tried to answer my questions I thought it only fair to reciprocate."

"Well it is a pleasure to meet you, Raina, though I wish it were under better circumstances." My voice is rough and I have to clear my throat a few times.

"So that's it then? You believe us, just like that?" Ryker incredulously scoffs.

"What other choice do I have?" Raina huffs as she bounces her leg to let out the nervous energy, much like Seros does. "As much as I would rather deny the last few days ever happened or pretend it was all a dream, I'm not stupid. And snake boy over here killed the spider for me so he's good in my book."

Seros beams at her side, going so far as to stretch his arm out on the back of the couch behind her. Much to my pleasure, she shifts just ever so slightly away from his arm, her thigh brushing against mine. Ryker sits across from me, eyes narrowed as he takes in the whole scene.

"Besides," she continues hesitantly, "if you're dropping bodies left and right, I can't afford to be one of them right now. Skye doesn't have anybody else and I refuse to let her grow up like I did," she finishes in a small voice.

Before I can press for her to elaborate, the little one comes racing down the stairs and into the living room.

"Mommy come see, come see! Rory has a brother!" The soft voice precedes her as Skye reenters the room, clutching a pair of identical stuffed tigers.

Raina jumps to her feet and is before her daughter before I can blink, kneeling before her as she attempts to keep her tone relaxed, though she fails miserably.

"Sweetheart, where did you find those?"

"On my bed."

Chapter 11
Ryker

With those words, Raina bolts for the stairs, Cain and I following right behind. Seros has the good sense to stay downstairs and guard the child. Taking the stairs two at a time, we find ourselves in the child's room. The first thing my eyes lock on is the window, slightly cracked open. Striding across the room I yank it open, gazing outside for threats. Somebody has to, now that my brothers are getting all worked up over a foolish human.

Eyes flashing a brilliant gold, I scan the area and find nothi....there! On the back fence, near the top, is a tattered bit of white cloth; no doubt torn from someone scaling the fence in a hurry.

I jump from the second story window, knees bent to absorb the jarring impact of the ground. I cross the yard in no time, the space pathetically small. I work the piece loose, returning through the backdoor to find Seros. His Quetzalcoatl offers him a better tracking ability of scent, whereas my Griffin is better at visuals.

As I return inside I see the human packing a suitcase. Good, be gone I say. Since stumbling across this pair of females my brothers have been distracted and distraction will get us all killed.

"Here, make yourself useful."

Tossing the scrap of shirt at Seros, I stride back into the living room with my head held high and settle in to watch the show as everyone bumbles about in a panic like morons.

"How could we have missed someone coming into the house?" Seros hisses at Cain.

"You know damn well that you and Ryker are the only ones with a leg up in this infernal realm," he growls back at him.

"You missed it because you were both so caught up swooning over the woman you couldn't see past your dicks."

"What's your excuse then?" Seros bites back.

I flip him off as I tune them out, settling back into my chair. Yes mine, I have officially claimed it. As the most comfortable seat in the room, my Griffin sensed the prize and demanded it as our own. My brothers often assume my behavior stems from how I was raised, but that isn't quite true. Not that I will ever admit it, but my Griffin has more control over me than is normal for shifters. Seros' episode the other day was a fluke for him, but nearly a daily problem for myself.

I recline back, deciding to capitalize on the opportunity to get a few minutes of rest. Heavens know I haven't had much over the last several days. It'll take them a while to get the humans packed up and if I have learned one thing during the wars, it's to get sleep when and where you can.

Chapter 12
Raina

Nope. All the nope, time to leave. I may usually be a little bit- some days a lot- paranoid, but seeing the guys' reactions convinced me I'm not crazy. Grabbing a suitcase, I start gathering any necessities and chuck them inside. It doesn't take long; I've never really felt this place was home, so there is very little here that I couldn't live without. Skye will probably be upset, but I'll be damned if we are bringing her tigers with. I may have no clue what's going on, but for all I know there's a tracker in its head or something. *Someone* obviously has a reason for leaving it in her room.

A small photo album, some clothes for the both of us, and my emergency wad of cash and I am ready to haul ass and get out of dodge. It should be quick enough; Skye is already pulled out of school and after this long of not showing up to work I've probably lost my job anyway. It should make me sad leaving, but I feel nothing for this place that never felt like a home. Within twenty minutes I'm ready to completely abandon the life that I spent five years building.

As I throw the suitcase in the back of my SUV and start buckling Skye into her seat, the opening and shutting of car doors causes me to look up. Squished into my vehicle are the guys.

"What the hell?" I take a moment to look at them. To *really* look.

Cain is in the front passenger seat, slightly hunched to fit. Seros slid next to Skye in the backseat, much to her delight. My daughter really has never opened up to anyone, but the smile on her face as she jabs her little finger into his cheek chanting, "Be a snake, be a snake, be a snake!" has my heart squeezing a bit tighter.

"I'm not a snake; I'm a Quetzalcoatl thank you very much! I'm much better than just a regular old snake." He acts dramatically offended, which only causes her to giggle harder.

Beside Seros is Ryker, staring at me with the same intensity. While my gaze holds only careful curiosity at this point, his appears laced with sheer hatred. *Well excuse me, but I certainly didn't ask for him to be here either!* His sharp elven features are pulled back into a sneer of disdain that I'm tempted to slap off of his face. Apparently he's going for openly hostile, which is just the cherry on top of this crap-tastic day.

So what if they are incredibly attractive? That doesn't mean I'm just going to let them hop in my car and come with me. Well, not *come* with me. Join me. But the other thought has merit.

As two more pairs of eyes snap up to connect with mine, it dawns on me that I may have said that last part aloud. Oops.

Pretending the last thirty seconds never happened, I climb into the driver's seat and turn to face the men inside. In such close quarters it is impossible to ignore the power radiating from them, setting them apart from other men. Like the air is charged with static, the fine hairs on my arms rise and goosebumps shiver across my skin. Their scent hits me then, both familiar and exhilarating; an earthy combination that reminds me of a walk through the forest. In this close of quarters I can't tell which scent belongs to which man, just the heady combination of wood smoke, evergreens, and lemongrass.

Nothing about them is triggering a sense of unease which is incredibly unusual. Typically I can't stand other people. Even with Marcus it was several years before I was comfortable enough to agree to his proposal. So then why do I feel so at ease with the three men before me? Drawing a shaky breath, I attempt to handle the situation.

"If you guys needed a ride home you really should have asked a girl first; climbing into a stranger's truck is usually a terrible decision you know. What if I'm really a serial killer?"

A chorus of laughter fills my ears, the sound doing funny things to my insides.

"As if a human could do us much harm," Ryker retorts, his voice holding an undercurrent of loathing beneath his mocking laughter, ruining the brief moment.

"You know, I didn't *ask* you to come! This lowly human has done just fine up until now so really, don't try and do me any favors. I won't tell anyone about your stupid, secret society, so you're welcome to leave. Heck I'm *asking* you to."

Silence follows my words as the brothers hold a whole conversation amongst themselves solely with their eyes, no doubt finally coming to the conclusion that they don't want to be locked in a car with a whack-job and should escape before I do something crazy like stab them or make them explode by accident. Or on purpose.

So when a large, callused hand cups my cheek, turning me to face him head on, I'm thoroughly caught off guard. Cain looks at me, trapping me in his golden gaze as he rumbles out, "If you truly want us to leave, we shall. I have no desire to do anything of the sort though, so please think carefully before deciding. I have no clue as to why I feel such a pull to stay with you, but I also find myself caring less than I should about it. Being near you feels right for now and my instincts rarely lead me astray. If it feels like I need to be here, then there must be a reason I have yet to discover. If you send me away I will respect that, but please don't make such a choice without thinking things through. You are obviously being targeted by someone, someone who is trying to either take your daughter or use her to hurt you. Are you truly sure you would like us to leave?"

My face heats as his words consume me. The intensity of his gaze mixed with his heavy words has me clenching my thighs together. The earthy aroma of these three strangers-that don't feel very much like strangers at all- in such tight quarters washes over me. His eyes darken with his sharp intake of breath and I could swear he knows exactly the effect he is having on me. And damn if the thought doesn't excite me further.

Choosing to swallow my pride, I shake my head. I'm out of my element here and need to keep my daughter safe, even if it means throwing three strange men into the line of fire. Actually, that's not a terrible idea. I could use them as human-shifter?-shields and get the hell out of dodge with Skye. It would probably take a kidnapper quite a while to drag Cain's massive body into a white panel van.

"Wasn't going to leave anyway," Seros mutters under his breath from the backseat.

The grin that beams across Cain's face, showing nothing but true, honest to the Gods joy, works to settle any reservations I may have still had. Nothing about this man comes across as deceptive, his intentions clear in his body language. Honestly, even

Ryker is clear about where he stands. Better the enemy you know than the one you don't. A look in the back shows two sets of eyes watching the display intently, Skye already asleep before our journey has even begun. I swear, the kid's narcoleptic.

Seros seems...agitated. Not angry per say, but displeased. I guess even if he feels the need to protect someone in danger, that doesn't extend to fraternizing with the humans. Ryker just looks livid. No ifs, ands, or buts about it. But neither says a word to object, so I put the truck into gear and pull away. I offered them a chance to leave; it's not my fault if they're too stupid to take it.

Chapter 13
Seros

All thoughts of tracking the intruder went out the window once Raina began to pack, my heart accelerating at the thought of losing her as soon as we've found her. I don't know what it is about this woman, but Gods do I want to find out. Never before have I met a female that stirred me up this way, consuming my thoughts and making my instincts go haywire. It's like I found a missing piece to a puzzle I didn't even know I was constructing until it fell into my lap.

I can tell Cain is having a similar struggle, but it appears he is right there with me throwing caution to the wind to cozy up with a human. While it isn't uncommon for shifter males to spawn children with humans, they cannot take them as mates or bring them home. They also tend not to reveal themselves, but I can't take that back. It'll make it easier if she knows about us anyway; we wouldn't have to lie to her when we left. All rational thoughts were gone the moment I inhaled Raina's scent.

Seeing Cain touching Raina so intimately gives me conflicting emotions. The need to protect her is at the forefront, but I know Cain won't hurt her. Even though centuries later he still punishes himself for what happened to Amara, I've never blamed him. Not only was it an accident, but truth be told I never really cared for her. Call me a callous bastard, but at least I'm honest.

Even though I should have been elated at the thought of finally obtaining a mate, it never felt like a good match. She was shy, timid, and spoiled rotten. She just didn't fit in with our group, brought nothing to the table. So when I found Cain standing above her body, a small, terrible voice inside of me rejoiced. We were free.

I've never done well with the shackles of responsibility, disappointing everyone left and right as a child. After I lost my family to Raiders, I lashed out at anyone and everyone that tried to decide what was best for me. I had already let my family down, I figured it was better to not let anyone else hold any expectations for me after that. All I was going to do was let them down anyway, so I pushed them away. It wasn't until I began my training that anyone noticed me for anything other than the trouble I caused, and it took me years to work through my hate and find myself again. If not for my brothers, I doubt I ever would have.

But underneath all of that need lies…jealousy? I have no reason to be jealous. My brothers and I have always known we would someday share a mate. Not that this human could be our mate anyway seeing as she's, well, human. Hell, we have had no problem sharing other women during our time in this realm. Never have emotions been involved though, just another pretty face and a hole to get us off. Nothing more than a night expected from anyone. So no, that can't quite be it.

Envy? Yep, bingo. I wish it was me. It's a fine line between jealousy and envy, but it's the line I find myself walking on. I wish I was the one leaning so close that it would take barely any effort to lean forward and kiss her, to see if she tastes as good as her scent leads me to believe. To slide my hand back from her cheek, fisting in her hair and swallowing her gasp of surprise.

Her moans vibrating into my chest as her hand slowly slides further up my thigh, inching closer and closer to where I want her...
Damn it, I need to stop!

The scent of arousal fills the confines of the space, not all of which is caused by me. The thought of Raina getting riled up by nothing more than Cain's hand on her cheek just adds fuel to the fire.

Raina splayed out on her back, Cain standing above her head; pinning her to the bed with one hand as he toys with her nipple with the other while I bury myself between her legs. Tasting, teasing and sucking until she comes undone for us.

Fuck, I need a cold shower. Shifting in my seat, I can already tell that no matter where we are headed, we won't get there nearly soon enough.

Eyes on the human, Ser. They like it when you listen instead of thinking about all of the ways you can fuck them senseless.

"So Raina, where are we headed?"

"Does it matter?" she counters.

"You don't have a clue, do you?" Ryker drawls.

"Shut up, Ryker, nobody asked you," she snaps back.

"How have you managed to survive this long with zero planning?" he continues anyway.

"How have you managed to survive this long without someone stabbing you in the kidneys?" Raina hisses between clenched teeth.

"Who says they haven't?" Ryker continues to bait her.

"Enough, Ry," Cain commands, glaring at the Griffin.

I stretch out my legs as best as I can as I settle in for what is sure to be a long ride of endless bickering.

"So what about the body Ryker so carelessly left lying about?"

Ry stiffens beside me, but doesn't comment. Cain wipes his hand down his face in frustrated exhaustion.

"Did you at least cover your tracks?" Cain asks Ry.

He nods sharply.

"Cat got your tongue?" I tease.

"That wasn't funny the first four hundred times you said it and it still isn't," Ryker says as he rams his elbow into my side.

"Aww come on, better than the manticore having you by the balls!"

Cain reaches back to smack me upside the head and cants his head towards the sleeping child, reminding us to keep the fighting in check.

"It's just a broken neck. Chances are the humans will find him and assume he fell," Cain decides.

"Oh, *just* a broken neck? Is that all?" Raina sarcastically asks. "You're right; us silly humans trip over our own feet all the time walking down the street and break our necks. It's just another Tuesday in Denver. What's one more body on Main Street?

"Good, it's settled then," Cain beams, completely missing the humor Raina was going for.

She shakes her head and quickly smothers a smile that I have the good fortune of catching in the rearview mirror. Orders be damned, I'm not ready to give her up just yet. She'll have to remain under observation for the foreseeable future. For research purposes of course.

Chapter 14
Cain

"Would you mind stopping by our house on the way out of town? That way my brothers and I can grab our packs and not need to return." My words seem to make Raina relax a little, as though she hadn't fully believed we intended to accompany her. That, or she plans to drive off the second we get out. The latter is more likely with the way Ryker has been behaving.

"You know you guys really don't have to come with us. You said you had some job hunting… other shifters? So won't coming with us instead get you into trouble?" she asks.

"See!? Even the human has better wits about her than the two of you right now. Let's just drop them off in a different town and get back to tracking the Rogue from Fifth Street," Ryker interjects.

"Fifth Street…and what?" Raina slowly inquires.

"Our mission is of no concern to you, *female*," Ryker retorts.

"Well *dickhead,* it seems as though you were already failing miserably before I came along so I was going to see if my theory was correct and give you a clue. But you're right, fuck me and my help." The acidity in Raina's voice actually gave my chastised brother a moment of pause.

While Raina and Ryker figured out their next move, I repeated the conversation in my head, my brain tripping over 'fuck me and my help'. Oh how I would love to do just that. The visuals her statement created made any thoughts of a clue disappear.

My heart beat picks up as the blood rushes from where I actually need it. I am painfully aware of how close she is next to me in the truck, of how little effort would be needed to reach out and touch her. Earlier, as I convinced her not to send us away, it had taken all of my willpower to keep myself still. As I felt her cheek in my hand, her body so small compared to mine, all I wished was to keep this fragile, beautiful creature safe. To pull her towards me and smooth away the jagged edges that left her jaded.

Ryker's whispered words pull me from my musings. "Elm. Fifth Street and Elm."

"That's what I thought..." Raina takes a moment to reign in her emotions. She fights down the sorrow and it is replaced by a steely resolve as she continues in a somber tone,

"What is soft, small and full of light?
What goes on for as far as you can see,
during the day or night?
What contains hope and the promise of tomorrow?
The answer you seek; your joy, my sorrow."

Her riddle hangs in the air as the weight of her words settle upon us. Seros is the first to speak and I suspect he had the answer the whole time, using the silence only to process what it will mean for us from here.

"Skye." He whispers it softly, the name more of a prayer on his lips than an answer. He glances at the sleeping child beside him, a look of pity in his gaze.

Chapter 15
Seros

"That's where her preschool is. It's where she....where I....." her words trail off.

All the pieces start to click along with something that seems impossible. "So wait a minute Raina...that means that *you* were the one that killed that man?" I briefly recall the man Ryker killed saying something about that, but it hadn't fully registered at the time.

As I remember the human blood upon the sidewalk, I realize my previous theories were all wrong. It wasn't some formidable shifter that killed a man without a scratch; it must have been Raina's blood that was spilled. I knew it had to be a separate incident than the Jorōgumo since they lure their prey to their lairs before killing them, but I can't picture the woman before me capable of killing a shifter male.

"The adrenaline did most of the work. I know I should probably be all torn up about it, but honestly, fuck that guy. He got what he deserved in my opinion."

"Are you still injured?"

She then scrunches up her face in confusion, "I'm fine. A few scrapes and bruises, but nothing that won't heal."

My eyes rake over her, searching for the injuries she speaks of. She obviously can tell what I'm doing and puts me out of my misery.

"Only marks left are some bruises on my stomach and sides, they always take longer to heal than scrapes."

I lean forward, stretching my seatbelt to its limits and pull her shirt up to assess the damage.

"Hey! Hands to yourself!" she snaps, swerving on the road as she tries to jerk her shirt back down.

I ignore the blaring horns as I make to reach for her again, but Cain bats my hand away and shoots me a murderous glare.

"What do you think you're doin?" Cain whisper shouts, still making a conscious effort not to rouse the sleeping child.

"She's hurt!"

"And undressing a lady that doesn't wish it is a quick way for you to follow in her footsteps," he threatens.

"You guys are freaking out over nothing. It's a few bruises, nothing I haven't lived through before," Raina says in an attempt to ease the tension. Little does she know, a statement like that only makes matters worse.

I bite my tongue and shoot frequent, furtive glances in her direction, trying to assess her movements to see if she has been wincing in pain all of this time and I was too blind to notice it.

I desperately try to refocus on the conversation that got us to this point and the more I do, the more I can't shake my growing theory. So this would mean a Rogue must be after Skye for a reason which means...

"Raina I have to ask...Skye's father...is he like us?"

Cain's head whips to face her, his eyes a torrent of restrained fury. I can't blame him, anyone that would allow his females to fend for themselves doesn't deserve to lay claim on them; human or otherwise. Even Ryker leans forward slightly as he awaits her response, feigning disinterest that contradicts his actions. Huh. I guess my brother has more interest in the human than he lets on.

I should expect it, after the human female his father kidnapped caused his kingdom to fall to ruin, it makes sense why he is being such a jackass to keep Raina at arm's length. But no matter how hard he tries, it looks like he can't completely quell his curiosity.

"I doubt it. I think I would have noticed a giant flying snake if it was around." She scoffs in my direction, but continues to pay attention to the road, following the directions Cain gives when he indicates where to turn.

"Quetzalcoatl. And not every shifter is like me. Heck, no one else is like me." I preen a bit in my seat.

"That sounds awfully lonely."

The pity in her words make me freeze. No one has said that to me before. All I ever heard were praises for my abilities, jealous murmurings that I thrived on. And before the disaster with Amara, the council's desire to have my brothers and myself procreate as quickly as possible to replenish our numbers. Well, used to. Now it's just condemning whispers, but never pity. And she's...right. But once I found my brothers it was easier to seal those feelings away, to bury them deep enough I didn't have to face them anymore.

"I have Cain and Ryker. As the last in their lines as well, we have made our own family of sorts." I shoot her a small smile that doesn't quite meet my eyes.

She has mercy on me and chooses not to push. "So what other kinds are there?"

"Ryker here is a Griffin," I use my thumb to indicate the brooding man beside me, "and Cain is a Manticore. There are many more common breeds, people who turn into animals you are familiar with. Bears, wolves, lions, hawks. Mythological shifters are quite rare. Besides the Jorōgumo we faced the other day, I had not seen one of their kind in decades."

"Well besides suddenly turning into a damn bear in front of me, how would I know if Marcus was anything more than I thought he was?" At the man's name I stiffen. This conversation may be necessary, but it doesn't mean I have to enjoy it.

"Did his eyes ever flash a different color? When we use our gifted abilities, our animal side slips out in small ways."

"Not that I can recall, honestly. Why do you ask?" she asks warily.

"Well it would make sense that if Skye is a half-breed, her father might be trying to take her back. Whether to protect her or sell her is a different matter." I can't contain the venom in my voice and it seems Cain is having similar feelings if the growl he lets slip is any indication.

She laughs. She actually fucking laughs. My brothers and I share a look as we all contemplate the sanity of the woman behind the wheel. At this point we have arrived at the house, but none of us have made a move to get out yet.

"Well then at least we can rule that out. He died shortly after we found out I was pregnant- car crash." Her tone is flippant, so at odds with the subject at hand.

"I'm sorry for your loss," Ryker of all people pipes up, his eyes meeting her.

"Thank you," she replies in equal shock, "it was years ago, so I've managed to make my peace with it by now. A part of me will always miss him, but I've come to realize over the years that I mourned the life I expected and lost more than the man himself. I will always be grateful to him for giving me Skye, but even when I agreed to marry Marcus, a part of me always felt off. He never hurt me, but I don't think I was ever truly happy either. Just content that it was better than what I had known until then."

"Regardless, his family could still be involved. If they found out they had a niece or granddaughter out there, they would be fools to do nothing." With Ryker's comment, any sense of relief she may have been feeling vanishes as her face blanches.

"What makes you say they'd be fools?" Raina asks, shields firmly back in place after their surprisingly tender moment.

"Unlike humans, our society practically revolves around females- either in protecting one, or obtaining one. Women are rare, so those that are decent spend their lives cherishing and guarding their daughters. Protecting and loving our mates." His voluntary information catches me off guard. Wasn't it not long ago he was shooting daggers at Cain and I when we admitted what we were?

"And those of you that aren't decent?" she warily inquires.

I choose that moment to break back into the conversation. "They sell them. They sell off their daughters and sisters for a high price, thinking of only what they can gain from females they cannot mate with." With this she shudders, fear for her daughter at the forefront once more.

Chapter 16
Ryker

"That sounds awfully lonely," her words breech my thoughts and I feel Seros stiffen beside me.

I can tell her words struck a chord with him, just as they did with me. All those centuries ago I watched on as my family was slaughtered, high on bloodlust. But as it faded and reality set in, so did the silence; so all-encompassing that it attempted to suffocate me. The ensuing madness sank its claws into me and tried to tear my mind apart, the scars so deep that they remain to this day.

I screeched and wailed, clawing at the stone walls of the cave I still resided in days later. I raged and lashed out, sometimes with hands and others with talons, until I was blissfully exhausted and drained. That night I slept alone in the mountains for the last time, waking with the dawn to seek purpose.

The sound of feminine laughter pulls me back to the conversation at hand. It is a charming sound I have yet to hear from this frustrating woman and I must say, the joy on her face does something to me. I am not used to seeing miserable, sullen females and this glimpse of what could be has my chest tightening a bit.

Hearing that Raina's husband is dead fills me with relief. As much as I don't want to admit it, she affects me stronger than any human has before. She gets in my head and distracts me. I hate it. I hate that merely the scent of her arousal has me hardening. I hate that my brothers are wrapped around her finger, just a bat of her pretty eyes and they'd probably come in their fucking pants right here and now. It's pathetic. I can't even accuse her of trying to seduce and use us since she has been adamant in telling us from the beginning that we don't have to follow her, as if she has no clue the effect she is having on us all.

Gods, what is happening to my life?

A female going through a pregnancy and birth alone is unheard of, let alone having a daughter to raise alone. This woman has been through much in her short years it seems and a good part of it was spent unhappy. Her home appeared decent enough, but there were no luxuries to be found. Besides being left to protect her young alone, this female also had to provide for them herself. My Griffin's feathers ruffle internally at the thought and I bristle, angry at my beast for the reaction. It already has shredded my mind, now it takes over my emotions as well?

"I'm sorry for your loss." And I mean it. Her very presence may piss me off, but I can appreciate loss. The Gods know I've certainly had my fair share.

Her heartfelt reply catches me off guard. I have done nothing but butt heads with this girl and try to push her away since we have met, but here she goes sharing something insanely personal with a *dickhead*.

As Seros takes over my part of the conversation, I catch Cain's intense gaze in the rearview mirror. As the leader of our group, Cain has a knack for knowing just where our mindset is at, a skill useful in keeping us from flying off the rails at times. Under his intense scrutiny I hold my chin high, refusing to cower before him. Whether or not the situation truly called for it, the proud nature of my Griffin would not allow me to shrink away or submit.

He can see my disdain at our current situation. He heard the sincerity in my comforting words, so at odds with my behavior up to this point. He allows me the mercy of a tip of his head as he shifts to face the frustrating woman beside him instead, breaking eye contact and freeing me from the spell.

I turn to open my door, ready to head into the building and grab my pack. No matter how much this isn't how I expected my day to play out, I may as well come to terms with it. We'll be stuck with the pair of females for the foreseeable future, so I best figure out how to deal with it. Shutting the door firmly behind me, I hear a muffled "Thanks a lot, dickwad." Turning back, I see Skye stirring awake and walk faster into the house before Seros can start laying into me. He has really taken a shine to that little one and me waking her won't please him one bit. A small smirk pulls on my lips as I can just make out the returned chant of "Be a snake, be a snake, be a snake," and can picture the tiny finger jabbing at my brother's cheek once again.

Chapter 17
Raina

With a slam of his door, Ryker has Skye waking up. I mutter under my breath before facing my remaining company. Cain just stares at me, asking for nothing, but promising anything. It's the kind of look a girl could really get lost in. Seros is already having his face assaulted by the new wave of energy catnaps bestow upon children. It's oddly comfortable now with Ryker's brooding presence temporarily gone.

Seriously, what is that guy's problem with me? I haven't done anything to him! Hell, he was the one that wasted some of my hard earned money, so if anyone should be full of malice it should be me. Fucker owes me three dollars. He seems like the type to not care about cheap, trivial things, but with money as tight as it is right now, it rubbed me the wrong way and I'm having trouble letting it go even if it *is* rather petty. I see that fact for what it is, but am helpless to simply forgive and forget.

We sit there for a few minutes more before Cain deems it time to head inside. I give a half-wave, planning on flipping the radio on to try and fail to get Skye back to sleep, when my door opens. With confusion, I turn to my left to see Cain standing there, holding my door open. The door behind me opens and Seros begins unbuckling Skye from her car seat. Normally the thought of anyone else doing that would have had me filled with anxiety, but with these men I feel much more comfortable and at ease. It's pretty alarming. I haven't drunken anything around them, so I doubt they slipped me a roofie, or whatever predators are using these days.

"Umm...are we going somewhere?"

"Inside to pack, remember? You can't think we would leave you out here unattended?" Cain rumbles.

"Worried that I'm planning to ditch you as soon as you get inside?" What I thought of as a joke has both men stiffening.

"...Were you? I thought we agreed we would accompany you?" Cain's voice holds a touch of misplaced panic.

"No, not really, it was a joke. We can just wait in the car, it's no big deal. I *am* perfectly capable of sitting in a car without someone watching me you know, I've been doing it for years."

The men release a breath I didn't realize they were holding. "We know you are capable of it, but you shouldn't have to be alone. Would you please join us?" Well, when he puts it like that it's hard to refuse. Good manners are hard to come by these days.

"We can pack while discussing our plan moving forward. Who knows how long we might be driving? This will give you ladies a chance to stretch your legs and for us all to map out a course. Did you have a destination in mind already?" Seros stands beside Cain, Skye's hand in his as they await my answer.

I am already unbuckling as I admit, "Not really, I was just going to keep driving until something popped out as a good place."

Cain offers me a hand as I step out of the vehicle. I'm not used to chivalry this day and age and as I take his offered hand to hop down, I find myself not wanting to let go too quickly. My left hand is enveloped in his much larger one. The calluses cause a delicious friction and I find myself taking an involuntary step forward. The heat he gives off is tremendous and I find myself drawn to it like a moth to a flame, a self-destructive part of me wanting to find out if it will burn me alive. I'm starting to second guess that roofie debate.

Much too soon, Seros begins to lead Skye towards their house, which has my feet following of their own accord. While I may be unusually at ease around these men, I have no intention of letting Skye out of my sight. Cain falls into line behind me and I let his strong presence reassure me.

The outside of their house isn't anything special. A few cement steps lead up to a single story white house, the tan curtains drawn shut. So when I take a few steps past the threshold I pull to an abrupt stop.

Now normally that wouldn't be too big of a deal, but Cain was following close enough behind me that he now crashes into my back, sending me flying face first towards the floor. At least it's carpeted. Arms thrown out in a futile attempt at self-preservation, I shut my eyes as I brace for impact.

Either this is the longest fall of my life, or I'm missing something here. Cracking open one eyelid, I find myself hovering just far enough above the floor that my fingers can't touch. Collar tight on my neck, I turn my head to see, shockingly, Ryker standing there with a fist-full of the back of my shirt. On second thought, no, I shouldn't be surprised. He probably jumped at the chance to choke me out, or to save his nice carpeting from my bloody nose.

As he continues to glare down at me, I default to my usual response in awkward situations-I babble.

"Thanks for the impromptu choking and all, but this probably isn't the best place. And I don't think you're doing it right. Not that I think about that often, well, until now—ooph!" I pull myself up, rubbing at my face. "Geeze, what's the point of saving me from falling just to turn around and drop me?"

Ryker throws his hands up in frustration and stalks from the room. Pulling myself to my feet, I seek out Skye. She is sitting on the floor of the living room, playing with a pile of colorful rocks. I rush over to take them away and put them back wherever she took them from. "Skye, we don't just grab things that don't belong to us! I'm sorry you gu—these aren't real right?" Turning a disbelieving look over my shoulder, I see Cain and Seros watching us closely.

"Of course those are real gems. What use would we have for fake ones?" Cain asks in genuine confusion.

I take a moment to really take in the room, making my way back to the entryway beside Cain and Seros, the way I attempted to earlier before face-planting in the entryway like a fool. Artwork lines the white walls, framed in gold. Crystal bowls make up a centerpiece on every table I see, overflowing with gems of every hue. Dark wooden furniture fills a dining room off to the left side and a glance through an archway in front of me reveals a modern kitchen in a similar dark finish. The living room set off to the right has furniture centered before an impressive fireplace. A plush looking white couch, trimmed in gold matches the walls. Two recliners flank the couch, the black leather contrasting sharply to the room's otherwise bright décor. The glass coffee table in this room doesn't hold a bowl of gems as the others in the house, but instead it appears to be filled to the brim with golden coins.

Attempting to pick my jaw up off of the floor, I slowly spin around to once again face Cain and Seros, only to find Ryker must have returned sometime during my blatant perusal of their home. The only flaw to be seen is a few cracks stemming from a giant hole in the wall next to the front door and the carpet is in need of cleaning in spots. Mouth agape, I try to find something to say and find myself failing; apparently it just takes a nauseating display of wealth to get my brain to shut down. But when Skye once again tries to reclaim a bowl of shiny, expensive rocks for herself, I finally regain a semblance of composure, something I'm sorely lacking the last few days.

Taking the dish from Skye once more and putting it back, I turn back to the crazy, mythological men that apparently don't know the value of a dollar around here.

"What the hell guys? I'm not saying your house looks terrible or anything, but walking up I never expected something like *this!*" I exclaim while gesturing wildly around me.

"Ryker likes shiny things," Seros says with a shrug, as if that explains everything. "If you were going to rob a place would you target the wealthy mansion or the rundown old house? This is only one of several houses we stay in when we have to travel to the human realm for assignments, so it's usually sitting around empty. We travel too much to stay in one place for long and I'd prefer it not to be ransacked while we are away."

Making his way towards us, he places an overflowing crystal bowl in Skye's hands and she runs off to the living room before I can steal her prize again. "Thank yoooooou!" her small voice calls over her shoulder. Well, at least she has manners I suppose.

Chapter 18
Ryker

I catch her scent before I see her and realize Raina followed my brothers into the house. Of course she did. I can't even get fifteen minutes of peace before being trapped in a car with her again. Rolling my eyes, I head back to the entryway just in time to see Cain crash into Raina's back and send her flying. With preternatural speed, I race forward and grab the back of her t-shirt, halting her descent. I swear, how this woman hasn't knocked herself unconscious yet is beyond me.

The last thing I expect comes out of her mouth, startling me into dropping her. An image is planted in my brain from her ramblings.

A naked Raina pressed back into the wall, my hand at her throat to keep her pinned in place. Her dark hair framing her face as grey eyes darken further with need. A slight flex of my grip, not enough to bruise, but enough to let her know who's in control of her pleasure as my other hand reaches down to lift her leg. With no preamble I slam into her to the hilt, giving her the barest of moments to adjust to my size before slamming into her again. She cries out and I swallow the sound, capturing her mouth with mine as she writhes against me in a futile attempt to break free and regain control. But I won't let her have it yet, no. This woman has had too much control over me and it's time to balance the scales...

"Geeze, what's the point of saving me from falling just to turn around and drop me?" she gripes.

Throwing my hands up in exasperation, I leave the room to head out the back door, needing some fresh air. I stand outside for a moment to take deep breaths of the polluted air and collect my thoughts. Gods, I need to get this woman out of my head. Or better yet, out of her clothes. Maybe a roll in the sheets is what I need to get her out of my system. The sooner we finish with her and her spawn, the sooner things can get back to the way they are supposed to be.

With one last disgusting inhale to collect myself, desperately making me wish to return to the fresh air of our home, I return inside to see a slack-jawed Raina inspecting our temporary shack. If she thinks this is impressive, her tiny human brain would most likely implode if she ever saw our permanent residence. Not that she ever could, humans are forbidden to cross over for obvious reasons. Maybe I'll show her some pictures, give her an aneurism. That would solve several problems for me.

My Griffin preens at her stunned expression though. I think the infernal beast is genetically programmed to provide for its mate and without one he just continues to amass and horde anything of value.

She snaps out of her reveling to converse with Seros and the little girl runs off with a bowl of jewels. Normally, I would take offense at an outsider being bold enough to run off with a piece of my treasure, but for some reason my Griffin doesn't even bat an eye at the child playing with his things. Peculiar.

I continue into the living room to sit in my chair-yes mine- to the right of the fireplace which gives me a perfect view to monitor the child. The others may be content to let her wander from their sight in the house, but since the child is obviously a target and possibly a half-breed, I'm not as foolish. This is exactly what I mean; the human's presence is making my brothers become idiots.

I wonder what breed she could be. Traditionally, a laboring mother will shift and give birth in her more powerful form, drawing strength from her latent abilities. The child will be born shifted and revert to human form as soon as the mother does- able to shift at will from then on. In the cases of a male impregnating a human female, the child is born human and tends to only ever shift if powerful enough to do so. That is why so many such children are left in the human world, many never any the wiser to their lineage. It is possible that Skye may never shift, but the blood still runs through her veins if our theory is correct and that makes her just as much of a target. Whether or not she displays abilities of her own, the dormant power could be passed along to any future offspring.

I will admit she is better behaved than other children her age that I have seen. She sits there content to pour the gems to the floor, sort them into piles, and make pictures out of them on the floor. As though I am a puppet to a higher power, I get up and bring over the dish of gold coins from the coffee table and set it down next to her as well. I return to my seat without a word, content on my perch to simply observe.

Skye stacks the coins into piles as high as possible before they collapse in a jumbled heap on the floor. "You have a really pretty house."

"It suffices when we are here. I prefer the view from the mountains though."

"If I lived here I'd never leave. My house doesn't have many shiny things," she answers easily, her eyes trained on the treasures in hand as she sifts them through her fingers.

"I take it you like shiny things?"

"I love them." At that she turns to face me, her once grey eyes lit up an electric blue as her unwavering gaze holds my eyes captive.

"Hey...guys?" I call without turning my head. "I think we can officially say we're right and someone is hunting for a shifter child."

Three sets of feet come running to see Skye readjust her stance in front of her pile of treasure, guarding it with eyes blazing. Raina takes a tentative step forward, but Skye merely stands before her gleaming treasure, eyes assessing the three people that stand before her.

"Are you feeling alright, honey?" The mother tentatively asks her daughter.

"Nothing's wrong, Mommy. This is mine now. Mine to protect. Mine to play with." Skye's eyes remain a vivid blue as her voice takes on an ethereal echo. "All begins and all shall end, but the ride can't start without the tokens."

Seros chooses that moment to reach out and gently pull Raina back a step. At a loss of what is happening, she complies with little protest. Seros steps forward with his palms up in a surrendering gesture. Skye watches on, content at the distance still between them. When he takes another step forward however, she growls. Honest to the Gods snarls like a feral animal. It's rather small and pitiful compared to Cain's, but certainly not what we were expecting. Her face contorts into a mask of rage temporarily, but quickly smooths as Seros backs up.

Quickly retreating, the three end up clustered together at the entrance to the living room, unsure of how to proceed. Deciding this is as good of a moment as any to see if I'm good with kids, I let my instincts guide my actions.

Slowly rising, making a conscious effort not to make any sudden movements, I grab another bowl of gold coins from beneath the side table. It's good to have an emergency stash. I slowly walk towards Skye, prepared to announce my presence, but find no need for it as a second later she hovers right in front of my face. Yes, hovers. Golden feathered wings tipped in the same bright blue as her irises sprouted from her back with barely a thought, shredding through the back of her t-shirt and leaving it awkwardly hanging from her collar to cover her front. The flying, pissed off child is hovering mere inches in front of me, warily eyeing me with suspicious intrigue.

What the hell is this little demon?

I hold up the offering, her eyes flashing towards it in appraisal and back to my face in record time. Hoping my intuition doesn't fail me, I speak strong and sure. "I have brought a pretty treasure for you to add to your collection. A pretty gift for a pretty girl. Would you do me the honor of accepting this gift and allowing my friends and I safe passage to leave?" I'm not sure where the words come from, but her presence just screams *other*. With old blood lines, formalities can play a key point in diffusing situations. Respect plays a major part in any diplomatic scenario. At least I managed to learn that much before my tutor's throat was ripped from his body.

Her voice still has that haunting resonance going as she responds, the voice sounding little like her own. "Your tribute will be accepted, though you still have much to atone for, Griffin. It will take far more than this to purchase your soul back from the Devil.

She snatches the dish of coins from my hands and returns to her pile, wings receding into her back and eyes returning to their normal swirling grey.

A collective breath is released as the four of us adults exhale as one. I sidestep towards my brothers, eyes still trained on the tiny girl that proceeds to play as though nothing has happened. Seros ensures the front door is firmly bolted shut and secure, then we head into the dining room to discuss what the hell that was all about.

Chapter 19
Cain

"What the hell was that?" the fiery woman beside me starts off.

We all exchange a look, replaying the last few minutes over in our heads.

"Well at least we know our theory was correct. Skye is a half-blood without a doubt so my best guess is that her father's family found out about her and is trying to take her back."

"So where do we go? I don't have too much saved up so I can't just keep running forever." Raina fidgets in her seat as she asks. I hate seeing her worry about providing for herself, it goes against everything I was taught, even if she isn't one of our own.

"Don't worry yourself about that now, this is actually good news. Now that we know what they are after we can prepare ourselves for it. We just have to wait for them to come to us." Having a clear mission helps to ease my tension.

"So use her as bait? I don't think so." Raina's eyes flash in outrage.

"Think logically for a moment. You know whoever is behind this won't give up so easily. They will send others, no matter where you relocate to. They've already upgraded from using humans to a Jorōgumo, so who knows what they will send next? A female child is too precious to give up so easily. So we bunker down somewhere and when they come, my brothers and I will eliminate the threat." I lift a shoulder in a half-shrug, this will actually be easier than the way we have been chasing our tails these last few months.

"Using humans?"

"The building the Jorōgumo's lair was in had shifters and humans alike inside, I could smell them even from the office we met you in. It stands to reason that whoever it is has quite a bit of influence."

"Officer Samael...God damn it! He was the one that gave me the therapist's card. Fucking traitor..."

"Then I will find this human and behead him for you."

"What?! You don't have to kill the guy! He could very well be being used and not have a choice. He *did* seem rather reluctant to give it to me now that I think about it," she quickly backpedals.

"So you're protecting this male?" I can't seem to stop the warning growl from slipping into my voice.

"No, I'm just saying you don't have to go on a homicidal rampage against everyone just yet. I thought you didn't want to start a war?"

Seros butts in, "Guys, we're getting off topic."

"Right, why would you guys go through all of this effort to protect my daughter? We barely even know each other."

How cruel has life been to this woman that basic decency is cause for suspicion?

Ryker chimes in, never missing an opportunity to offend our guest. "Our mission is to return or eliminate Rogues. Make no mistake human, your presence here is tolerated because it benefits us, not because it is enjoyed. The second we have our target we will be on our way."

Why the hell is he being so hostile? It's not like Ryker hasn't taken his fair share of human women to his bed before, so what is it about this one in particular that brings out the worst in him?

"Speak for yourself," I spit the words at him through gritted teeth, finally fed up with his treatment of the woman, my blood becoming heated.

"Excuse me?" Ryker looks at me in surprise.

Instead of immediately answering him, I turn to Raina. "Would you please allow my brothers and I a moment to speak alone?"

She gives a slight nod and rises from her seat. Eyes trained on her as she heads to join her daughter in the living room, I'm gifted a lovely view of her ass in tight, dark jeans. My blood heats for a completely different reason now, but it isn't enough to dispel my anger.

"You may be miserable, but that doesn't mean I am. Even if the child had been human, I would have continued to safeguard these females."

"What happened to *'Let's watch them for two days and then be on our way',* Cain?" Ryker argues.

"Plans change," I grit out, trying to restrain my growing ire. "Especially now that the child is one of us."

"So let's take the kid to Caspian to decide what to do with. We don't need the human for that," he bites out.

"We are *not* killing a mother to kidnap her child, for fucks' sake! You should be ashamed of yourself; would you speak to any other female at home this way? Now that you have seen for yourself that the child is one of us, would you return home without a second thought if she had a home? Food? Leave her at the mercy of the Raiders should they discover her, in this realm or ours?

No brother, I have no plans to abandon them to fend for themselves." Silence follows my speech as my words hang heavily in the air.

Seros breaks the weighted tension first, "And don't think I haven't noticed how you watch Raina when she isn't looking. You may lie to yourself brother, but your actions betray you."

"...She's human. I can't. Not after everything th—" I cut him off, everything finally becoming crystal clear.

"You are not your father. Do you hear me? Your father started a war he couldn't finish, going so far as to bring a human into our realm which is strictly forbidden. You have done nothing of the sort."

"He changed. The human blinded him to the world around him; he couldn't even be bothered with Mother anymore. How can a human keep you from your mate? They are nothing but distractions. That's why we've always kept it to no more than a night with them when we are here. Admit it, you've both been more careless since they arrived. They will get us all killed," he presses.

"Why Ry, I didn't realize you had gotten so weak in your old age. Scared of a human? Need me to save you from the scary little girl?" Seros taunts.

"As if I would be scared of a couple of females! I'm just concerned that if we're all thinking with our dicks where Raina is concerned than none of us will have a clear head to keep us from walking into a trap. And what about when this is over? When we find the men after the child and dispose of them? If you aren't willing to separate the two, Raina will take her child and leave as soon as she has no further use of us," Ryker vehemently retorts.

"Or if her family is actually just trying to bring her home to protect her..." Seros grudgingly starts to see Ryker's point. "Raina would never let her go without a fight. They'd either kill her or bring her with them and she can't cross over. They'd keep her just to use her and use Skye against her. Even if they have an allegiance to the little one, it won't extend to Raina."

"Exactly, we will lose them either way. So no point in falling for a pretty face if we can't keep her anyway." Ryker grins, believing he finally won the argument.

"Ah, so you admit you want to keep them too?" With my smug words, the grin fades from my brother's face, but I choose to press on. "Just stop, Ry. Stop lying to yourself and lashing out at the rest of us. You know as well as I do that the council has not found any other female willing to mate us after what happened with Amara. And they never will. Why should they? I ruined everything for us...." I take a shaky breath to ground myself, but press on. "So you'll never repeat your father's mistakes. You won't cast aside your mate for the attentions of a human; you won't ignore your children for a pretty new plaything. So why not see where this goes? I personally have no intention of standing aside and letting them be taken from us without a fight, consequences be damned."

"Here, here! All in favor of keeping them around?" Seros asks the room, face alight with enthusiasm with his hand thrust into the air above his head like an exuberant child.

He really did jump on board with the idea from the beginning, didn't he? I chuckle, but raise my hand in support as Seros and I wait for Ryker's decision expectantly. He pauses for a moment, really letting the conversation play through his head and mulling over his options. Finally, he lets out a weary breath and agrees.

"Fine. We'll let this play out, but when it blows up in our faces expect me to be there with an *I told you so*."

Chapter 20
Seros

Hopefully now that Ry has started to accept the situation he will be less of a dick. He's always a pretty high strung asshole, but Raina seems to really draw out his inner dick. Snickering to myself at the poor word choices floating through my brain, I head towards the living room to check on the girls that have turned our lives upside down. I stride into the room and see Skye right where we left her, letting her newfound treasure run between her fingers. Raina sits on the couch eyeing her daughter, a pensive look upon her face. I plop down right beside her and throw an arm over the back of the couch in an attempt to lighten the mood.

"Well good news, Ra, we're keeping you."

"Ra?" Her face scrunches up in confusion as she turns to face me.

"Like the Egyptian sun God? It makes perfect sense really. You created the Skye, and you light up a room. Besides, there aren't a whole lot of ways to shorten Raina, anyway."

"You're ridiculous," she snorts in reply, "and that was pretty cheesy. You vastly overestimate my personality; sunshine and rainbows aren't really my thing."

I revel in the comfort and familiarity of the conversation. During our banter she has leaned back against the couch and into me slightly, so naturally I doubt she is even aware of doing so. The innocuous gesture has a smile tugging at the corners of my lips. As suspicious and defensive around us as she was before, seeing her let down her guard a bit pleases me immensely.

Good, our little human shouldn't fear us. We'll need to figure out a way to keep her safe while we're away. We'll also need to find more excuses to come back without raising suspicion. So much to do.

"No, Ra, you vastly underestimate it." We sit there for a moment or two in companionable silence before I feel her tense beside me and move away.

"What do you mean *keep me*? Who says you get to keep me?" she asks in irritation.

I frown in confusion, not understanding the sudden hostility. "We voted on it. It was unanimous by the way, in case you were worried about Ryker. Don't worry, he'll come around."

"I hate to tell you this, but you don't get to just *keep* people. What does that even mean? Keep me for what? Is it a shifter, human slave thing? If getting your help means agreeing to a life of servitude then forget it. I'll take my chances on my own." She huffs and stands up, moving to scoop up Skye-who has turned her ruined shirt into a kangaroo pouch to hold her horde- and heads towards the front door.

Panicking, I jump up to call for Cain, but he is already walking towards us. His peaceful expression is quickly replaced with confusion as he reads the room. Raina takes a step back, eyeing him warily as she asks, "Are you going to keep us from leaving?" Fear laces into her voice as she stares at the towering man blocking her path. Can't say I blame her, Cain is a behemoth of a man. Thank fuck he's on our side.

"We would never hold you here against your will, Raina," his tone belying nothing but naked truth and open curiosity. "But why do you wish to leave? Did something happen?" He turns to me for answers, but Raina beats me to it, twisting my words like she wants Cain to hit me.

"I won't trade our freedom for your help. I don't know what you mean to keep me for, but I'll have no part of it. So if you'll excuse me, we'll get out of your hair. No need to be our living shields, I've got this."

A hurt expression flashes across Cain's face, but he conceals it quickly. "Who asked you to relinquish your freedom in exchange for our protection?"

"Seros said you voted to keep me. I won't trade one set of kidnappers for another."

Awareness dawns upon my brother's face as the pieces fit together, turning his seething glare on me before finding a softer expression for Raina.

"My brother chose his words poorly, you misunderstand. The three of us agreed that even after the current situation is resolved, we will not simply abandon you as Ryker claimed. There are no strings attached, no deals to be had. You owe us nothing and are free to leave whenever you wish, but know that we will still be around even if you choose to do so. We still must hunt the Rogues regardless if you stay in our company. And as one of us, we still have a moral obligation to shield Skye from harm in the absence of her family's care. It's simply a matter of if we are protecting her from inside the house or out."

Raina processes Cain's words thoroughly, weighing her options. Finally, she comes to a decision. From the way she straightens to her full height before speaking, I brace myself for the incoming litany of complaints.

"You're right. I jumped to conclusions and even if I don't fully understand what's going on, being here is probably our best bet for now. I hate being in someone's debt though, so if you can promise me when this is all said and done that you won't stop me from leaving if I choose, then I will do what I can to help out so that we can call it even. I don't have much in the ways of funds, but I will pitch in what I can and you can send me a bill for the rest."

Wait...did a woman just admit she was wrong? Is this what it feels like when Hell freezes over? It's more temperate than I was expecting if that's the case. I let out a heavy breath I didn't know I was holding, her decision to stay for now filling me with relief.

"Bill? For what? We have no need of your money, keep it for the two of you." Cain seems incredibly lost at the direction the conversation has taken.

"Your security services. Food, hotel, or whatever. Who knows how long it will take you guys to catch these people?" Her sincerity is insulting, truth be told.

"Ra, the only services you have to worry about me providing don't come with a bill. They come with me." I shoot her a wink right before Cain's hand comes up to smack the back of my head.

"Will you shut up before you get us in trouble again?" Cain growls at me.

Rubbing the sore spot, I grin unabashedly at the beautiful woman before me, choosing to leave the room before I can inflict any more damage.

I make my way back to my room, taking the hallway that sprouts off from the other side of the living room. I'm grateful that Cain was able to talk her into staying. I almost chased her off and we haven't even had her for a day! I'm used to seducing women, not courting them. Thank fuck there are three of us, women are a lot of work.

I flop heavily onto my bed, the dark blue comforter cushioning the impact as I sink into it. Thoughts of the fiery woman that has much too quickly become the center of my focus run through my mind. Taking a deep breath, I attempt to clear her from my head, but it's futile.

The exhaustion from the past few days catches up to me quickly and I don't fight the pull of sleep, grateful it's strong enough to fight my racing mind. After a quick nap we can plan our next move, but I'm helpless to resist the temporary peace that claims me.

Chapter 21
Raina

Now that the confusion Seros' words caused are resolved, I'm anxious to make a plan. I've never done well with the unknown. As much as my days are usually uneventful-minus the usual frustrations or minor injuries- I secretly thrive on the routine. With the last few days flipping everything I knew on its head, I am more than ready to try and regain a bit of control back over my life. Though, his parting words caused me to choke on my own spit in surprise. I'm used to the flirting attempts of Elijah from work- though I guess I can kiss that job goodbye- and from the skeezeball at Skye's old school who stalked me home, the one that I am pretty sure ended up as that body the guys were fighting over.

I mean really, who does something as creepy as that? Was that reason enough for the guys to kill him? If they'd kill a human for something like that, how safe are we really with them?

What I'm not used to is the heat that flared to life at Seros' words. Instead of cool indifference or uncomfortable aversion, he stirred something to life. He more than likely is just a notorious flirt; he certainly looks the part, but that knowledge does nothing to cool my rising temperature.

I attempt to resolidify my thoughts and brush away all of the emotions to be practical. They've already threatened to kill me several times. While I may have a better shot with them than whoever is after Skye, I can't let my guard down completely.

Who's to say things won't change in an instant and they'll decide I'm not worth the trouble?

"Skye, sweetheart, what's going on?"

"I'm playing? I promise, I won't make a mess," she emphatically promises, completely missing what I was asking.

"No, I know that. I meant, are you feeling alright? Your voice... I don't think that happens when the other three shift based on their reactions."

"Oh, Mommy, don't worry. You can't forge the sword without the fire, but it's cool on the other side. I know how to listen, it's going to be ok and then you won't be sad anymore." Skye doesn't even make eye contact, focused solely on the gem she's rolling between her fingers.

"I don't have a clue what you are talking about."

Skye absentmindedly reaches out with her free hand to pat my cheek. "Patience, Mommy. You always tell me to be patient."

Sighing in frustration, I set Skye down to return to her game- if that's what you could even call it- checking to see if she's alright and finding nothing but a chipper little girl playing away. With a kiss on the crown of her head, I leave her to play while I try to deal with everything else. Would have been nice of Marcus to give me a clue that I might be raising his demon spawn, no matter how adorable said demon may be. I don't much care for being blind sided.

Turning to face Cain, I find him quickly averting his gaze. He looks down sheepishly, rubbing the back of his neck, clearly awkward.

"I'm sorry about Seros. He can be a bit too much at times, even for me. I'll talk to him about reining it in while you're here," he says as we meander our way back to the dining room, stopping to kick off my shoes by the front door.

I hope the display of comfort will help to ease a bit of his tension after how he reacted to the thought of me taking off. Not that I'm ready to confront that yet, I just met these men. Yet here I am, lusting after them like time means nothing. I desperately need a cold shower.

"No it's alright, I shouldn't have freaked out. You three, well...two, have been nothing but helpful and kind to me since the beginning. It's just that no one I have ever met does anything without getting something in return. I keep waiting for the other shoe to drop."

"I assure you," he continues, "no one will be dropping any shoes on you while I'm around."

The utter seriousness of his face pushes me over the edge and I double over laughing, only feeling mildly guilty at his expense. If you don't laugh, you cry sometimes and I give myself a little leeway to be slightly hysterical as everything starts spiraling out of control. It's a good way to pass off my hysteria so as not to end up as dead as the last human to cross their path.

I couldn't get this lucky if my life depended on it. Not just one, but *two* incredibly attractive, nice guys? Well, and one guy that probably *would* be attractive if he pulled his head out of his ass. I don't think I'd even know what to do with one.

As I pull myself back together, the last few chuckles die off in my throat as I take in Cain's heated expression. His eyes smolder with heat, the normally golden irises darkening. That's not exactly what I was expecting; I figured he would be ticked off at me laughing at him. The tension between us starts to grow so thick that I don't think I could wade through it to leave even if I had wanted to.

Wasn't I just lusting after Seros a minute ago? What the hell is wrong with me? Have I been alone for so long that anything with a dick is starting to sound like a good idea?

But any thoughts conflicting my mind vanish as his hand cups the side of my face, reaching his thumb out to trace a path across my bottom lip as my breath catches. Back and forth, his finger elicits a shiver down my spine and my eyes close of their own volition. His hand tenses in response, and I fear he's going to pull away. It would be better if he did, so as not to further complicate an already overly complicated situation.

Unconsciously, my tongue darts out to wet across my lips, catching his thumb in the process. Just as I'm about to apologize for licking him, Cain's mouth crashes to mine. Fierce and unyielding, he consumes me with his very presence. Where before his thumb stroked my lip, now his tongue darts across, seeking entry. Against my better judgment I comply, parting my lips to taste him, knowing I'm going to regret it, but stuffing the logical part of my brain down into the deep recesses of my mind. Our tongues clash and he releases a low growl from his chest, the sound vibrating into me and shooting straight down to the building ache between my legs.

As if he can sense my desperation for contact, he backs me up from the foyer to the table in the middle of the dining room. As he grabs my hips, I feel the heat of his hands sear through my clothes. He lifts without effort, placing me onto the edge of the table without breaking the kiss.

Screw it, I'm an adult. I can sleep with the bodyguard if I want.

Giving in to the devil on my shoulder, I part my legs and grip the front of his shirt, drawing him closer still. I practically purr in approval as he grinds himself against me, his obviously hardening length putting pressure right where I need it. I slip my hands under the back of his shirt, feeling the smooth skin and hard muscles beneath as I pull him even closer. The fire inside of me building, I begin to slide my hands up beneath his shirt over his taut muscles when....

"Hey, Mommy, I'm hungry," Skye calls from the other room.

Aaaaaaaaaannnnnndddddd cockblocked. Like I was tossed in the lake, the cloud of lust clears. I go to hop off the table, but Cain hasn't budged from his stance between my legs and I'm stuck in a compromising position, the rational part of my brain coming back enough to worry about one of the others catching us like this. Breathing heavily he stares down at me, his pupils blown large enough that his eyes are nearly completely black.

With a gentle push to his chest, he snaps back to himself, lifting me off the table easily and setting me back to my feet. His hands linger on my hips for a moment, but too soon he releases me. Taking a deep breath to collect himself, he speaks first. "Come, let's see what we have in the kitchen."

Ok not quite what I would have gone with, but to each their own I guess. Oh wait, food- right.

"Alright honey, hang on," I call out to Skye.

As Cain leads us from the dining room to the kitchen, my face heats with embarrassment as I replay the last few minutes in my mind. What the hell am I doing? I just met this guy, these *guys* and here I am sucking face and making myself at home. Obviously I've been alone for too long if a couple of sexy words and a face stroking has me this worked up and horny. Heck, maybe I just need to pound one out so I can think straight again.

A sharp intake of breath draws me from my musings as Cain's nostrils flare and he pins me with a look. Oh shit, I must've thought part of that out loud again. I really need to get a better handle on that.

Choosing not to comment on it, I bend down to rummage through his fridge. Expecting cold pizza and beer, I am pleasantly surprised to see it decently stocked. Trying to think of what I can make with minimal mess or effort, I begin to whip up a stack of grilled cheese sandwiches; a simple, easy staple when you have kids.

Rummaging through the cupboards, I pull down two plates; one for Skye's to start cooling down, and the other to stack up the rest. I may be nice enough to make extra for the guys-it *is* technically their food and kitchen after all- but that doesn't mean I'm going to give them the wrong idea and serve it to them. They have legs, I'm sure they can figure it out.

Leaving the stack on the counter, I take Skye her plate in the living room. I consider the fact that I should probably make her eat at the table, but with a shrug figure it will probably be better for her to not be there as we map out a plan. She obviously knows there is a problem, but I can do my best to shield her from too many details.

I head back to the kitchen, but find it empty. Frowning, I go to check the dining room and find all three men sitting there, eyes watching as I enter the room. Well that's awkward and uncomfortable.

Reaching across the table, I snatch up the last sandwich before they can take it. I made them, I should at least get one, after all. Though, with the size of these guys I probably should have figured they would eat like horses. After a considerable silence, I decide to take the bull by the horns.

"So what's the plan? You said we wait for them to come to us; are we going to stay here?"

Ryker is the one to respond, but not to answer any of my questions, like usual. "Thank you for making lunch."

Ooooooookay? Today is officially the weirdest day of my life. We've gone from three men bombarding me at my house to having an asshole act like a decent human being. Talk about whiplash.

"You're-erm-welcome."

Smooth Raina. Very smooth.

"This place is nice and all, but I think the safe house in the Rockies would be a better choice. Less people around so if we need to shift it won't be a big deal," Seros answers me, nostrils flared as his gaze rakes up and down. "Besides, it has a great view."

"Rocky Mountains?"

"Yes, have you been? They're gorgeous."

"No, but I've always wanted to."

"Perfect!" Seros turns to Cain for confirmation, practically bouncing up and down like a kid at Christmas.

"It'll take a few hours to drive there from here, so we may as well sleep here tonight. We will take turns on watch, three hour shifts, and leave just before sunrise." Cain leaves no room for argument based off of his tone.

"Ok, what time does my shift start?"

The three men pin me with a look before Ryker snorts, obviously unable to contain himself. "It doesn't. You cannot possibly think we would leave a human female to guard us as we slept?"

Seros and Cain shoot him a loaded glance, but it's Seros that turns to placate me. "Consider the three of us your bodyguards, so it is our responsibility. If it makes you feel better, you can start thinking of ways to repay us?" He waggles his eyebrows at me, coaxing out a laugh rather than be insulted.

"Far be it from me to object to getting a full night's rest."

With a plan of action in place, everyone stands to excuse themselves from the table. I expected everyone to go about their day for a few hours before bed, so I'm rather surprised to hear three sets of heavy footsteps follow me to the living room. I stoop down to pick up Skye's empty plate and check on her, but she is content being left alone for now, using her sparkling stones as teetering building blocks. I let her be and return to the kitchen to clean up the mess I made. When I turn around, only a few feet of distance separates me from three intense stares.

"Can I help you?" I demand, hand cocked on my hip as I stare right back, refusing to back down from whatever life changing news they are planning to spring on me next.

"You're still not panicking and your child just grew wings. I don't understand," Cain admits as he analyzes me.

"Compartmentalizing. Deal with the priority problems first, stuff down emotions to deal with later and then don't go back to deal with them unless you're ready for a good life-altering cry. I don't feel much like dealing with all of that quite yet."

Cain cocks his head and just continues to consider me, like *I'm* the strangest thing in the room.

"It's just...we aren't used to having a female around. It's kind of nice." Seros looks sheepish and glances away quickly.

My slight irritation ebbs away. "Oh, well...thank you. So, what do you guys usually do for fun around here? We have some time to kill before we need to head to bed." Maybe I should have thought about how that would sound before I spoke. That, or my subconscious enjoys flirting with the devil.

My face flames and I quickly search the room for anything to look at except the men in front of me. If I thought they were staring at me intently before, it's nothing compared to the smoldering gazes locked onto me now. What the hell have I agreed to? Maybe they're right, the revelations are leading to an impending mental breakdown.

"I do believe we could think of a thing or two to pass the time..." Cain's eyes burn molten gold as he leisurely looks me over; much like a lion would study a gazelle, moments before he pounced.

With the reminder of our shared moment not long ago fresh in my mind, my face burns brighter under his scrutiny, dishes forgotten. Doesn't he care that his brothers are literally standing right next to him? Of all the people to put me out of my misery, I never expected Ryker to be the gentleman that offered me an escape.

Stepping forward, he offers me his arm in a regal gesture. I waste no time in latching on, willing to accept the hand of the devil himself if it would pull me from the confusing intensity of this room. He leads me back to the living room, escorting me to the couch without a word. He leaves the room and returns within minutes, two books in hand. Handing one to me, he turns and perches in his chair, opening his book without a word to me or a second glance. I follow suit, opening my book without even checking the title first.

Hours pass by without any further incident from Skye and all of us hesitant to disturb her. At some point I must have resituated, stretching out on the couch with book in hand. I'd just reached a particularly interesting part when I feel my feet being picked up and Seros slide beneath, placing them back down onto his lap. I choose to ignore him for now, enthralled in my story and happy to escape the chaos of my life for however long I can. Avoidance and denial, my best friends right now. I make it about five more minutes before getting distracted again.

Seros has one hand on his phone, scrolling leisurely as the other idly rubs my foot. I can count on one hand how many times in my life I've had a foot rub before and still have fingers to spare. More than the act itself, the fact that it seems he is doing it absentmindedly has my heart clenching. How can I already be so comfortable around these men who are practically strangers? I've known these men for what, a day now? But time seems of little consequence as I take in my surroundings.

With Seros at my feet, a book in my hand to match Ryker nearby and my daughter playing peacefully nearby, I feel more at home now than I did in any of the years spent in that rental house with Skye. And if I were to truly admit it to myself, I feel more at ease now than I even did before Marcus died. Is it just because they are some sort of supernatural species? Their presence lulling me into a false sense of security? But if that was the case and Marcus was in fact some kind of shifter, why wasn't I this content around him?

Chapter 22
Ryker

None of my brothers have ever been as keen on reading as I am. So when I see Raina take to the book I offer without a second thought, my chest swells with elation that I try to temper down. Just because we plan to keep her around, that doesn't mean I have to get too attached. My brothers may think this will all unfurl with ease, but I'm not so easily convinced. Even if we keep her permanently, we can only see her while we are here in the mortal realm and she can't follow us home. She's upgraded from fleeting to temporary as far as I'm concerned.

We read in companionable silence for hours and I foolishly allow myself to begin to hope I can get Raina to see me in a new light, though I try and temper the feeling, lest I end up as pathetic as Ser. I've spent nearly every moment in her company pushing her away and trying to get her to hate me; so now that we've decided to keep the females, I have my work cut out for me to undo the damage. I'll be damned if we finally keep a woman around just to find myself excluded, no matter her semi-permanent status.

Seros makes his way into the room and sits with Raina on the couch, a bit of envy rising up at the casual comfort they share. But I temper it down as well. The best things in life are the ones not easily handed to you, and I have dug a bit of a grave I need to pull myself out of already.

Cain comes into the room to announce dinner and I rise first, but it isn't the pretty woman I approach, it's her carbon miniature. After a slight detour to the drawer of the end table, I slowly approach our newest mystery. I offer the small, yellow cinch backpack to the child, my face serious.

"If you're going to have your own hoard now, you'll need a way to carry it around. Unless you plan to stay in this living room forever?" She shakes her head and takes my offering.

I move to help her load the bag, but she turns on me with a sharp hiss. Hands up in a placating gesture I step back, not willing to push my luck. After her pack is loaded with every last piece, she secures it onto her back and looks up at me expectantly. For what, I couldn't hazard a guess. With a quirk of my brow I stare down at her in confusion as I wait for her to elaborate.

"I have to pee," she finally states.

Oh, hell no.

I turn to holler for her mother, but she is already there, taking her hand and following the directions Seros gives to find the bathroom. I lead the way to the dining room to await their return.

Cain has really outdone himself, no doubt in an attempt to show off. My brother definitely has a knack for the culinary arts and I'm grateful for it. If it wasn't for him my brothers and I would be living off of pizza and take out. The table is filled with a wide array; no doubt he was worried about finding something they liked.

The girls return and look at the table in awe. Skye moves to snatch something off the table, but Raina bats her hand away gently, reminding her of her manners. The little one sees something she likes and takes it, the camaraderie blooming in my chest. Maybe she is a fellow Griffin? No, the wings are wrong.

We take our seats and enjoy the feast until we can hardly move. The poor child is half asleep sitting up, her head lolling to the side and snapping up repeatedly. Seros notices her state as well and grins at me from across the table. My brother rises, making his way over to scoop her up.

"I'll put her down and you can sleep in my room," Seros volunteers far too eagerly, his gaze on Raina.

"Take the couch then, Ser. Hands to yourself," Cain decrees.

Pouting, he proceeds down the hall towards his room, Skye already asleep against his chest as he grumbles about hypocrites. With her shifter nature rising to the surface, she must be able to sense her brethren already. Otherwise I doubt she would have allowed my brother-a near stranger- to carry her so soon after her attempted kidnapping.

Raina rises, darting her confused gaze after Skye as she thanks Cain for the meal and begins to follow her daughter. Just as she is about to leave the dining room she pauses and turns back to me.

"Do you mind if I borrow your book a bit longer? I'd like to see how it ends," she asks a bit timidly, sounding nothing at all like the woman that threatened me with a bat earlier.

A sly grin encompasses my face. "Not at all, keep it as long as you wish."

With a grateful nod she makes her way to retrieve the book and heads towards Seros' room, my eyes helpless to follow the sway of her hips as she saunters away.

With a resigned sigh, I turn to Cain. "She's going to be a handful isn't she?"

He flashes me a devilish grin in reply, "Or three."

Chapter 23
Cain

"Time to go." I shake Raina awake, the little one stirring with her.

"What's going on?" she asks in a raspy voice still heavy with sleep.

"Apparently dead humans aren't as common as you led me to believe. It's all over the news and Seros assures me we need to get out of here, so wake up. We leave in five."

She blinks a few times as my words sink in, but to her credit she doesn't question anything further or fight. She and Skye are ready to go in precisely five minutes without a word of complaint and we hit the road.

The hours fly by without incident, only needing to stop a few times. Raina insisted we take her vehicle instead of renting one, much to my chagrin. The vehicle was a tight fit for us all, but Raina wouldn't budge. *'Money might not mean anything to you guys, but I can't afford to replace it when this is all said and done and I doubt you'll want to drive us back when I get a new place.'* The woman really doesn't understand I have no intentions of letting her go, but after her reaction to Seros I choose to bite my tongue.

I have been around many children in my youth, but the little one continues to take me by surprise. As her mother continuously fretted over her young during the drive, the child kept brushing off her concerns.

"I told you Mom, I'm fine!"

"So much has happened the last few days Skye, its ok to be upset or need to talk. You had wings for Pete's sake!"

I don't know who this Pete is they refer to, but I don't like him already.

"I like my wings, they're pretty. And everything is happening just the way it's supposed to."

"What does that even mean?"

"Patience Mommy, you always forget your patience. You don't trust anything, but you have to. The pretty kitty wants the bird, but first the cage must be broken."

Most of their conversation was lost on me, but it passed the time. By mid-morning we were pulling into a parking spot and I eagerly maneuvered out of the car to stretch out my cramped muscles.

The breathtaking view as we approach the base of the mountain will never grow old to me. There is just something about the massive mountains towering above, the stillness of the forest, that makes me feel small. That in itself is a feat. I inhale the sense of peace, letting all of my problems and worries fade away as I exhale. The clear sky, dotted with the occasional falcon and hawk searching for their breakfast, allows me to see for miles. The crisp air smells of pine and morning dew and I allow myself to just bask in the moment.

A hand brushes against the back of mine and I look down to see Raina sidled up beside me in my distraction. Maybe Ryker is right, I didn't even hear her approach. I'll have to be more alert from now on; I will never be able to forgive myself if any harm befalls the females in my care. It would truly destroy me at this point; there's so little left intact.

Determination washes over me and I begin to lose the temporary tranquility I had felt. But Raina remains content, oblivious to my internal musings, as she takes in the scene for the first time. I continue to stand beside her, letting her enjoy the scenery and calm while she can, knowing full well that moments like this are rare in life.

All too soon it is time to carry on. With a gentle tug of her hand, I lead her back to the SUV where the rest of our group is gathered and waiting, Ryker tapping his foot impatiently. Opening the back hatch, I divide up the backpacks, handing one to each of my brothers as I also grab Raina's suitcase.

"Well, let's get hiking boys and girls."

"Wait, we're climbing the *mountain*?" Raina appears surprised. Where did she think we were going?

"Well yes, it wouldn't be much of a safe house if anyone could just stroll up to it."

She sets her face in determination, but doesn't speak again as she begins to follow us, Skye's hand in hers. Once the little one begins to tire, Raina hefts her onto her back and continues on, keeping pace with my brothers and I. Hours tick by, but Raina never complains, though she does begin to slow a bit. I offer to take a turn carrying Skye or to have us break for a bit, but she adamantly refuses.

"You guys are carrying all of our stuff, I'm not going to make you carry us too. I refuse to be any more of a burden than I already am."

Gods, this girl. The corner of my lip twitches with a restrained smile at her independence. The majority of shifter females spend their lives being worshipped and coddled, so they mostly grow into spoiled, entitled women. It's a breath of fresh air.

We finally approach a smooth section in the rock wall, marking the entrance. I walk straight through and hear a squeak behind me. Sticking my head back through the concealment, I see Raina looking even more pale than usual.

"You just...how did you...what the hell?" Ever eloquent, this woman.

"A concealment, one we had to pay a pretty penny for, if I do say," Ryker explains.

Seros elaborates, "It's what makes this safe house so secure. Only someone strong enough to sense enchantments will be able to tell anything is amiss and even then they would have to be able to get through the rest of the traps to approach the house. But then they would have to face us, so really they would just be making their deaths harder on themselves." He winks and confidently strides through the wall to join me.

With only a brief hesitation Raina walks forward, arm outstretched in distrust of the illusion. She joins us, Ryker right behind her. The lights strung up across the cave ceiling offer enough light to follow the tunnel onward, deep into the heart of the mountain. We continue down the tunnel for a few minutes and when I approach the first trap I pause, waiting for the rest of my party to catch up.

Handing the suitcase to Ryker-as he glares- along with my backpack, I take Skye from her mother and place her in Seros' already waiting arms. Of all of us, she is most comfortable with him and we will need her to fight us as little as possible in the coming minutes. I then turn to Raina, worry halting my words in my throat. How will she react? What if she runs? What if she looks at me with disgust from now on, if she even stays? Swallowing my fears, I brace myself for her rejection.

"From this point on, we will need to shift and carry you to the house. There are too many traps to coach you into avoiding. Please," my voice drops to just above a whisper, "don't be afraid. I would never hurt you." I glance down as memories of Amara threaten to overwhelm me. How can I promise the woman before me such a thing? I *could* hurt her, so easily. She's soft and breakable, too fragile for what she's about to face.

A soft hand across the scruff of my cheek lifts my head to focus on her grey eyes, "I may not have known you long and it's probably stupid of me to trust someone so easily, but I do believe you will never intentionally hurt us. I'm more comfortable around you three already than I have been around anyone else in my life. So whether I'll end up regretting it or not, only time will tell. Shift away, Spartacus."

"Spartacus?" My brow wrinkles in confusion.

"Have you seen yourself in a mirror lately? I hate to tell you this, but looking like a gladiator doesn't exactly help you pass off as a human anyway. You look ready to wrestle a lion before you have even had your coffee."

With a smirk, I step back from her, missing her touch immediately. Her words make me chuckle, not even realizing how close she is to the truth. I take off my shirt slowly, maintaining eye contact with her as long as possible. I see her throat bob as she swallows and revel in satisfaction as I pick up on her sudden arousal, shooting Seros a smug look.

Aware of the child though, I turn around before slipping off my pants, leaving me in only my boxers. They may end up destroyed, but I can at least attempt to salvage whatever clothes I am able.

With barely a thought, my bones begin to break and morph and I relish the slight pain it brings. Maybe it's a sick, twisted sense of self-punishment, but the pain I feel in order to become my beast helps to ease my perpetual guilt.

My shoulder blades burn as my reddish-black, leathery wings burst free and I fall forward as my body morphs into that of a massive lion. Coarse, tan fur covers my body, but the shaggy mane that frames my face is that of my normal white-blonde hair. My spine begins to heat as poison spreads through my veins. With a sharp sting I can feel my scorpion-like tail bursting free, small barbs leading up to the tip. My claws scratch the stone floor and I shake out my mane as I settle into my manticore form.

Raina remains rooted to the spot, eyes wide, but she doesn't retreat. My eyes barely have to look up since I stand nearly as tall as she does. With a shaky hand, she steps forward and reaches out as if to stroke me, but pulls back at the last second, a question in her eyes.

In response, I lean my head into her hand and her fingers tangle into my mane. She lets out a soft sigh and continues to work her fingers through the hair with less tension.

With bold confidence, I butt my head against her rib cage-nuzzling and circling as I rub myself against her, marking her with my scent. She laughs at my antics and I doubt I've ever heard a more beautiful sound. The last time I heard that laugh I had nearly claimed her right there on the table, more beast than man. Her searing kiss as she came alive beneath me fresh in my mind, a low growl emanates from my chest. As if she can sense the direction my thoughts have taken, she leans down and places a gentle kiss on the top of my head.

"So how are you supposed to carry me like this? Do you want me to ride you?" I swear, she must say these things on purpose.

I crouch down to allow her better access. She settles herself onto my shoulders and Ryker comes over to readjust her so that she sits just above my wings before he quickly releases her and moves back to where he left the bags. Her legs drape down my neck and her fingers tangle in my mane to steady herself.

"Well I guess that answers that question," she chuckles, and I can just imagine the mischief sparkling in her eyes.

When a grunt sounds out, I turn to see Ryker clutching the backpack Seros chucked at him. "I am not a pack mule you know." His eyes darken to match his venomous tone.

"You're the only one that can hold things well while turned, so suck it up," Seros taunts.

Seros chucks off his shirt before arranging Skye onto his back, her treasure still secured in her pack, and playfully asks her, "Well kid, still want me to 'be a snake'?"

Her little hands clap out their excitement "Yeah! Be a snake! Be a snake!" she chants.

With a chuckle, Seros begins to transform. He forces his wings free first to keep Skye from sliding off, the silver feather tips catching the small, dim lighting. Scales shimmer across his skin as his body elongates, becoming a massive serpent. His face contorts, rearranging into that similar of a dragon, as he finishes his shift.

Skye pets his neck, incredibly at ease. "You're very pretty." She tightens her grip around him, securing and bracing herself as if she knows what's coming.

"How is she ok with all of this?" Raina asks under her breath in disbelief.

"Children are more adaptable than adults. They tend to roll with the punches better, so to speak, since they don't already have a preconceived notion of what the world should be. They still believe in magic." Ryker answers her anyway, picking up on her whispered words even from the distance between them.

"When did you become the wise one?" she asks him.

"It's not much of a challenge in this crowd," Ryker rolls his eyes and begins to change, not even bothering to strip first, so I turn so Raina will be able to witness it.

His hazel eyes flash gold as his lion tail flicks behind him, the bottom half of his body looking very similar to mine-though his fur is more gold than tan. He falls forward and catches himself on the talons that have replaced his hands, still gripping some of our bags. His short brown hair and elven features are exchanged for the head of a proud eagle, not a single white feather out of place. His sharp beak matches his fur and even with all of these changes it takes only one glance at his expression to know that it is still Ryker; even his griffin looks high and mighty.

His matching golden wings burst forth and he ruffles them out, folding them gently against his body. With a cock of his head, he keeps his eyes trained on Raina, awaiting her reaction. He may be the most opposed to keeping her around, but even he knows that you can only push humans so far before they break. I stalk forward, bringing her within reaching distance should she choose, just as curious to see if being surrounded by all of our beasts will finally be what it takes to break her. I settle down on my haunches as the two engage in a stare-off.

"Even your Griffin looks pissed off, Ry," she finally states with a teasing air.

Ruffling out his feathers with indignation, he turns, whipping the tuft of his tail across her face and causing her to sneeze. Eyes glinting with satisfaction, Ryker uses his talons to gather the rest of our bags and flies off down the tunnel without a backward glance.

I rise and begin to run in pursuit, gaining momentum to leap into the air. I feel Seros launch after, his lithe body cutting through the air and surpassing me in a blink. Raina clutches her legs tighter around my neck and her fingers grip my mane as I twist and turn, avoiding poison laced darts and pressure points. The narrow chamber forces any flying being to have to touch down in certain sections and one wrong step will release any number of miseries. Poison gas, a spike filled pit, a cave in, you name it.

I leap and crawl, fly and barrel-roll, until finally the cabin looms ahead. Seros and Ryker have already arrived, the latter returning to his human form to unlock the door. I release a breath as similar to a snort as a lion can manage at the absurdity. As if a lock will stop anyone that gets this far.

The two story cabin is our hidden treasure. This tunnel empties out into a mountain oasis of sorts, a humongous open grotto deep within the mountain. Illuminated in a subtle glow from strange plants, it truly is as magical of a place as we have ever been able to locate this side of the veil.

Veins of crystal snake through the rock walls, picking up the glow and reflecting it around the open space. Fresh water pools inside, fed from the ceiling above and twisting off to empty through a narrow exit. A soft breeze follows the path of the water, keeping the air from growing stagnant. Beside the small lake is the smooth flatbed we chose to build our safe haven. With as large as this space is, we were able to make it two-stories high and not come even close to the top. We have plenty of space to stretch our wings and roam. With the fresh water and a selection of edible vegetation we could stay here indefinitely if ever necessary. The only other entrances are where the water pours in from above, and where it trails away. Both spaces are so narrow that I doubt even Skye could slip through. Nonetheless, we rigged traps near each location on the off chance something figured out a way to slither through.

Rolling my eyes as Ryker unlocks the front door, I revert back to normal with Raina still perched on my shoulders. She lets out a startled yip, but my hands on her legs keep her from falling off. Turning my head to quickly nip at her inner thigh, I let her slide down my back. She straightens with a blush, her dark hair windswept and hanging loose down her back. I lean in, prepared to kiss her once again, but Seros slips in out of nowhere and my mouth lands on the back of his head instead.

Sputtering in indignation and eyes squinting in anger, I see Seros has turned around and is grinning in amusement. He dances out of my reach before I can throttle him, grabbing Raina's hand and pulling her into the house. She looks back at me with heat in her eyes and a smile on her face. Life is certain to be more fun now that she's around.

Chapter 24
Seros

I see Cain lean in to kiss her and who can blame him? That girl is sex incarnate. But it isn't fair for him to start a round two when the rest of us haven't even gotten a round one yet. Determined to win her over, I head over to steal her away. Cain glowers at me, but he'll get over it. If we really do intend to keep her, than he needs to learn to share after all.

Pulling her into the cabin, I lead her on a tour of our second favorite home. With no electricity, convenient appliances serve no purpose here. Even the lights we strung up in the tunnel have a hidden solar panel powering them. Instead of a stove, we cook over a fire pit behind the house. Thus, the kitchen is more of a collection of pots and pans, plates, seasonings, and some boxed or canned food we've brought back with us. The lounge area takes up the majority of the first floor, boasting cushions and pelts- it really isn't practical to haul a couch up a mountainside. We pass Ryker and Skye sprawled out on the floor as Ry attempts to teach the little one some type of card game, using coins as incentive. Lovely, he's teaching her to gamble already.

A small bathroom completes the downstairs and I lead the way up to the second floor. A hallway with four doors, I take her past the bedrooms and lead her to my favorite room in the house- the weapon's room.

Floor to ceiling, not a space is spared from displaying weapons of every variety. We spend more time in the human realm than other soldiers, so we have perfected fighting in human form over the years. Some are more practical than others- things like daggers, swords, or bows and arrows- but some are there simply because they look badass and I insisted. Flails, chain whips, maces, grenades, halberds, and even caltrops line the walls or on shelves. I tried to convince Cain to let me buy a flamethrower to add to the collection, but he shot me down. He's just no fun, the big mope.

Raina looks around in awe. Not all women appreciate weapons and tend to shy away from the violence they represent, but I should have known Raina would continue to surprise me. Reaching out to caress a golden bow, she pulls her hand back just before making contact. I've noticed her doing that a few times now- getting caught up in the moment and pulling back at the last second with hesitation.

"Why are you always doing that?"

"Doing what?"

"Wanting to touch something, then stopping yourself," I clarify.

She pauses for so long I think she may not answer, but then a soft voice full of pain meets my ears. She lets out a weary sigh and refuses to meet my eyes, focusing on anything else.

"You know, you're actually the first person to ask? I guess no one paid that close of attention before, or maybe they just didn't care."

I don't respond because what the hell could I even say to something like that. She takes the bow from the wall, running her fingers over it and toying with it to give herself a reason to avoid looking at me.

"My first memory is of sitting on the ground beside a brick building and all I could focus on was how cold it was. I couldn't have been much older than Skye at the time. It was raining, but I sat there anyway because I had nowhere else to go. I didn't know where my parents were, or where home was; I just knew I was supposed to wait. I sat there for the longest time waiting, but no one came. Eventually, I couldn't even picture my parents' faces anymore.

"After a couple of days I realized no one was coming, so I started walking, searching for something, but not knowing who or what it was. I stumbled across a young couple and reached out to them to ask for help, but couldn't find the right words. I didn't know exactly what I needed, just that I didn't have it."

She pauses for a moment, releasing a shaky breath. "The man backhanded me and I went sprawling on the ground as he left the *filthy street urchin* behind." My hands clench with restrained fury, but I don't interrupt.

"A few days later I was picked up by a policeman and taken to an orphanage since I couldn't give them my parent's names to find me, but I'd rather have stayed where I was on the streets. I may have had a bed to sleep in, but the people there were cruel. If you tried to take any food before it was offered, the women in charge would smack your hands and drag you off to bed by your hair without dinner. Same went for if you were foolish enough to touch anything around the house. It wasn't ours and that fact was made abundantly clear. We were allowed to live there, but far from wanted. Even our parents didn't want us, so why should someone else?

"What we were offered was just enough to keep us alive as it was, so the more you acted out, the weaker you grew. The other children were just as bad; instead of banding together, they turned on each other. If you fell asleep, they would steal whatever you had, so you had to sleep with one eye open.

"Once I was a teenager, things got worse. Any hope of being adopted was long gone by that time; people only want the little ones after all. After puberty, it wasn't your things you had to worry about at night anymore. But if the caretakers caught you fighting someone off you were both punished. They would smack us across the face and force us to spend a day locked in the basement for making their lives more difficult.

"One day I was called down to the main office along with a few other girls around my age, I was about fifteen at the time. There was a man there, saying he was interested in having us. At first I thought as the other girls did, that he meant to adopt us, but as soon as the caretaker went to lock the door, reality sunk in."

She trails off, trapped in a nightmare, and I give her time to work through it. At this point I'm shaking, my anger kept in check by sheer willpower alone, so it's best if I don't open my mouth to make things worse. Her fingers follow the lines of the intricate engravings, eyes unseeing and glazed over.

"I fought him off and even managed to break his nose. The other girls weren't as lucky as I was though. I managed to get away relatively unscathed, busting out the window of her office with a chair and running. I left the few things I had behind and scavenged on the streets to get by until I could find work. Nobody wanted to hire a dirty kid with no address or phone number to put on an application, so it took a while.

"Eventually I got a gig at a coffee shop and that was where I met Marcus. Three years later we were married, and I didn't have to flinch at every sound anymore. I had somewhere safe to sleep and there was always food in the house. They were the easiest years of my life. But then it all came crashing down when he died and I had somebody to protect now.

"Growing up in Georgia was no picnic; there's a reason they sing about the devil down there and it has more to do with the residents than the location. I pretty much picked out our new home at random, closing my eyes and jabbing my finger onto a map. Once I opened them, it just felt right. Figuring it had to be better than this hellhole, I went for it.

"So I moved to Colorado, got a job at a bookstore, and raised Skye." A single tear slips down her cheek as she rushes through the end, clearing her throat.

"So to answer your question with a long-winded response, that's why I flinch. I was never allowed to touch things before without being punished and even after a decade, old habits die hard." She shrugs as if it were no big deal. "Sorry if it annoys you."

I yank her towards me and hold her so tightly that I worry I'll crack her ribs, but I can't let go. I clutch this girl to me as if she were a lifeline when it should be the other way around. I wish I could hold her close forever and shield her from anything that dares think to make her suffer like that again. I feel my brothers enter the room and realize they must've been listening from the hallway. Cain moves to embrace her from behind, jaw clenched so tightly I worry it'll snap.

Ryker awkwardly pats her shoulder, unsure of how to offer comfort. Not that I have any damn clue how to respond either in this case. I'm not sure how long the three of us stand there like that, but I'll be damned if I'm the first to pull away. It's Raina though that squirms for release, wiping at the silent tears that trail down her face in a quick attempt to hide the fact she was crying.

"Sorry, sorry. Here you three are trying to help us and I make things awkward."

Red rimmed eyes look up to me and I feel my heart cinch tighter in my chest. Gods, but this woman has me already. I would take on the Devil himself if it would make her smile. If there were any thoughts before of returning home without her, they'd be gone now. I lean down to place a chaste kiss on her lips, holding the contact for only a heartbeat before pulling away.

"Don't ever be sorry. Especially not for the actions of others."

Running my hand through my hair until it's sticking up in every direction, I try and collect my tumultuous feelings. Heading downstairs, I settle in next to our newest resident shifter, still no clue as to what she could be. With the wings and treasure hoarding, my best guess would be Griffin or possibly some mixed breed of dragon.

"Hey kid, want to teach me that card game?"

"Okay!" she exclaims in excitement.

We stay like that for a while-it's hard to tell time without the sun or clocks- until our hunger has us raiding the kitchen. Settling on my hidden stash of cookies, we head back to lounge on the cushions. We eat in silence, the others still upstairs, until she finally speaks; when she does, my heart just about breaks after already being through the wringer.

"You'll take care of mommy right? When I leave?"

"Leave? Skye, what do you mean?"

"I'm different now, I scared everybody. The bad people want me back because I'm bad people too." She says it with such honest sincerity that I'm pretty sure my jaded old heart is going to mutiny after making it feel so much after all these years of neglect. These girls will be the death of me.

"Sweet girl, no. You're not a bad person, you're like me. I won't let the bad people take you from us. Cain, Ryker, your mom and I won't let that happen. You remember what I did to that spider? I'll always protect you, if it's the last thing I do." I reach out to pull her into a hug, but whether it is for her or me I can't tell.

"The kitty? And the angry bird?"

A sharp laugh escapes me. "Yeah kid, kitty and angry bird. You're one of us now and we protect our own."

I distinctly remember her calling Ryker 'Griffin' during her freak out over her treasure horde. Maybe whatever happens when that creepy voice thing happens, she's not really aware of?

"So I need to learn to fight too? So I can save you guys?"

A huge smile breaks the tension of the room. "You sure do! The angry bird is always getting into trouble and it's up to us to help him."

With a fierce look I'm sure she inherited from her mother, Skye stands and raises her tiny fists. She punches and kicks the air until falling on her butt and we both erupt into cathartic laughter. She breaks into a huge yawn and it dawns on me just how much hiking she did today before needing to be carried.

"Come here little warrior princess, you need some rest. You can't learn to fight if you can't even keep your eyes open." I rearrange the cushions and pelts to make a comfortable spot to recline and let her lean against my side in the crook of my arm.

"I don't mind summer, but forever is too long to burn," Skye mumbles, half asleep already.

One minute the kid and I can carry on a complete conversation and the next she's spouting nonsense. Whatever this poor girl is going through, I pray her mind is strong enough to survive it. I've never heard of a half-breed finally shifting only to have her mind torn apart during the process, but I've also never heard of them only partially shifting either. We had better figure out a way to get her to finish her shift soon in case that has anything to do with it.

I run my hand over the top of her head, smoothing her hair until she starts softly snoring. Raina stands at the base of the stairs, leaning against the wall and just watching.

Stretching out to get more comfortable, I open my other arm in invitation as I look at Raina with one eyebrow raised. She hesitates briefly, but ultimately crawls towards me and situates herself in the crook of my other arm, her head lying on my chest and her arm draped across my stomach to gently rub circles on her daughter's arm. I lower my hand and it brushes against Raina's hip, tugging her closer.

It's been far too long. My people used to be very fast and loose with affection, tending to naturally congregate and sleep together for warmth. We're attracted to the body heat and rarely slept alone. As our numbers diminished and with the loss of my family though, all of my nights have been cold. We never keep the human women for more than a brief one night stand, never letting our guard down or caring enough to stay the night. Even if we would have considered it, Ryker would have lost his shit. So this right here? Soothes a part of my soul I had buried too deep to remember was suffering.

After some time, I feel her hand still and the gentle rise and fall of her chest, her breathing steady against me. Raina didn't make it long either before she succumbed to the sandman's lure. With the unfamiliar comfort, I drift off to sleep, sleeping deeper than I have in years as I follow them into peaceful oblivion.

Chapter 25
Raina

I wake up and take a minute to orient myself. A steady rise and fall beneath my cheek, my hand on warm muscled skin. I glance from the corner of my eye and see my hand must've slid up Seros' shirt at some point during the night.

What the hell am I doing?

I disentangle myself slowly so as not to wake him and peek over at Skye. Pleased to find her still asleep, I tiptoe my way outside. I have no way of knowing what time of day it is, but the peaceful calm reminds me of just before dawn rises while the rest of the world sleeps.

I make my way to the edge of the pond, settling myself on the smooth expanse of rock and letting my legs dip into the cool water. Time ticks by, minutes and hours meaningless here. It's like we are in our own little world, away from the struggles of life.

I sense someone approaching behind me, but I don't even startle this time around. Whatever the reason, I'm done worrying about it. Whether or not I understand what I'm doing, I've given up the thought of them turning against us if I'm not careful. These men feel like...home. A sense of ease settles around me whenever they are nearby that I'm not used to, that I've never felt before. They've never given me a reason to think they might hurt us, not even Ryker-the pompous-butt-munch-, and now that Skye is one of them, I'm confident that they will do whatever they can to at least keep her safe. That's enough for me.

As if summoned by my thoughts, Ryker sits down beside me, keeping his feet clear of the water. I wonder if that's because of the being part-cat thing? Even though half of the time spent in his presence has been in hostility, he appears to be making more of a concentrated effort to not be such a tool. We sit in comfortable silence and absorb the serenity before us, each lost in our own thoughts. After a long stretch, I'm the first to shatter the peaceful illusion.

"Do you ever feel like it's just too much?"

"What is?" He asks as his hazel eyes fill with cautious curiosity.

I shrug, "Life? It's just...too much. It's overwhelming. It's like no matter what you do or how hard you try, it's never good enough. No matter how many monsters you kill, two more take their place. No matter how good a person tries to be, they still die before their time. We spend our whole lives fighting either the world we were born into, or internally against ourselves. We live, we struggle, we die. What's the point? I just found out there's an entire secret society of people who can change into animals and I'm barely even surprised. Life loves to throw curveballs at you just when you get comfortable, like a giant cosmic 'fuck you', just because it's bored."

He doesn't answer at first, just takes my hand and tugs me against him, capturing my mouth in a fierce, bruising kiss. It's over just as suddenly as he pulls back and practically shoves me away from him in disgust, leaving me surprised and confused. He releases my hand as if it burned him and leans back to stare at the roof of the cave high above us.

Ryker hasn't exactly been shy in making his distaste of me known. Sure, the last day he hasn't been too much of an ass, but

I figured that was more of Cain's doing than anything else. Now the tingling feeling on my lips has me questioning which way is up since my world is flipping upside down. I'm getting closer to that impending breakdown every day and I'm not sure what kind of person I'll be when I pick myself up afterwards.

The gold flecks in his eyes blaze bright, nearly overshadowing the swirling green and brown of his irises. With a sigh, he finally answers and it takes me a moment to recall what I even asked.

"Nearly every day. Every day I fight to keep my Griffin from taking control, sometimes I struggle to even change back. Some days I don't know why I even bother resisting him-things are easier when I'm like that. I don't need to worry about anyone else, there's no existential crisis and I can just let go. I can stop being *me*."

His tortured expression kills me, feeling his pain, but he remains steadfast in his perusal of the rock and continues, adamantly refusing to meet my eye. The crack in his carefully constructed mask reveals nothing except for raw pain and aching wounds.

"But then I'd miss moments like these, the ones where someone is willing to listen and helps to ease the internal torment. Sometimes you need to just not be alone and it makes a world of difference in shouldering your burdens. And if the misery can be lessened, then it can be replaced with something else; something akin to purpose, something worth fighting for. If you have a reason for being, you can focus on that to distract yourself from the pain.

"You're not quite what I was expecting, but that's not necessarily a bad thing. You're not alone now, Nymph, my brothers and I will help shoulder your burdens."

The endearment throws me, not understanding how we got here suddenly when five seconds ago he shoved me away from him like I was disease ridden.

Not wanting to ruin the moment, but unable to stop myself from asking, "Don't you hate me though? Why would you want to ease my troubles when just days ago you made it clear you wanted to get rid of me as fast as possible?"

"I don't hate *you,* I hate what you represent. Hope; a chance for my brothers and I. In my experience, hope is an incredibly dangerous thing and mortals are far too breakable. My brothers are choosing to ignore that."

"A chance for what?"

When he does answer, it's just above a whisper, so quiet that I'm not sure I heard him correctly. "...forgiveness."

As I consider his words, feet swishing in the cool water, I consider how much my life has changed over the last week, and it hasn't all been for the worse. Chaotic sure, but not necessarily completely terrible.

"We got off on a bad note and I take full blame for that. Give me a chance to explain?" Ryker asks, refusing to meet my eyes still.

I nod, but quickly realize he isn't watching me so I make a murmur of agreement, settling back on my hands to try and get comfortable. Ryker takes a harsh breath, no doubt working up the nerves to say whatever it is he wants to say.

"There is a reason the Griffin Kingdom was coveted and constantly attacked- our beasts have a hoarding problem. Anything shiny catches our eye and we must have it, consequences be damned. Jewels and treasure filled our halls, so we constantly had to be wary of thieves. Our bloodthirsty nature quickly settled into our bones, the trait passed on through the generations.

"One day we went too far. My father, Zeid, came home one day, a pretty young woman clutched in his talons. Hair of spun gold reflected the sunlight, her white dress giving the impression of an angel. I remember it as if it were yesterday because that angel heralded the beginning of the end.

"It wouldn't be long before we would come to realize that the pretty female my father snatched was the daughter of another land's king. The illegitimate offspring half human, the girl had no abilities to call upon to save her from my father. I was born to three fathers, but once Brice and Adrien learned of my father's infidelity to their mate they fought against him, only to lose to cheap tricks and low blows they never thought Zeid was capable of.

"Zeid toyed with her for weeks; my mother, siblings and I cast aside in favor of his shiny new toy. Caught up with her as he was, my father was too distracted to see the attack before it came. Fire rained down from above, feathers incinerating and preventing escape by flight. My brothers tried to protect Mother in my fathers' absence- but they were no match for an army of dragons.

"Though half human with not enough power to ever shift, no king would stand by as his blood was stolen from him, human bastard or not. Chaos reigned as all who faced the onslaught perished. But I was petty and spiteful, more so back then. I saw the attack coming from my position in the mountains, I could have warned him. But no, I wanted father punished for prizing a human more than his own blood. If his blood matters so little to him, let his spill. Let it coat the land and paint it with his sins."

Hesitantly, I reach over and cover Ryker's hand with my own, offering silent comfort that I'm not sure he even wants. When he doesn't immediately pull back, I take that as encouragement to leave my hand there, but don't push for anything else.

"I retreated into the labyrinth of caves in the mountainside, watching from afar as they were all slaughtered. Blood poured across the earth, watering the land. 'Let the flowers bloom red in the wake of destruction,' I decided, as if I were the authority on such things. A load of horseshit. I would be the king of nothing and damned myself to become the prince of nothing but betrayal and bloodshed.

"What they said was certainly true, our bloodlust was passed down through the generations, but instead of dwindling away as it diluted over time, it festered."

He finally turns to look at me, pleading with his eyes for me to understand. "I'm a monster, Raina. Not the sort that goes bump in the night, but the sort that will walk up to you in broad daylight and tear your throat out without a hint of remorse. Why on Earth would you choose to stay in our company?"

I have the distinct feeling that the next words I choose will be pivotal in my standing amongst them, at least in his eyes.

"You're not the only one with blood on your hands, Ryker. If you're a monster for killing without remorse, then so am I. Just a handful of days ago in fact. Now I at least know *why* you've been acting like a jackass, but that doesn't give you free reign to be one. Unless you at least try to do better, you're simply making excuses. A shitty upbringing doesn't excuse shitty behavior. You recognize it, so you have the ability to rectify it. So I'll stay for now because I really don't think you're as much of a monster as you believe yourself to be."

The break in his armor seemed to only last a few brief moments, gifting me a glimpse behind the chilled facade he had kept rigidly in place up until now. A coat of ice I now understand is worn to numb the pain that never seems to abate.

Instead of sneering or scoffing at me, a slight hint of a smile graces his features briefly. "Well, Raina Adams, here's to shattering preconceived notions." He tilts his head in understanding and it feels suspiciously like I passed some sort of test that I was unaware I was taking. But all good things must come to an end, even ones riddled with confusion.

A loud explosion rings through the air and Ryker tackles me to the ground, lying on top of me to shield me from the falling debris as pieces of rock break loose from the ceiling and tumble down along with an onslaught of dust. Our eyes lock momentarily before we are scrambling up, racing towards the house. Cain is already barreling out the door, eyes frantic as he searches for us. Once he spots us, he lets out a breath of relief and ushers us inside, placing his hand on my back when I'm close enough to pull me in the rest of the way. I hurriedly seek out Skye, finding her in Seros' arms, burrowing her face into his neck. His eyes bright silver and flashing with his anger, he quickly checks me over and looks to Ryker for confirmation.

"She's fine. The girl?" Ryker asks, tone clipped and all business.

Seros nods, but the increasing testosterone flooding the room screams that they aren't too happy with anyone daring to attack their home. All three men fall into battle-ready mode instantly, something I wonder how much practice it took to perfect. I move to stand by Skye and Ser, feeling like deadweight and hating it.

Cain takes charge, expecting immediate compliance.

"Ryker, gather intel. Fly out there and see what we are dealing with." With a sharp nod, Ry is off. "Seros, you'll stay here with the females. Keep them out of the line of fire." They lock eyes, a thousand words seeming to pass between them.

"What can I do?"

Cain doesn't even hesitate as he responds, "If Seros falls, grab Skye and run. We'll find you."

I hate that my role is to abandon ship, but at least I was given a task more than 'sit there and look pretty'.

"And what about you?" I ask. He takes a step towards me, letting the back of his fingers trail down my cheek.

He replies with a wicked smirk, "I'm going hunting."

Chapter 26
Cain

Shutting the door firmly behind me, I charge forward, my body breaking and knitting itself back together. My paws stir up dust as I run, my clothes a tattered memory destroyed as easily as our temporary peace. Adrenaline floods my system as I leap over rocks and water in my pursuit of Ryker. He returns to me moments later, shifting as he still hovers ten feet in the air and lands at my feet gracefully. The downside of losing our human form is losing the ability to speak to one another. After all of these centuries together we have learned many ways to communicate without switching back and forth, but some things are quicker to just say.

"About fifty feet down the tunnel, at least a dozen men. Two bears, a falcon, tiger, wolf and the rest still in human form." Report finished, he shifts back into his Griffin.

We brace ourselves, hearing assorted traps set off and smiting a couple of the un-shifted humans. Idiots. The falcon breaks through first and Ryker is off like a jet after him. The bear shifters lumber through in tandem and once they spot me they start running forward, murder in their beady, black eyes. I pounce onto the larger of the two, jaw clamping around his throat and tearing. Blood coats my nose and mouth, the scent spurring on my savagery.

I'm tossed to the side as large paws swipe me off of my enemy's kin. Rolling to my feet I tense up, raising my tail and ready to strike venom into the bear's belly. Pain explodes in my side as sharp teeth sink into my flesh, sinking deep through the layers of muscle. Blood coats the striped beast's muzzle as I shake him off. We tangle in a flurry of claws and limbs as my attention is pulled to the new, more dangerous threat. A snarl is ripped from my throat as I am finally able to sink the tip of my tail through his hide, pumping venom through his body until he drops; dead as suddenly as he arrived.

Wasting no time, I am once again on my feet assessing the area, ignoring the pain lancing through my side along with the steady stream of blood slickening the ground beneath my paws. Ryker is engaged with the other bear and I am grateful for the momentary reprieve to allow my wounds a chance to close, willing the process to hurry the fuck up. Human shaped bodies litter the floor, dead before they had the chance to shift, though some of the blood is positively human; Ryker most definitely is not playing around today.

Not to be outdone, I take a running start and launch into the air, my leathery wings hoisting my heavy beast into the air, coming down on the back of the remaining bear. Pushing his face into the stone, I sink my teeth into his neck and jerk, effectively breaking his neck. His body goes limp, all fight in him gone.

Ryker and I face each other, doing a mental tally of the felled intruders. As though it dawns on us at the same time, we whip around to see the wolf busting through the door of the cabin. With inhuman speed, we race back to where Seros and the girls are cornered, fear pulsing ice through my veins. With every beat of my wings and heavy footfall churning up dust beneath me, I will myself to push myself just a bit faster. A wave of power assaults me, alerting us to Seros' transformation as he fends off the beast.

It's a tight fit with us all crammed inside, so I shift back, worried about adding new fuel to my nightmares. I can't effectively use my beast in these tight quarters without risk of injuring those I care about, nor am I willing to risk it.

Nothing could have prepared me for the scene unfolding before me, and I've seen plenty of incredible things in my many years. I expected to see Seros in serpent form, his Quetzalcoatl coiled around the females as he struck down the wolf with his fangs or something of the like. But no, my brother remains in human form with Skye tucked behind him against the wall, frozen in place. Not even a breath or a blink as he remains paralyzed.

But that isn't even the biggest source of shock. The wolf is also frozen…midair. Paws outstretched and muzzle wide in mid-attack, chest not even rising or falling as his snarl is frozen on his face. Standing before him is the most beautiful creature I have ever seen.

On all fours, Raina faces the wolf with her once grey eyes now a bright electric blue. Long dark hair gently billows behind her, at odds with the stillness of the room. Her torso remains human until just below the swell of her breasts, coarse fur of a lioness similar to mine covering her nipples and extending down to cover the rest of her body. The exposed human skin is tattooed with golden hieroglyphs that shine brightly in the dim lighting. Her arms gradually morph at her elbow and legs have been replaced with paws like mine, though her tail still has a tuft at the end like that of a natural lion. Feathered wings are spread out behind her, primarily golden with accents of the same bright blue of her eyes tipping each feather, the same as Skye's.

I've heard tales, but I never before have seen one with my own eyes, thinking like the rest of our world that they had gone extinct long ago. A Sphinx. Rumors of their abilities have circulated, blending fact and myth until no-one knows the truth anymore. But I guess we can at least say for certain now that they have the ability to freeze time for short bursts.

I stare at Raina in awe, trying to piece together everything I know about her. The riddles, how she managed to kill a man with no skills besides adrenaline. How could she not have known? How could a creature as strong as hers lie dormant for so long? Skye's freak out protecting her treasure triggered her own shift, so is that what it took for Raina? The threat to her daughter causing her protective nature to flair to life? Why wouldn't that have happened before?

I feel the energy shift as Ryker emerges behind me, human as well. I want to turn to see if he has the same stunned expression I know I must be sporting, but I cannot tear my eyes away from the mythical creature in front of me. Unlike my brothers and me, Raina retains the use of her human tongue.

As she speaks, her voice echoes with ethereal resonance, much like Skye's had done. "Who sent you here? Where can they be found?"

The wolf then lets out an inhumane shriek of agony as he is forced to shift midair. Instead of the usual, naturally smooth transformation, his body spasms and jerks as his bones crack and break, seemingly shoved into their new positions by force.

Gods, how powerful is *this woman?*

As the lupine figure gives way to a panting, sweating man, I stride forward to hold his wrists in restraint. Now that his paralysis has been lifted, I don't want to risk his attempt at retribution.

He is lanky, black hair in need of a trim and smaller than Ryker. I am able to restrain both of his wrists in one hand as the other comes up to grip his sneering face.

"I do believe the lady asked you a question."

Eyes flitting between us in fear, he seems to make the wise decision of obeying. "The Atwoods. There's a concealed entrance near the base of Thunder Butte about four hours south of here."

Raina lets out an incredulous snort and fights to hold in a laugh as her voice returns to normal. "Thunder Butte? Seriously?" She loses her battle and breaks into a fit of immature giggling.

"Byo͞ot, not butt. What are you, five?" the wolf asks, exasperated even in the face of what could be his death.

"Really Raina? Is now seriously the best time?" But I can't help but smile down at her.

"Sorry, sorry." She clears her throat to compose herself, but when she goes to raise a hand to her mouth her eyes widen in shock. "What the fuck?!"

She attempts to get a full look at herself and just ends up spinning in circles, chasing her tail. In all honesty, it is an incredibly endearing sight to witness.

"Raina," I keep my voice level so as not to startle her, "calm down."

"Calm down?!" she shrieks. "In case you haven't noticed, I'm a damn flying lion! And I'm naked!"

Ryker steps closer, his voice low and full of desire. "Oh trust me Nymph, we noticed." He takes his time; gaze raking over her form, causing a shiver to run down her spine.

"If you two are quite finished, we still have a hostage to deal with you know," Seros interjects.

Skye is clutching his leg, peeking out from behind him. I spy no fear in her eyes, only curiosity as the scene plays out before her and a tiny, satisfied smile playing at the corner of her lips. When Ser notices the direction of my attention, he quickly slaps a hand over her eyes to shield her from the abundance of nudity shifting results in.

"Let's just kill him and be done with it," Ryker suggests, his usual go-to method of handling problems, as he makes to grab us each a pair of pants to pull on. I pass off control of the wolf's wrists to Ryker as I tug mine on, quickly resuming my assumed position of warden.

"We should see what other information we can get from him first," I decide, tightening my grip on the man turning my attention to his face. "What purpose do the Atwoods have for Skye? What was your mission?"

The man shoots daggers through his eyes, hate bleeding into his tone. "You're just going to kill me anyway, so why should I tell you shit?"

I backhand his face and blood trickles from his mouth. "You'll tell me because I have yet to decide if I should let you run back to your masters with a message or if I should let my brother tear you apart where you stand. I suggest you try and motivate me before my patience runs thin."

Before he can answer though, Raina seems to lose control over her beast and it recedes, leaving her standing there stark naked. I'm pretty sure I've forgotten how to even breathe.

A strangled sound slips out from the man in my grip, which had considerably tightened around his throat involuntarily while I fought the urge to throw Raina over my shoulder caveman style, take her upstairs and fuck her raw.

I spin him around to shield her from his view, reluctantly loosening my hold to allow him to speak. When he does, he doesn't seem vindictive or scared, just resigned to his fate. "I was assigned to bring the small shifter home where she belongs."

"To shield her or to sell her?"

"I wasn't told things like that. Mr. Atwood just emphasized she was to be returned to him unharmed, or any wound inflicted on her would be tripled on us."

I look at my brothers as we consider his words. Seeing them come to the same conclusion, I release the man. His face wears a mask of confusion and shock, but he is wise enough not to speak.

"You will return to your boss and inform him we are coming. We will meet with him ourselves to decide if he is a threat or an ally. No more men will be sent out to hunt her while he waits for our arrival in two days' time. Now go!" The man wastes no time changing forms, his wolf hauling ass out of the cabin and back from whence he came.

"Get your things; we're leaving in half an hour."

Chapter 27
Ryker

A Sphinx. A Gods-given Sphinx. I thought they were all long gone, died out centuries before my birth. How could they have survived with no one knowing? I watch the woman beside me in the truck in my peripherals. We have been driving for roughly two hours and no one has commented on what transpired in the mountain and it's driving me mad. Are we all just supposed to ignore the elephant in the room?

This changes everything. Not a human, but a shifter female. A *Sphinx* at that! Once word gets out, men will come for her left and right. Some will attempt to court her- the thought makes me bristle with fury- and the Raiders will come at full force to try and take her; a prize of this magnitude won't be ignored.

That also means... a mate, should she choose us over others. A possibility for a future where beforehand there was none. Of course she'll choose us! How could she not? She knows nothing of our history with Amara and we are some of the rarest species still living. I may have tried to push her away in the beginning, but she understands now that I've explained things to her. Things will be different now that we know what she is.

"I thought you said we weren't going for two days?" Raina asks Cain.

"And that's why we arrive early, so we don't give them time to set up a trap or gather forces," he nonchalantly replies.

"Oh." She sits in silence for a bit before continuing, "What if they don't mean well? Do we run? Where would we go?"

"Then we kill them," I shrug as though it's obvious. "Besides, now we don't even know if it really is Skye's father's family. You're a Sphinx, Raina. You passed down your form to your daughter, so Skye's father could just as well have been human."

She considers it and shifts uncomfortably beside me in her seat. I can only imagine her thoughts; everything she thought she knew about her life turned on its head. I subtly cover her hand in mine, letting the touch imbue her with strength. She pulls back slightly from my touch and I fight to control my frustration.

The rest of the journey to Thunder Butte flies by in relative silence. Before long, we are approaching a flat expanse of rock wall that makes the most obvious choice for an entrance. I let my hand trail against the rock, searching out the tell-tale signs of a concealment enchantment. A bit farther back than I first guessed, I locate it and wave my group forward.

I take the lead, letting my Griffin's superior eyesight scan the area for danger. As we approach a bend in the tunnel, I raise my fist in signal for the others to wait. Inching forward for a better view, I find the large cavern illuminated by electricity. Lights hang from the ceiling in even intervals, giving a perfect view of the room ahead. There are a few men walking about and I strain my ears to hear their conversation.

"Heard Tibald found the mother too. Looks like we'll get something to play with after all, eh?" The lecherous laughter trails off as they move deeper into the cave and I have to fight to remain in place. A glance back at Cain and Seros reveals murderous expressions. Obviously they picked up on the conversation as well.

We creep further inside, sticking close together. I hear it before I see it, a sharp exhalation of breath as a dagger is whipped end over end towards Cain. I dart out a hand and catch it mid-flight, a hairsbreadth from making contact with Cain's rib cage.

Seros has always been more adept at stealth than any of us, but he takes even me by surprise. Just as my hand clasps around the dagger's handle, Seros rises up behind the blade's owner and snaps his neck in one swift motion. With otherworldly speed, he fells two more opponents before I even see them approach.

A slow clapping from above has my head jerking up to see a man in his forties or fifties standing on a metal walkway about thirty feet in the air. I feel the air crackle with energy as Cain shifts behind me, guarding the females.

Seros shouts to the man above us with bravado. "We hear you're looking for us? Well here we are! Give us the old song and dance so we can get home in time for dinner."

The fucker chuckles, amused by those beneath him. "I have no interest in the lot of you, I simply wished to meet my granddaughter. Can't fault a man for seeking his kin, can you? And imagine my surprise to find out my son was keeping this beauty from me as well! We have much to catch up on."

"Marcus was your son then?" Raina's voice betrays no fear of the man that has wreaked havoc on her life this last week.

"Once maybe, but he lost that title when he left. Dropped off the face of the earth without a word for Gods only know why," the man drawls, not a hint of unease in his voice.

"He died... that's why," she deadpans, devoid of any emotion.

"No child, he left several years before that and now I see why. He chose to keep you for himself, that selfish bastard. To betray his family and abandon us. No, his death was a mercy- he never would have gotten off so easily if I had found him first." Disdain finally creeps into his voice, likely wishing to spit on Marcus' grave. Can't say I fault him that one, sadly.

Fury contorts Raina's features, but she manages to hold herself together for Skye's sake. "So you don't just want to get to know her or protect her. You just want to use her."

"Silly child, she couldn't be safer than she would be with me. I have no intention of letting a single hair upon her head be harmed before the selection of her future mates can begin. If her mother is any indication, she will be quite a beauty when she comes of age. What purpose would it serve me to allow harm to come to my investment? She's the only good thing Marcus ever contributed to the family and she will more than cover his loss. Now, thank you for delivering my grandchild. Hand her over and you can be on your way."

"I'm not leaving her here with you, you psycho! She is not just some prize to be auctioned off," Raina snarls.

"You're more than welcome to stay as well human, I'm sure we can find a use for you as well." Even from here I can see the glint in the man's eye.

Wait...human? He doesn't know what Raina is yet? I turn to meet Cain's furious red eyes, stark against his lion's tan face, to see his matching clarity. Either the wolf never delivered the message or he chose to keep Raina's status to himself. Hopefully Raina doesn't say anything foolish to give away our advantage.

"A thief is condemned to death.

He may choose between three rooms.

The first is full of blood, the second one poison.

The final room contains a single woman.

Which does he choose?"

She presents the riddle with a deceptively calm demeanor, as if she were possessed.

"The woman, obviously," Mr. Atwood scoffs. "What is your point?"

"I only came out of courtesy to see why you were so determined to take my daughter away from me and now that I know…" She turns as if to leave and I see the man tense.

"Stop her!"

Soldiers charge into the room, but I don't even get a chance to move more than a single step before Raina's fury is unleashed. Her black hair billows behind her as energy is cast from her body, electric blue eyes beaming in the artificially lit chamber. There goes our element of surprise.

Her hand outstretches languidly as though she has all the time in the world. Maybe she does. Golden hieroglyphs burn across her exposed-still very human- skin as she renders the rest of the room motionless.

Mr. Atwood's eyes practically bug out of his head as his face freezes in shock. Is that what I looked like when she transformed the first time? Wait a minute…why hasn't she shifted? We may be able to use a shadow of our abilities in human form, but something of this magnitude should be impossible. Forget Gods-given…the Sphinx must be a race born of demons. The sheer power she is radiating would be enough to knock a mortal unconscious.

A translucent blue air shimmers across my vision and when I reach out to touch it I'm met with resistance. The force field surrounds our group, a similar version surrounding Mr. Atwood.

Her voice contains the same resonance as before, a sound like a thousand souls whispering at once, echoing across the chamber.

"Your honesty does nothing to redeem your failed trial. The sentence, you have chosen." With that, every soldier in the room explodes simultaneously, leaving a pile of sand where bodies once stood. The silence is deafening, my heartbeat so loud it drowns out any small sound.

Mr. Atwood stays frozen behind the shield Raina created over him, hardly daring to breathe. No fear shines in his eyes, though, only rabid hunger. The display of Raina's power has only fueled his desire and I'm sure he will stop at nothing now to have her. This foolish woman has done nothing more than paint a target on her own back to match her daughter's ever growing one.

With a flick of her wrist, Raina releases the barriers, eyes still trained on Skye's grandfather. Just as she is about to annihilate the man, Skye's hand reaches out to grab her mother's shirt.

Little eyes blazing, Skye speaks with the same haunting quality of her mother. "The fates aren't yet finished with Gabriel. He must live."

"He's a threat." Her voice starts to lose its resonance, returning to that of our conflicted female.

"He's a necessity. I need you to trust me, to trust *them*, until the time comes."

Torn with indecision, Raina pauses for a moment before finally nodding her agreement. She lowers her hand and the symbols marking her skin fade from view. "Leave. This is her mercy, not mine. You will not find it again."

Eyes wild, Mr. Atwood -Gabriel?- doesn't move at first. He looks full of hunger, like he would rather leap from his perch to descend upon his newly found victims. The look in his eyes has my talons emerging, the desire to claw his eyes out enough to have me start stepping forward.

Snapped back to the reality of his situation, he backs off the walkway above us and retreats into the shadows. The action leaves me on edge; not having a clear line of sight on my opponent goes against my training. Cain must feel the same way because he stalks forward, murderous intent clear on his face.

Raina reaches out a hand to twine her fingers through his fur, offering comfort while still looking as if she wants to rescind her agreement with Skye. "Trust goes both ways, Cain. If you want us to trust in you three, then you need to be willing to offer us the same."

I pipe up, indignant. "You're taking battle strategy from a *child!*"

"In case you failed to notice, she's not a regular child. She obviously knows more about what's going on than the rest of us somehow. If she's wrong, then you guys can mutilate the fucker to your heart's content, if you manage to beat me to him. Until then, I need you to take a chance that someone might actually know something more than you."

More frustrated than I've ever been in my life, I snatch up Raina's hand in a fierce grip and tug her back towards the exit, the others following right behind. I lead the way with Raina in hand, Seros carries Skye behind us and Cain guards the rear. Within minutes, fresh- well, fresh compared to the cave- air envelops us as we leave the tunnel. I don't stop until we reach the truck, all but shoving Raina inside. Once we are far away from here we will talk, but for now I can focus on nothing except getting this woman and child as far away from this place as possible. That, or marching back inside to rectify her deadly mistake, consequences be damned.

Chapter 28
Raina

What the hell is happening to me? I wasn't really in control of my actions back there, but I remember all of it. It was as though someone hijacked my body and made we witness myself kill a room full of people in the blink of an eye. And they fucking *exploded!* The power rushed through my body like I have wielded it my entire life and knew exactly what I was doing. A thousand voices whispered in my head, making me feel like I knew everything, yet nothing, all at once. Maybe I'm schizophrenic and this is all in my head. Maybe I'm as mad as they claim Ryker to be. Maybe Ryker's not even real and he's my psychotic alter-ego or something. How can I tell if I'm crazy or not?

I'm crushed in the middle of the backseat between Skye and the yet-to-be-certain-is-there Ryker. The latter has yet to take his eyes off of me the entire trip, his unwavering scrutiny burning through me as though if he looks hard enough all the secrets and mysteries of the universe will be answered on my face.

Seros is driving recklessly, his agitation evident in his speed and sharp turns. I have no clue where we are going and yet, I don't find myself caring all that much. As long as we put as much distance between us and Gabriel Atwood as possible, location doesn't really matter. Speaking of...

I turn to face Skye. "How did you know his name was Gabriel? He never told us," but I'm pretty sure I already know the answer.

"I just knew." She shrugs. "They told me I had to listen, that it was really important, so I did."

"Who told you that angel?"

"The Whisperers. They're my friends. They talk to me sometimes so I'm not lonely. They tell me stories, or tell me not to do stuff if they think it's dangerous."

"So when you said I had to trust them...you didn't mean Cain, Seros, and Ryker?"

"Nope."

"Honey, why haven't you ever said anything? Why didn't you tell me?"

"They said it wasn't time yet. Mommy wasn't ready, but one day they would talk to you too, I just had to be a good girl and wait. I had to follow the rules, or I would lose the game. I don't like to lose."

So I'm not going crazy, or if I am it's genetic. Those voices that spoke for me, that gave me that rush of power that consumed me, are also in Skye's head. Not long after, Skye drifts off to sleep, the long car ride taking its toll on my narcoleptic, creepy little demon child. Good thing she's cute.

Turning to face my guys- no *the* guys, not mine –I figure it is as good of a time as any to finally talk about this. After I shifted at the cabin we had an unspoken agreement not to talk about it yet, I needed time to process. But after killing a room full of people-which I still weirdly don't feel bad about, I *should* right? That's the sign of a serial killer or something?- I doubt I'll get any more of a reprieve. May as well go for broke and lay all my cards out on the table, or however it goes.

"Soooo apparently I'm a flying lion serial killer. You sure you don't want to just ditch us on the side of the road yet?" I joke, trying to lighten the mood with all of the social skills of a potato.

Although, a small part of me is actually worried they might say yes. Helping a woman and child is one thing, but this is a whole ball of crazy I doubt many people want to get mixed up in.

Seros answers, "You aren't getting rid of us that easily, Ra. I just happen to *like* flying lion serial killers. Why else do you think I keep Cain around?" He shoots me a wink in the rearview mirror.

"Give yourself a little credit there, Nymph; you're much more fun to look at than Cain." Ryker chimes in beside me, his hand falling possessively on top of my thigh.

"I've told you before, I have no desire to leave. If anything, recent events have clarified my feelings on the matter. You're a Sphinx, Raina. That is unheard of where we're from. Not only are you a lone shifter female, but everyone thinks your kind doesn't exist anymore. So that pull I felt from the beginning must have been a part of me recognizing you two as one of us." Cain rumbles out.

"So what happens now?" I ask, the seemingly innocuous question holding the weight of our entire future.

"We take you home, where you belong," Cain declares.

Ryker butts in, "We can't do that! What do you think will happen as soon as the others learn about her? She's unmated. Males will come at her left and right, trying to court her. And what about when the Raiders find out a mother *and* daughter Sphinx have surfaced?"

"Let them try. Anyone who would dare to take them will meet a face worse than death," Cain booms, much too loud for the confines of the truck.

"Tell that to *Gabriel.*" Ryker sneers.

Seros follows his declaration with one of his own, "Besides, they can't court her, she's ours. We voted!"

"Umm...don't I get any say in this?" Seros slams on the brakes and we jerk forward, three sets of eyes turning to bore into my soul.

"Are you saying you don't want to stay with us?" Cain asks with a sliver of pain in his voice.

"I never said that." I give him a sympathetic smile.

Whatever pain he deals with seems to slip out from time to time and I'd love to take some of that burden away. "I just meant...ours? Us? You make it sound like if I stay I don't have to pick one of you. *If* I even pick anyone at all. I still haven't said I even want to be in a relationship yet, let alone whatever being mated means."

"You don't," Seros explains. "Things are different for shifters than you are used to, Ra, we aren't like humans. You get your pick of the lot, even if you pick them all.

I mull this over for a minute, processing. I'm not blind; the three men I've been spending so much time with are incredibly attractive and I'll admit to having my mind in the gutter when I'm around them, but the thought of a serious relationship hadn't really occurred to me until now. A fun time boning the body guards sure, but long term?

Once the thought takes root though, I can't shake it. How am I supposed to choose? Seros was the first shifter I met-I am *not* counting the spider- and he threw himself in to protect Skye and me without even knowing us. He always finds a way to lighten the mood and I find myself enjoying his company, loving the way I feel instantly at ease with him.

Cain has never made his feelings a secret. From the beginning he has made his desire known. And that kiss...my cheeks flush at the memory. I've never felt that way about someone before. I find myself wanting to understand the pain that flashes across his face, leaving this beast of a man unsure of himself.

And Ryker. Even if it was a rough start and I used to think he was nothing more than a raging asshole, he's starting to grow on me. A little bit. Our conversation alone at the grotto let me get a glimpse of his pain. He opened up to me in a way I doubt he does for many people and that personal moment changed the way I once looked at him. The pain he carries entices me as much as the man himself; like calls to like after all.

One of my biggest concerns is how I could wreck everything so easily. I've come to like this unusual company, this little family of misfits we have started to form in such a short time. They brought me and my daughter into their group and cared for us like one of their own. Now that I know we are one of them, that instantaneous comfort level and ease I felt around them makes sense. I don't want to destroy this small haven I've found by complicating things, by turning brother against brother by picking someone to slake my newly found raging libido. But now that I think about it... even after my make-out session with Cain, he never acted jealous when I spent time with Seros and Ryker.

If I don't have to choose? If I could keep going like we've been, getting to know each of them, reveling in their touch? Is it so crazy that it's enticing, that I'm considering it? It just feels...right with them. Gods, maybe I *am* broken. First I hear voices in my head, then I turn into a murdering psychopath. Now I'm thinking of keeping three men for myself and it doesn't even feel wrong? I've gotten greedy it seems. I don't know that I could even handle one of these men full time, let alone all of them.

"So you mean to tell me I could kiss Ryker right here, right now and neither of you would get jealous?" I challenge, testing the waters.

Ryker's eyes darken with heat, but it's Seros that answers. "Not at all. Actually, watching you get riled up would just spur me on. Seeing you overtaken by lust, losing yourself to the moment, witnessing your pleasure in the throes of passion. Letting you come crashing down around him, only to step in and have you writhing again beneath me. Driving you to the brink of insanity over and over again, pulling you back at the last moment until my brothers and I are the only names you can remember..."

His words light a fire inside of me that causes me to shift in my seat, clenching my thighs together to try and add pressure where I need it. If it wasn't for the sleeping child, this conversation would probably lead down an even more dangerous path. As if he can sense my turmoil, Ryker's hand tightens on my thigh where it still lay after all this time.

The air is charged with sexual tension so thick I can barely breathe. I'm practically choking on it and between you and me, I can think of a few things I'd prefer to choke on right about now. Cain's eyes darken and his nostrils flare like he knows the effect they have on me with just their words. Wait a second...

"Can you..." my cheeks heat with embarrassment, not sure how to voice my question. "You said shifters tend to have heightened senses, right?"

Cain nods.

"So you can...I mean, you know when..."

He looks at me confused, but Seros jumps in to save me from having to actually voice it. "Can we tell when you're getting hot and bothered? Smell the pheromones in the air?"

I nod quickly, part of me not wanting to know.

"Of course we can. Any shifter worth his salt would be able to," Seros answers with a shit-eating grin.

I cover my face in my hands, groaning. A chorus of laughter at my expense surrounds me and I can't even think of a way to casually play it off at this point. Choosing to focus on literally anything else, I turn to Ryker, knowing he's easy to pick a fight with and distract me.

Removing my hands from my face in favor of wringing them on my lap, I make sure to clarify, "So you only suddenly want me because I'm the unicorn of shifters, is that it? Oh shit, are there unicorn shifters?"

He snorts derisively, "Don't be preposterous."

"About the unicorns or about your hidden agenda?"

"Both. And it's not hidden, I've been quite clear. I don't care for humans, but I had already begrudgingly started to accept your place with us before I knew better. Now, it just makes things simpler."

"Shut up Ry, you're making it worse," Seros mumbles from the front seat.

He isn't wrong. I very obviously shove Ryker's hand off my thigh and choose to ignore him completely, but secretly grateful to him for the reprieve from my embarrassment.

Turning towards the front seat full of men I don't currently loath, I answer, "Well then...I guess we head for home."

Chapter 29
Seros

The drive to the forest portal in southern Colorado was difficult with the raging boner I'd given myself. I couldn't help it, the mental images drawn up at Raina's challenge ran rampant. I shifted in my seat for the hundredth time, trying to adjust myself and just making myself more miserable with each brush against my dick.

I understand Ry's concerns. She is gorgeous and powerful; a man would be stupid not to try and gain her favor. Add in the fact that she has a daughter and people will be knocking down the door in an attempt to claim her. Let them try. I was serious when I said she was ours. Whether or not she has officially chosen us as mates yet, I already consider her ours. If only Ryker can pull his head out of his ass and quit making it more difficult than it already is.

I've never felt this kind of pull before, not even with Amara, so it can't be solely the fact she is a female shifter like Cain believes. Whatever it means, it draws me to her like a kraken to the sea and I will dive in willingly. Let me drown, so long as hers is the last face I see.

We unload our packs from the vehicle and at her insistence, Cain places Skye up onto his shoulders, her fingers clutching the pale hair to secure her place. The child can practically see over the tree line at such a height. This little girl already has us wrapped around her little finger and I swear she knows it. Tiny yellow backpack of jewels still secured to her back, we head out.

We hike through the forest for a while, following the sound of rushing water. Before long the waterfall we seek comes into view and the sight is truly magical to behold. The sun is already setting, the dramatic colors reflecting off of the water. Trees flank the pool beneath, framing it in. The rock face stretches up high enough that you need to crane your neck back to see the top. The stone is mottled greys and reds, darkened where the water splashes onto it. Soft moss spreads up and out, the forest trying to claim the small mountain.

"I could just stay here all day, it's so peaceful," Raina sighs beside me.

Taking her hand, I give it a gentle squeeze in agreement. This is one of my favorite portals so I'm glad it was the closest one. We take a minute to absorb the sight, letting the image brand into memory. This is the end of a chapter in her life; once we step through everything will change even more than it already has. I wish I could just keep her here in this moment with me forever, suspended in time, but I know that's a selfish fool's dream.

This woman has been through too many hardships in her young life and I want to offer her any peace I am able. Things will never be simple for her, not once word gets out about what she and Skye are, so I make a vow to give her more of these moments of beauty and respite in a storm of chaos, however brief. Life is too hard to just constantly fight for survival and miss out on all the moments that remind us to live.

All too soon, Cain begins the trek to the base of the waterfall. I keep her hand in mine and lead her forward. Cain appears to vanish for a moment as he slips behind the curtain of water, but we are right behind him. A few steps farther into the hidden cave and a smooth wall signaling a dead end comes into view, a subtle glow around the edges only visible to our kind.

With eyes flashing red in the dim light, Cain presses his palm flat in the center of the wall and pushes. His hand sinks through the rock, swallowing his arm as he continues onward. Skye's eyes flash briefly as she makes contact, her body passing through with no resistance.

Once gone, I lead Raina forward to repeat the process and notice Ry take her other hand and step forward with us. Stuffy bastard sure came around quickly once her claws came out. She cocks her head to shoot him a glare, but doesn't let go I notice.

I cannot see them, but I can feel the power bleed through me as my eyes change from green to silver, the portal playing with our latent abilities to allow us through. I push forward and before long Cain and Skye come into view, waiting for us on the other side.

A sharp gasp at my side has me smiling as I turn, enjoying the stunned expression on her face. Even after centuries, the sight of our home never gets old. The sky appears trapped in a perpetual sunrise; purples, pinks, blues, and gold swirling above majestically. The Great Forest looms ahead, trees taller than any in the human realm. Their rich, vibrant greens create a canopy that can pull you into your own world once inside, refusing to let you see anything except its own majesty. The forest has a life of its own and it's a vain one.

Off to the side, you can make out the sea on the horizon, the clear water reflecting the sky above it like a rainbow pool. The air is fresh and crisp, unsullied by pollution. Mountain ranges can be seen beyond the forest, their snow capped peaks piercing the clouds. I could stand here for days and never grow tired of the view.

Unfortunately, our home lies in the mountains so we need to go through the Great Forest to get there. While the journey may be beautiful, the majority of shifters have made their home beneath the forest's branches. My brothers and I removed ourselves from society after Amara's death, choosing to live on the outskirts of civilization rather than face the harsh judgment of our peers on a daily basis. While they may respect us as warriors, they will never forget that we failed our intended. That also means that they will get a good look at Skye and Raina on our way and Raina will hear every horrible thing from our pasts as they try and turn her against us.

Gritting my teeth, I begin the arduous journey home. The others fall into step with me as we head down the slope towards the tree line. We walk on, careful to listen for others, but content enough to make idle small talk. We share a few humorous stories with each other and glean more of an insight into the minds of our females, even Skye joining into the conversation. Yes, ours. I refuse to think of them as anything else, mated or not.

The tree canopy blocks our view of the sky, allowing only filtered light to flit down to the forest floor. The trees are so wide that it would take three Cains just to hug one. The dirt floor offers subtle trails to follow from frequent use, lined with plants and flowers I don't know the names of.

It will never cease to amaze me how well behaved Skye is. I may not have been around many children, but I doubt one as small as her is usually so quiet and tame. Half the time it's easy to forget she's there, probably listening to things we should be more careful to discuss in her presence. I'll have to do better about that. You're not supposed to say *fuck* around kids, right? Or ogle their mother. Yeah, I need to watch it more.

Obviously I became too complacent on our casual stroll because by the time I picked up their scent it was too late. We are already surrounded and they are closing in fast. I shift in a blink, destroying my clothes and not even alerting my brothers. Any second wasted may cost us and I'm sure they will figure it out.

I coil around Raina, Cain coming over to deposit Skye in the small cocoon. Ryker shifts and jets into the air to try and assess the situation while Cain remains human, our voice should we be able to talk our way out of this without bloodshed.

The pack of wolves close in, noses to the ground in search of whatever brought them here. Two guesses what that could be. Their alpha breaks the line to approach us, shifting mid-stride. Great, of all the people we could stumble across first, it had to be him. Goddamn-cocksucking-fuckface-wolf-twat. Raina's rubbing off on me.

The grey wolf is traded for a man slightly smaller in stature than Cain. He runs a hand through his brown hair, pulling it out of his eyes. As usual, he doesn't bat an eye at his blatant nudity, his physical strength on full display. Shifters are much less modest than mortals, but we've made a conscious effort around Raina for her comfort.

"Cain, didn't expect to see you three back so soon. Or two. Birdbrain finally run off on ya'? Weren't you on a long haul mission? Find any good Rogues to execute?" The deep voice of Callum asks.

"We had an interesting mission, yes. Now if you'll excuse us, we need to make our reports." Cain attempts to brush off Callum and leave, but a firm hand catches his arm.

"Why the rush? You wouldn't be hiding something now, would you?" His eyes narrow in challenge, nostrils flaring as his brown eyes bleed to black.

"I hide nothing. I have with me what is mine and I fully intend to keep it that way," Cain draws himself up, bracing for a fight.

I really should have expected Raina would never be able to just stay quiet.

"Excuse me, but we really need to be going. It's a long walk and I desperately need to pee soon. So if you two could quit fighting over who's dick is bigger, that'd be great. It was nice to meet you, though."

Well, that's one way of handling it I hadn't thought to attempt.

At the sound of her voice, Callum's head whips around to face her, locking her in his sights. Several low growls fill the air and I tense a bit tighter around the girls.

"Nice to meet you indeed. My name is Callum, to whom do I have the pleasure of addressing?" I snort as much as my reptilian face will allow, his instantaneous switch from bully to gentleman making me laugh. He shoots me a quick glare, but then returns his focus to Raina.

"Just a girl, no one special. Now if you'll please allow us to pass, we have places to be, things to do." She brushes him off casually, but Callum is not one to be dismissed.

"If these men have convinced you that you are no one special then let me be the first to apologize on their behalf. I've never seen you around here before, who is your family? Are you visiting from another settlement? A beautiful woman such as yourself deserves better than to roam the woods with murderers and monsters, why don't you allow my brothers and I the honor of escorting you instead?"

I can feel her tension in the way her body stiffens against me. "Then I guess I'm exactly where I should be. If murderers are so looked down upon, then you should probably not sully yourself with my company," venom spitting from her words.

Instead of answering her he turns to Cain, a look of rage contorting his face. "I see you haven't changed. This female needed to defend herself? And where were you that she had to take matters into her own hands, huh? I don't know where you managed to steal her from, but I'll be damned if I let her stay with you pathetic lot."

Turning to Raina he softens his words. "Come with me dear. I won't allow any more harm to befall you. My brothers and I will take you back to your family and discuss arrangements." He reaches out a hand in offering.

"I'm fine thanks. I'm not going to just run off with a pack of strangers, that'd be pretty fucking stupid. Don't you know that's how you end up dead?" Gods, I adore this woman.

"I assure you, no harm will befall you in our care," his tone less calm now, his frustration at not being instantly obeyed bleeding into it.

"Oh, it isn't me I was worried about. The last time I was surrounded by a pack of strangers, I killed them all. I'd hate to have more blood on my hands so soon."

"You killed an entire pack?" he asks, bristling. "By yourself? Not likely."

"Oh, it's very likely. Now I would say it's been a pleasure, but I hate liars. Honestly, you've been a dick to my guys since the moment you got here and my patience is wearing thin. So if you'd just go ahead and leave, that'd be great."

Façade dropping, Callum faces off with Cain, shoving his chest. "What the fuck did you guys do, huh? Couldn't find your own female so you go out and steal one? Turn Raider on us? I should just kill you now and save everyone the trouble." His body vibrates as he fights for control, wrestling his wolf back.

When he tries to reach past me to grab Raina's arm, all hell breaks loose. I snap at his outstretched hand and my movement gives him a glimpse of Skye. Eyes bugging out of his head, Callum stares at Skye and Raina as though they offer salvation.

Callum shifts, his wolf aiming for my throat, but he doesn't make it far before Ryker is plummeting out of the sky towards him. Ry's talons sink into the wolf's flesh, drawing blood. He carries Callum higher into the air before flinging his body at a nearby tree. Callum's body hits the trunk with a loud snap, bones breaking from the impact. But he is the Alpha of the region for a reason and pulls himself back to his feet, fighting through the pain.

His brethren charge in, half aiming for my brothers and the others straight for me. Cain lets his manticore burst free and faces off against several wolves at once, clawing and tearing into them. A few manage to get in a lucky hit or two, but Cain makes quick work of them. Ryker still faces off with Callum, circling and seeking an opening.

I strike out as our enemies approach, pumping venom into their systems as my teeth pierce flesh, but I cannot fight as freely as I am used to while staying wrapped around the girls like a barricade, keeping them from getting hurt in the crossfire. Sharp fangs scrape against my scales, attempting to tear me apart, but finding no purchase. My scales are harder than armored steel, they will have to try harder than that.

Tail whipping out to knock them away, my brothers and I make steady work of the wolves. A sharp cry has my head whipping around in time to see Callum's jaw latched onto the base of Ryker's wing, attempting to rip him apart. Cain bounds over, roaring in rage as he comes to our brother's aid.

As the two collide in a tangle of snarls and fury, clawing and rolling in an attempt to pin the other, I feel tiny hands scrambling over the coils of my body.

"Skye! Get back here!" Raina shouts, frantically giving chase to her daughter.

The little girl darts straight for Cain, a look of sheer outrage on her angelic face. "You knock that off RIGHT NOW! That is *my* kitty so stop hurting him!" She puts her hands on her hips as she stomps her foot and glares at Callum.

Raina and I catch up to Skye, Raina picking her up and pulling her away. It seems as though Skye has claimed Cain as a part of her collection of things and doesn't much care for people touching what belongs to her.

Callum barely even reacts and I wonder if he heard her. But Skye also has inherited her mother's temper in addition to her abilities, because she doesn't back down.

"I *said* STOP!" Her tiny body trembles as it is replaced by the form of a mini- sphinx. The tiny humanoid lion cub lets her wings rip her away from her mother as she joins the melee.

As she gets close enough for Cain to see her, a look of pure terror crosses his face and he falls back into his human form, not risking the baby Sphinx harm by accident. His fist takes Callum by surprise, not expecting the change in opponent. The action snaps Callum into awareness and he pauses, taking in the sight of the tiny shifter. He immediately changes as well, beholding her with reverence.

"You...you're a...." He struggles to find the words, still in awe.

"Sphinx. Yes," Cain growls out, reaching out to scoop up Skye against his chest.

She struggles to break free, but Cain holds firm, not allowing her any closer to the enemy before us. She hisses and spits like an alley cat, claws swiping as she tries to attack Callum to defend Cain's honor or something equally as stupid.

"The woman is one as well? How? Where did you take them from?" Callum asks, never taking his eyes from the mythical sight before him, though admittedly less hostile.

"We didn't *take* them from anywhere. Or anyone. You may not like us, wolf, but we have too much honor to join the Raiders. They were being hunted by the father's family in the human realm and we brought them here for safekeeping." Cain gives him too much information for my liking, but I refuse to shift yet to object, not trusting the man.

"Father? The woman is mated then?" he asks, a bit deflated.

Cain hesitates to answer, weighing his options. ".....No. The father is dead. The little one's grandfather found out about her and is trying to reclaim her."

The answer has him perking up instantly. "Oh, she's not is she?" He turns to eye Raina over. "Perhaps this man only wishes to protect his kin? Perhaps he is interested in coming to an arrangement?"

"No. He's interested in an arrangement alright, but only one that involves coin and cage." Cain continues to rein in Skye as she fights to break free of his grasp, paws running through air as she squirms. Finding no escape, she continues to growl and hiss at Callum, attempting to look ferocious. That's probably my fault, after telling her we protect each other. I really should have been more specific.

"And you allowed him to live?" Callum grunts out his disapproval.

"There were.....unusual circumstances," Cain hedges, not divulging the full story. Better to play some things close to the vest.

"Well then, I guess this changes things," he says with a cocky grin. "Without the red tape of a family to pre-approve matches, this lovely lady gets her pick of the lot." He returns to give Raina his full attention, Cain instantly forgotten. I wrap myself around her in claim, hissing at the man.

"Now, now filthy snake, where are your manners? Just because you found her first doesn't make her yours." Turning to address Raina he asks, "You've never been to the homeland then, only ever the human realm? I'll make you a deal. You allow me to show you around, stay in the main settlement for a few weeks at least to get to know your options and I'll back off. Something as rare as a Sphinx shouldn't be saddled with the first ragtag group she meets."

"And if I refuse?" Raina inquires as low growls rise up around us, the fallen pack healing and ready to begin fighting anew.

"More will come. Once word spreads that we have not one, but two Sphinx in our midst, you won't find a moment of peace. Between the men vying for your attention and the Raiders, your group will constantly be challenged. Without a formal match in place, any unmated male has the right to contest this group's supposed claim on you. But if you present yourself and take control of the situation, they will be respectful of your decision when the time comes and leave you be."

"And you? You wish only to show me around for no reason other than civility?" Raina scoffs.

"No gorgeous, I intend to show you how much better your life would be by my side. I'll introduce you to your choices and prove I'm better than them all." He practically purrs.

"My men will come with me, that's non-negotiable. And after I've met your people and rejected them, you will leave us be," Raina declares.

"Fine," Callum answers in a clipped tone. "But that still won't stop others, just my people."

As he extends a hand to escort Raina, I tense around her in reflex. I don't like this, not at all. She's ours. But... what if she chooses to leave us? Could I let her go? Not without a fight, that's for damn sure. This girl came crashing into our lives and replaced everything I knew with chaos, but I wouldn't change it for the world.

A soft hand comes to stroke my side, offering comfort. I meet her tender gaze and I know deep, *deeeeep* down, that my worries are pointless. She may not have said it, but Raina has come to care for us too. Letting out a weary sigh, I shift back to wrap an arm around her waist, pulling her into my side as she blushes furiously at the nudity all around her.

"Lead the way then, mutt."

Chapter 30
Cain

"As if pissing in the woods wasn't awkward enough, I have to do it with about twenty people listening in," Raina complains from where she's hiding on the other side of a tree.

I can't even bring myself to smile, I'm that enraged at our current situation. I thought we would have had more time before Callum found us, Gods be damned. I hate this more than I can say, but the fucking mutt has a point. If we don't let Raina publicly court suitors, than every group within a hundred mile radius will be at our door to challenge us for her hand. Not that I won't gladly slay them all if I must, but I can't freely fight and still keep an eye on both females with that many threats surrounding us.

Skye refuses to shift back and has instead perched on my shoulders like a damn pirate with a parrot, her sharp claws digging into the bare skin. I barely notice the scratching unless she moves, but she is pretty good about staying still, one eye always trained on the wolves at our side or Callum ahead of us.

We paused to pull on new pants before following the filthy dog, an attempt to make Raina less embarrassed. We decided to forgo the shirts; they'd just be pointless anyway. I hope Raina never loses that human sense of modesty; if she were to start strutting around town half naked, I'd have to remove the eyes of every man that dared look at her.

Our journey is made in tense silence as we approach the main settlement. Nestled in the center of a vast clearing, people mill about. Small groups gather around fire pits roasting their lunches, small boys practice fighting in shifted and human form. High above us in the branches lies a city in the sky. Rope bridges connect homes, a labyrinth stretching into the canopy above. People saunter about without a care in the world. This settlement holds at least two thousand shifters between the tree houses- colossal buildings that defy logic nestled in the branches- and nearby dens, but it takes little time for word to spread.

As soon as we break the tree line into the clearing, several boys look up, darting off to find their fathers. A not so hushed whispering starts up at the sight of my brothers and me- my actions haunting us even after hundreds of years. What am I thinking? How can I consider subjecting Skye and Raina to a lifetime of being pariahs? Maybe Callum is right and this is for the best…they deserve better. After the life they've led they deserve men able to give them everything, not a failure like me.

As if she can sense my thoughts, Skye brings her face down to nuzzle against mine, purring and offering comfort. How strange, a man such as myself needing the reassurance of a kitten? It's as though she imbues me with determination and strength, though. I stand taller, ready to take on the world if it pleases this small child.

As people begin to notice the tiny shifter on my shoulder the whispers turn into an all-out deafening roar as people begin talking over each other and pointing at our party. Callum strides forward, commanding the crowd to settle. Unfortunately for us, Callum isn't just the Alpha of his pack, but also of the Great Forest's main settlement.

"Listen up! I'm not going to repeat myself so you all best shut it now!" He gives the crowd a moment to calm down and pay attention.

"While many of you have your own strong opinions about this lot," he turns to shoot us a glare himself, "they have done our society a great service this day. While on an extended mission in the human realm, they managed to stumble across two members of shifter kind we thought long lost from us."

He pauses for dramatic effect. "Not just one, but *two* Sphinx!" The crowd erupts into anarchy and it takes several minutes, along with some shouting, for Callum to settle them down enough to hear him.

"An unmated mother with a daughter, no other family that we are aware of as she was raised in the human realm. She has agreed to settle here for the time being as she is introduced into our society. Now you all know our laws! In the rare event a family is not present to pre-approve potential matches, the honor falls to the female herself to weed through applying suitors and we will all follow that. We struck a bargain to have her even consider someone from our home. She will court potentials and if she finds them lacking, they will be able to leave whether or not mates are taken without a fight. I hear one word of anyone raising a hand to her or her child and the price will be that same hand. Understood?"

The crowd takes on an excited air as people begin running about, sharing the news with those on the outskirts that missed the announcement.

"If you'll follow me milady, I will escort you to a place to stay for now." Callum offers his arm with a flourish and Raina eyes it with distaste, but grudgingly accepts.

We follow Callum's lead to an unoccupied treehouse smack dab in the center. *Of course-* I think, rolling my eyes- *surrounded on all sides so we are unable to run off with them in the dead of night.*

We get settled in, Skye insisting on picking her own bedroom within and slinking off to make it her own. I hope she finds something to color all over Callum's perfect walls with.

Now that Callum has taken his leave and Skye is arranging her new room, we're able to settle down to talk in private.

"Holding in there, Nymph?" Ryker inquires from across the room.

"It's all just a waste of time in my opinion. Why would I suddenly decide to shack up with a bunch of strange men?" Raina replies.

"Uuhhh... you do realize that's exactly what you did with us, right?" Seros teases.

Blushing furiously Raina attempts to salvage things and fails. "Well that's...different."

Laughing, I reach out to run the backs of my fingers along her cheek. "It's all just a formality. I may not like it, but hopefully we can hurry this along and finally go home. If you enjoyed the portal, than you'll adore the view from the mountains."

"I never even said I wanted a mate. Why can't they just all leave me alone?" she huffs in frustration.

"Little Muse, have you seen yourself? You are not only gorgeous, but fierce as well. A true treasure. Any man who does not seek your favor is a fool. Besides, if you want to leave before the few weeks are over, you just need to declare your intendeds. There is no rush for things to escalate beyond that if you don't wish them to. You are the one with the power here, no matter what others lead you to believe."

"Little Muse?" Raina asks with a quirk of her brow.

"You inspire me to be a better man Raina, whether you intend to or not."

"How could you possibly be better? You're all already so freaking perfect," she murmurs and I doubt she realizes she uttered her thoughts aloud.

Smirking, I carry on. "We will humor them for a few weeks as agreed, then we will leave regardless of an announcement and I will cripple any man that tries to stop us."

"How many people do I have to meet?" she asks with resignation on a sigh.

"As many as needed until you formally announce your mates, or three weeks passes."

"I can tell them to go fuck themselves if they try anything right? I may have agreed to this charade, but I'm not going to just let people touch me whenever they want." She glowers, no doubt mentally preparing herself to knee a man in the balls.

"If any man dares to attempt such a thing, all you need to do is gift us the name," Ryker promises.

Moving in to invade her space, I let my hand fall to her hip, dragging her flush against me. I lean in as if to kiss her and veer off at the last moment, letting my lips whisper against her ear. "I happen to recall you liking my touch, and I want to....very. Much." I pull her earlobe into my mouth and suck gently before releasing it again. Pressing my growing need against her stomach I continue, "Aren't you going to stop me?"

She trembles beneath me, sliding her hands up to my chest where they become pinned between us. "Do you want me to?"

she asks with a slight bit of uncertainty in her voice that I can't believe I heard. How could she be unsure that we want her?

Seros comes up behind her, fisting his hand into her hair to lean her head back and kiss the length of her exposed neck. He slowly licks upwards from collarbone to jawline, stopping to murmur in her ear "You can go ahead and tell us to go fuck ourselves Ra, but we might just take you with us while we do."

She shivers between us, unable to speak. In answer, she grinds back against Seros, eliciting a sharp hiss as he presses closer against her. She reaches up to tangle her hand in his hair and tug him closer, but just before his lips crash into hers the vixen repeats my move and adjusts to whisper in his ear. "Or maybe I'll just do it myself while you watch and not let you join the fun."

She adjusts herself and twists free from our grasp, moving to stand beside Ryker who watched the entire exchange like a hawk. She leans against his shoulder, eyes sparkling in triumphant amusement as his are alight with rare humor.

A knock outside has me stiffening and Ryker tucks Raina behind him as Seros moves towards Skye's room. I thought we would have had more time, but I should have known. With a sigh, I approach the door, anger simmering beneath the surface.

While I try to put on a reassuring front for Raina's sake, this whole scenario makes me want to do nothing more than bash a few heads in and whisk her back to our home. But alas, the games must be played if they are to be won and Raina is a prize worth fighting for.

Five men stand before me, shifting nervously. "We were told by Callum that interested parties were welcome to approach?" Gritting my teeth I don't even bother answering, just turn back to shout for Raina.

She appears in the doorway with confidence, holding her head high and letting none of her previous nerves show. My chest swells with pride; she allows herself to be vulnerable around my brothers and me, but not this group of –I sniff to check- foxes.

"Hey." Short, sweet and to the point, my girl.

"Hello there. My name's Ethan. These are my brothers, Finn, Hiro, Cam, and Leo. We were wondering if maybe you would join us for dinner?" He offers a shy smile.

Raina glances back at me as if asking permission. Silly female, if I had my way I'd lock her in the house until the three weeks had passed. I bury my feelings instead and offer her a nod of encouragement.

With a sigh, she turns to address Ethan. "Sure. Where should I meet you?"

"We can escort you now if you'd like? With as much walking as you must have done I imagine you might be hungry." Ethan beams with excitement, the bastard.

"Oh. Ok just...hold on a minute." She turns her back on the men- something I really need to get her to stop doing- and asks me, "Would you be willing to watch Skye while I'm gone? I'd like to keep her somewhere safe while I'm stuck meeting people."

Her trusting words impact me more than she could ever know. For centuries I've heard the condemnation in other's tones, the cruel words they've spoken since Amara's death. They may have trusted my skills when they had need of them, but it was always made crystal clear that they didn't trust me around their families anymore. A centuries-old wound being stitched together with seemingly innocent words.

"It would be my honor, Little Muse."

She heads inside to say her good-byes to her daughter, leaving me in the entryway glowering at the foxes. They shift uncomfortably while we await her return.

"Lay a hand on her and it will be the last thing you ever do."

"Is that a threat, old man?" One of them bolsters.

"No, it's a promise."

"We could take you. Our fathers have told us all about your group and I must say; I'm not impressed." Cocky little fucker is just itching for a fist in the jaw I see.

"Then I guess it's a good thing it isn't me you have to worry about." Let them find out the hard way what they are walking into.

Before they can ask me to clarify, Raina reappears. Dressed in a simple purple t-shirt and dark jeans, she looks just as likely to take a walk as she does to kick some ass. Much to everyone's surprise, she stretches up on tiptoe to kiss my cheek on her way out.

"Well lead the way boys; I could use something to eat," she commands.

"I think that you'll find us to be men, my lady, not boys." Ethan quips.

"Eh, that's debatable. Shall we?" Raina counters.

With a sly grin, I return inside. If ever before there was a woman I didn't have to worry about taking care of herself, it was Raina. While I may wish to be able to hide her away and fight her battles for her, it is already abundantly clear that she would resent me for it. Raina is a woman who likes to stand on her own two feet upon a mountain she climbed herself and I respect the hell out of her for it.

Let the boys play their games, she will re-write the rules.

Chapter 31
Ryker

Raina startles me with a kiss on the cheek before moving on to do the same to Cain and is out the door for her *date*. Gods, how can Cain be so calm about all of this? We should just convince her to publicly claim us and be done with it. But no, here we sit in the wolf's den and offer up our female as a snack. This is ridiculous.

Shoving away from the wall I leaned against, I begin to pace the main room. Cain returns from the threshold, calm and at ease.

"What the hell, Cain!? How can you let us just stand by while they make off with our woman?"

"Ah, finally come around I see," he chuckles. "Don't you trust her?"

I pause my pacing. "Trust her? What does that have to do with anything?"

"Everything. You saw what she did to Atwood's men; do you really think she can't handle anything they throw at her?"

"She shouldn't have to," I spit through clenched teeth.

"No, I agree she shouldn't, but think about the time we've spent with her. She's not like the other females around here, Ryker. She's like…us. She wants to fight, to contribute to the group. She would hate thinking of herself as dead weight or that we didn't think she could survive five minutes without us after the kind of life she's led." Bastard makes a point.

"Why can't we just make her claim us already so that we can get out of here?"

"She's not ready to." He shrugs nonchalantly, but I can see the worry in his eyes as well, "and if you keep pissing her off, it just makes the possibility that much more out of reach."

"What if...she doesn't want to? If she chooses to go with the fox clan or worse, Callum?"

Seros joins the conversation, obviously overhearing the whole thing. "Then we kill them. She can't very well take mates that are dead."

Laughing, I address my brother, "You sound like me now."

Grinning unabashedly he taunts, "Then I guess you aren't just a birdbrain after all."

Skye enters the room, still in Sphinx form. She's been on edge since our encounter with the wolves and flat out refuses to change back.

"Well boys," Cain states, "looks like we're on babysitting duty today." Turning to address the child, he continues, "want to show us what you've done with your room?"

The rage that takes over Skye's face fills me with foreboding. Until recent events I've rarely been around children, but one look at this small child and I see the disaster brewing already.

Dear Gods, give me patience.

Chapter 32
Seros

Holy fuck am I tired. If yesterday someone had told me what the last few hours of my life would have been like, I would've laughed in their face. You would think that after the last week of my life, nothing could surprise me anymore, but you would be very, *very* wrong.

As soon as her mother left, our smallest companion flipped the fuck out. Where up until this point she had been a child so well behaved and quiet, now we had a raging she-demon.

In response to her mother's departure, Skye's eyes blazed with power as she began destroying the room. Waves of unfiltered power were cast out, splitting furniture and cracking the walls. She lashed out with claws and teeth, tearing apart cushions or flesh, it didn't matter. Any time my brothers or I tried to grab her she would fly out of our reach with preternatural speed, evading us and hissing.

She still has a human face, why the fuck is she hissing and biting?

When we did finally manage to get a hold of her, she would sink her teeth into the flesh of our arms, slashing her claws at our faces and chests until she broke free.

"For fuck's sake kid, knock it off!" Ryker shouts.

Unwilling to risk hurting her, we refused to shift, making catching her all the more challenging without our wings. Shouting in frustration, Ryker stalks outside to calm down, leaving

Cain and I to deal with the child. Since our current efforts aren't working, I decide to throw a Hail Mary and try another approach. It couldn't exactly make anything worse at this point if it failed.

"Skye, *talk* to us! Tell us what's wrong so we can fix it!"

Apparently actually talking to kids like they're people instead of shouting at them and chasing them around actually works. Huh, go figure.

"This is all *wrong*! It's not supposed to happen this way!" she screams while yanking the window covering down with a swipe of her claw.

"What do you mean, Sunshine?"

"Mommy is supposed to stay with you and we're supposed to go home. They *promised*!"

"Who promised you Skye?" Cain growls out.

"The Whisperers! They said if I was good and I did what they told me to, than mommy and I would get to go to our new home and mommy would be happy again. But I've *been* good! I promise! So now they have to keep their promise too!"

Cain and I exchange a look. If this was a normal child, then the talk of hearing voices and a stranger's promise would be incredibly alarming. But after hearing Skye and Raina speak with the haunting quality of thousands of souls as they wielded their powers and the brief mention after the disaster that was Thunder Butte, it's clear there is much more to the Sphinx race than we know.

"What *exactly* did they say, Skye?" I ask cautiously.

She sighs then begins to recite the words as if scripted. "*As the spider falls to the snake and the wolf howls at no moon, Gabriel will rise. Through fire and darkness the reason known. On the mountain torment end, dawn smiles on the rain. Listen child and heed our words; at home with the light, freedom is born."*

"Ro-Ro killed the spider and mama hurt the wolf in the cave. We met Grandpa Gabriel. You said your house was on the mountain and mama's name is Raina." She looks at us as though we are idiots and honestly, it's starting to feel that way.

"Skye..." Ryker tentatively attempts,-when did he come back in?- "there's no reason to be so upset. If I heard you correctly and that prophecy means what you think it does, the *fire and darkness* still needs to happen before we get to the mountain part."

She purses her lips for a moment, considering his words. "Okay, but it better not take long. I want to go home."

"So you want to live with us?" I ask.

"Well, duh!"

I let out a soft laugh; hopefully her mother feels the same way since the rest of us are already in agreement. Now to just figure out what that prophecy means.

"Hey Sunshine, why didn't the Whisperers tell that to your mom? If they can speak inside your heads, couldn't they just have told her what we're supposed to do?"

"Mama's not ready to listen, so they speak to me instead. '*She's a stubborn one*,' they say," the little Sphinx replies.

Ha! That's certainly accurate. Maybe these Whisperers know a thing or two after all.

"Mommy just needs to come home, she belongs with us," she pouts.

"I feel the same way, kid."

Chapter 33
Raina

Ethan, Finn, Hiro, Cam, and Leo lead the way to the center clearing and offer me a seat near a fire pit before settling in themselves. Where were all of these gentlemen back home? Is chivalry just a shifter thing?

The smell of roasted meat fills the air as people walk past, staring and whispering. I despise being the center of attention. These people live in a magic world, can turn into flying bears and shit and they really don't have anything better to do than stare at me?

I size up the men around me. Ethan and Finn must be actual brothers, their features are too similar not to be. With bright red-orange hair, emerald eyes, a smattering of freckles and lean builds, they hardly come off as threatening.

As we settle into our seats around the fire pit I have to wonder, Ryker made so many snarky remarks about the lowly, little human world. So why then does it just feel like I'm on a camping trip? They don't even have electricity? I'll have to rub that in Ryker's face later.

Leo takes a turn addressing me, taking the lead away from Ethan. "So tell us about yourself Raina, how are you?"

Oh great, time for the Q and A portion of the afternoon. Yay me.

Leo is a sweet, summer child. His blond hair and orange eyes compliment his tan, smooth skin. His smile and eyes appear innocent and honest, as though he has never faced a world of hardships or grief. His kind gaze makes me feel a little guilty about being such a bitch. After all, it isn't his fault that his words fill me with dread.

"I was human until a few days ago and now apparently everybody's after my magic cooch. So just super thanks for asking, you?"

Leo and Hiro choke on their food, sputtering and faces turning as red as Finn and Ethan's hair. The aforementioned Irish twins pound on their brother's backs as Cam just stares at me with the biggest grin on his face.

"I like her!" Cam laughs as his brothers try to compose themselves.

After Hiro regains his decorum, he passes me a plate of meat and vegetables and I take it eagerly. Whether or not it's poisoned, having something to fiddle with to keep my hands busy and a reason to look away from the intense scrutiny of the five boys is a blessing.

Hiro is slight in stature with dark hair, eyes and glasses. He gives off an air of intellect and rationality, so I assume he is the most level-headed of the bunch. So far he hasn't said a word, just observed and, well, choked.

I pick at my food only to be surprised that it is actually pretty delicious. Well, at least something good came out of this. I continue to eat, waiting for someone else to pick up the conversation where I left off.

"I think I speak for all of us to say we're surprised. You're not quite what we were picturing when they told us about you," Ethan admits.

"Disappointed?" I ask with a little too much excitement.

"Not at all. It's a nice change of pace," he continues.

"Oh."

"Well jeez princess, don't sound too excited or anything," Cam teases.

Where Hiro seems mature, Cam appears his polar opposite. The only thing the two have in common is the dark hair, but Cam's is wild and windswept. The mischievous spark in his blue eyes promises trouble. He looks like a good time full of bad decisions, but I've made enough of those lately already.

"Well can you blame me? I spent my entire life thinking I was human and struggling to survive just to have my husband die and raise my daughter alone. Someone tries to kidnap my daughter and a jagamuffin attacks us. A flying snake kills it and three men stow away in my car. I turn into a flying lion of death and make a bunch of guys explode, just to be pulled through a magic rock. And after all of that unbelievable nonsense, the only thing on anyone's mind is who I want to bone. Not any of the important stuff, just who gets to sleep with me? So excuse me if I find this entire thing ridiculous."

I continue to eat in silence as they absorb my rant. It's really not these guys' fault that I'm dealing with any of this, so I feel a little bad for unloading on them like this.

"A jagamuffin?" Leo eventually asks, face scrunched up in confusion.

"You know, huge spider monster with acid face?"

"OOOOOOOHHHHHHH a Jorōgumo!?"

"Yeah that's what I said."

"No it's not."

"Tomato, tomahto," I shrug.

He laughs and some of the tension dissipates around the circle. We've all finished eating and the boys stack up the dirty plates in a bin nearby.

"Can we show you around?" Ethan asks. He seems to take point for the most part, so I figure he's the leader of their group.

"Alright, but I don't want to be gone for too long. I need to get back to Skye."

"Well then we better walk quickly if you're going to see everything."

They take me around the settlement and I'm surprised to discover shops with people in the middle of glass blowing or wood working. It's fascinating to behold. At first glance I had assumed this was a rustic place to live, but after taking a closer look I find it thriving and surprisingly comfortable.

"Hey wait! That place sells clothes?" I'm practically bouncing up and down with excitement.

"Well...yea. With as many large or winged shifters that we have living around here, we go through clothing pretty quickly," Finn answers this time, confusion lacing his tone at my excitement.

After ending up naked last time and Skye shredding through her shirts with her wings, this place is going to be my new best friend. Wait...

"Do you guys take regular money? You know, human dollars?"

"A stupid currency. No, we take gold coins, like everyone else in this realm."

I deflate at his response. I don't have a fortune saved up by any means, but I figured I could at least get a few things. Unfortunately, I don't have a sack of gold like a pirate Santa Clause to throw over my shoulder, so I'm even more poor here than I was at home.

I start to walk away, ready to continue our tour, when a hand lands on my shoulder. I jump, startled, and the hand quickly retreats.

"Do you need something? We would be more than happy to buy it for you," Ethan asks and his tone belies nothing but honesty.

"I couldn't ask that of you guys, especially since we just met! No, I don't need anything, it's just nice to know it's here if I need it." I give them my best nonchalant grin, ready to move on.

We carry on with our perusal of the bustling marketplace. People still stare, but I pay them less mind then I did before, caught up in my own browsing. We didn't get a chance to explore the whole settlement, just branches off of the main clearing and the market area. But as I should have come to expect in my life, every time I feel content, the rug is pulled out from beneath my feet.

"Well, well, fancy meeting you here little lady."

I stiffen as Callum's voice reaches me and the foxes instantly pick up on my unease. Coming to form a loose circle around me, I feel the heat of their bodies as they surround me. I'm touched at the friendly gesture from people I hardly know and haven't even been all that nice towards.

"Ah little foxes, you think to hunt the hound, eh? Amusing. Sphinx, would you care to join me?" Callum rumbles, authority oozing from his pores.

"Not particularly. You *did* tell me to spend time getting to know people and that's exactly what I'm doing. Also, I do have a name you know."

"Ah yes, Raina correct? I do believe the deal was I would get a turn showing you around as well." He looks down with a wolfish grin, ever the predator, but I have claws of my own.

"It was never specified it would be the first day. I'll play your games for now Wolf, but they'll be by my rules. You may intimidate lesser men, but I'm not one of them."

"Careful kitten, the hunt just makes it that much more enticing for me." He reaches out as if to caress my cheek, but a firm hand grips his wrist, halting the movement.

"Pardon me Alpha, but I do believe your own words were *'I hear one word of anyone raising a hand to her or her child and the price will be that same hand'*. I'd hate to see our leader lose such an appendage by *accidently* forgetting his own rules." Cam faces down the wolf with no visible fear in his eyes.

"Yes...how careless of me." He strikes Cam across the face so fast I barely see the motion, just Cam reeling from the force.

"Good thing that only applies to the girl," caution lacing his words.

Before the other boys can jump to his defense, I'm there shoving Callum back a step. I'm sure I only even managed that much because he wasn't expecting it of me.

"What the hell, Wolf? I knew you were some kind of leader around here, but no one mentioned you were a tyrant. You get off on smacking people around?"

"Give it time Sphinx, you'll learn exactly what gets me off," he practically purrs, ignoring my outrage.

"Hard pass. I've dealt with enough abusers in my life; I've no interest in adding another."

"You think these little foxes can protect you from me?" He laughs, the sound echoing around the clearing. Finn and Leo come closer to me, stepping slightly in front of me. It's sweet, but pretty pointless right now.

"I wouldn't ask them to, I can hold my own thank you very much."

"You have fire Kitten, I'll give you that. You'd do well by my side; we could rule with our power unmatched."

"I highly doubt that," I deadpan.

"Maybe this will convince you..." He shifts into his wolf and lunges for Hiro, as if mauling people in front of me is akin to bringing me flowers.

Running on instinct, I fling out my hand, freezing him in place before he can tear into Hiro's throat, a hair's breadth away. I feel the power flow through me, so overwhelming it threatens to drown me. I fight to keep control, not wanting the voices from before to hijack my body and kill everyone around me again. I feel a drop of sweat trickle down my temple, a sign of my exertion and I've only just barely started to use any power.

I manage to hold onto my sanity and slowly stalk to the beast before me with deceptive nonchalance, not wanting him to know how little I actually know about what I'm doing.

"You're a monster, Callum. While the rest of us may be able to change into beasts, yours is twisted with corruption. I rescind my previous offer, consequences be damned. Try what you will, but I have no interest in being alone with you. Ever. Leave, while I can still contain my power. If you stay, I guarantee you won't live to regret it."

I let my power ebb away, Callum falling gracefully to his paws before returning to his human body. He straightens up fully naked and, yep, hard. Obviously instead of being frightened of my power, it just managed to turn him on. Great. This might not be such a blessing surrounded by people that are more beast than man.

"I will return soon Kitten, very soon." With malice and promise in his gaze, Callum takes his leave, sauntering off as though he didn't have a care in the world.

With a collective sigh, the boys around me visibly relax. "Are you alright Raina?" Hiro inquires, genuine concern on his face.

"Me?! What about you?"

"Just fine, thanks to you." Hiro blushes a bit, but refuses to look away.

"Yeah, you guys didn't need to make yourselves targets like that though, I could've handled him."

Finn scoffs, "What kind of men would we be if we stood by and did nothing?"

"Living ones? If that guy is anything like I imagine, then he won't forget you standing up to him so easily."

"Good, let him remember. He may have our fathers browbeaten into submission, but that doesn't mean we are," Cam boasts.

"So it's not just me, Callum really is that much of a dick?"

"Damn straight he is. He struts around acting like top dog and making sure everyone stays in their place. Outdated thinking if you ask me," Leo chimes in.

"So what in the hell was that anyway!? You fuckin' froze him!" Ethan bursts out, obviously flustered.

"If you think that was impressive, than you should have been there when I blew up the last guys." I burst into laughter then because apparently, I'm demented that way now.

With a smile, we head for the house my guys- I mean, *the* guys- and I are staying at. As we approach the door I hesitate, not knowing what's expected in this circumstance. I resolve myself to handle it the way that I normally would have before all of this happened, back when I was just a girl that nobody wanted.

"Much to my surprise, I actually had fun tonight. Thank you guys and…I'm sorry for coming off as a bitch in the beginning. But I'm going to be honest; I'm not going to take on some mates just because a society I barely know anything about thinks that I have to. You guys stood up for me and I will gladly return the favor if it comes up, but I don't want to get your hopes up. Can we just leave things as…friends for now?" Wow, that sounds more cringe-worthy out loud than it did in my head. Grimacing, I await their answer.

"…friends sounds nice, Raina. To be honest, we only came because our fathers forced us to," Ethan looks away sheepishly, rubbing the back of his neck awkwardly.

Finn picks up where his brother lets off, "I don't think any of us are actually ready to take on a mate yet. But I would be honored if you'd consider us friends and allies. The way you stood up to Callum was ballsy and to be frank, exactly the kind of thing we need to stir things up around here."

Grinning ear to ear, I nod and say my goodbyes. This went way better than I expected the afternoon to go. Turning to open the door, I freeze in shock at the state of the room. It's like a tornado ravaged the room, everything destroyed. Panicking, I race inside to find my daughter.

Exhaling my relief, I find her and the guys in one of the rooms branching off the central space. Seros stands before Skye, palm facing her as she kicks and punches it, her face is contorted in concentration.

"What the hell happened here?!"

"MOMMY!" Skye rushes over and throws herself into my waiting arms, hugging me in a tight embrace.

The men look between each other as if deciding who gets to be the unlucky winner. Apparently, Cain draws the short straw.

"Skye missed you."

"What does that have to do with everything getting destroyed?"

"She missed you...a lot?"

His hand rubs the back of his neck awkwardly, just like Ethan's did moments ago. I have to wonder if it's a shifter thing or just uncomfortable men in general. After a solid minute of glaring at them, Ryker finally breaks.

"The child, how would you phrase it- 'spazzed the fuck out'? Apparently there is some prophecy she refrained from sharing with us and we were going off course."

"What prophecy?"

"*As the spider falls to the snake and the wolf howls at no moon, Gabriel will rise. Through fire and darkness the reason known. On the mountain torment end, dawn smiles on the rain. Listen child and heed our words, at home with the light freedom is born,*" Skye recites. "Mama, I'm sorry for being naughty, I just want us all to go home."

"Sweet girl, I don't think we can go back home."

"Not that one silly, our new home with Ro-Ro, Kitty, and Ry," she explains.

I can't say that isn't a tempting fantasy, but things don't usually work out like that for me. Ry's right, hope is a dangerous thing.

"That's a pretty big decision to make so soon, sweetheart."

"Nuh-uh it's easy mama. We're supposed to stay with them."

"What makes you say that?"

"The Whisperers said so; they picked them out for you. They said you were going to need all the help you could get, so they bound them to you or something? I don't remember all the words, there were a lot." Skye shrugs, unconcerned.

She can remember that long, confusing prophecy, but not this? Kids, I'm telling you. If these 'Whisperers' are as powerful as they seem, then why can't they just cut to the chase and tell me what the hell any of this stuff means?

I'd nearly forgotten the men in the room, my focus solely on my unusual daughter, so I jump when a hand lands on my shoulder.

"It makes sense. That pull we've all felt from the beginning? It's like nothing I've ever felt around other females we've come across. There's something different about you, Raina. I just wrote it off as curiosity at first and later because we'd never met a Sphinx before. I hadn't considered a binding, they haven't been done in thousands of years to my knowledge, but it fits," Ryker confesses to the room, looking not quite sure of himself.

"This is perfect!" Seros bounds across the room towards me, overflowing with excitement.

Once he is right in front of me he takes Skye out of my arms and hands her to Cain. Before I know what's happening he is kissing me breathless, pouring all of his feelings into it. It's over just as quickly as it started and I sway a bit on my feet. Chuckling, he reaches out a hand to steady me.

"Easy there, if that was enough to make your knees weak, then you'll love what comes later," he flirts with a wink.

Where before I might have blushed furiously, now I just hold his gaze with heated curiosity and anticipation. Before I can let my better judgment stop me, I grab the front of his newly donned black t-shirt and tug him back to me. Seros comes willingly as he meets my fervor with heat of his own, one hand on my hip and the other on the nape of my neck as he keeps my body pinned flush to his. My hand moves of its own accord, tangling in his dark hair to hold him in place.

A not-so-subtle cough to get our attention comes from one of the others. Seros begins to pull back and I can't stop the sound of protest from slipping through my lips. Grinning down at me, he places one last quick kiss upon my lips before pulling away completely.

Cain and Ryker watch the whole event unfold with restrained lust, more in control of themselves than I am apparently, but Skye has a huge smile plastered onto her face. Oh great, there's that blush I thought I got out of. What the hell has gotten into me?

With red cheeks I ask, "So what's a binding?"

"A soul binding is old magic, meant to tether two people together. If your mate was on the brink of death and you were lucky enough, you could complete the ritual to tie their life to yours, extending their life. It was rarely done though. That connection also means that if one mate died then the other would be pulled into the afterlife as well. Not many people were willing to put their lives in the hands of another and it took a vast amount of power to even accomplish in the first place," Ryker informs.

"Oh shit, you must hate me," I say, blanching.

"Why would you say that?" Seros asks, offended.

"If you really are bound to me, then the next time I trip over my own feet I'll probably end up falling off the side of a cliff and taking you all out with me!"

Cain, who had been silent up to this point, "Then I shall keep you away from cliffs." I roll my eyes, but smile.

"Ry, back me up here. You of all people can't want this."

Instead of answering he crowds me, backing me against the wall. His hands come up to brace against the wall next to my head, caging me in. I should probably be frightened, but my survival instincts have obviously drowned in lust and left me to my own devices.

"Before, no. Now?" He leans closer, his breath warm against the shell of my ear as his voice drops to a low whisper. "There are a great many things that I want to do Nymph, none of which involve leaving you behind." He nips my ear and pulls back, his hazel eyes flecked with gold.

I swallow, mouth dry and skin tingling. Blood rushes through my veins to my quickly beating heart, heating everything in its wake as I struggle to regain my composure.

"If it binds two people together, how can all three of you be tied to me?"

"Well obviously you're too much of a handful for just one person, Ra. These Whisperers must know how clumsy you are and thought you could use the added help," Seros teases, laughing at my expense.

"So what does this mean then?" But I think I already know the answer.

"That you're stuck with us, like it or not, Nymph."

"You're ours, Little Muse."

"Come hell or high water we're yours, Ra."

Tears spring to my eyes, but I fight them back, not wanting to ruin the moment. For years I've been searching for something I couldn't name, miserable and alone. Now, standing here in this destroyed tree house with my daughter, with three men who look at me as if they would burn the world to the ground if I so desired, the perpetual ache finally subsides. After all these years, I've finally found what I've been looking for.

    Home.

Chapter 34
Cain

I begin clearing away the heavier debris and broken furniture from the room. It'll need to be replaced, but that can wait, we have bigger priorities to focus on. Who are these people able to place a soul binding spell without our knowledge? What does Gabriel have to do with anything? And for the love of the Gods, where did Raina come from? Even though any of these questions should have been at the forefront, what I actually ask is far from it.

"So how was your *date,* Little Muse?"

Skye glares and stomps off, slamming the door to her room, much to her mother's surprise.

"It was actually pretty fun," she nonchalantly declares, looking after Skye's departure in confusion.

Mine isn't the only growl to fill the air, disapproval evident. I stop cleaning to give her my undivided attention, dropping the broken couch with a thud.

"Details," I grit out.

"Lunch, a tour of some shops and joked around a bit. Oh, and Callum showed up." She fills us in as she assists in cleaning up the damage, crouched down and filling a trash bag with smaller debris.

Dropping all pretense, I stride over and lift her easily, bringing her to a table that survived Hurricane Skye. I settle her onto it, our position very similar to our last table experience. My hands settle onto the table beside her thighs, pinning her in place and forcing her to lean back to stare at my face. The vulnerable position thrusts her breasts in the air and it takes an immense amount of self-control to remain focused on what led to this.

"And what happened when Callum arrived?"

"Cam sent him on his way, but he really didn't have to, I could have handled him."

"Oh, of that I have no doubt." I make a mental note to find this Cam later. Raina may not know what Callum is capable of yet, but he certainly will be. I'll need a better account of events to know what to expect.

Ryker interjects, "Not too much fun I would hope," his eyes narrowing in suspicion.

Raina obviously listens to the devil on her shoulder far more than she should. "Oh, plenty of fun. Lunch, skinny-dipping, followed by a good old fashioned orgy. Isn't that how dates are supposed to go?"

She bats her eyes at him, all faux-innocence that even I can tell is done to get a rise out of him. Ryker must be more upset about things than I first thought because his face darkens a few shades as he makes to storm out the front door, no doubt about to massacre a skulk of foxes.

Raina shoots a panicked look my way, pushing me back so she can jump down from the table. She makes it across the room just as Ryker is about to tear it off of its hinges, slamming her palm against the wood to shut it. Ryker whirls around to face her before gripping her hip and changing their stances, pushing her back against the door while he fixes her with a glare.

"You may not want to claim us, but that doesn't change the fact that you're *ours*. Sleeping with anyone outside of our group is unacceptable and the sooner you accept that, the better," Ryker growls out, his control fraying at the edges.

I take a step closer, prepared to wrench him away from her if need be. When he loses control, Ryker is without a doubt the most savage of us all.

"Ry, we talked about this. The harder you pressure her, the further away you push her. Stop."

Raina cants her head to the side, perfectly at ease and unaware of the danger she's presently flirting with. "Why Ry, if you keep that up, I might just think you care," she teases.

Ryker tangles his fist in Raina's hair and tilts her head back, baring her throat. I take another cautious step forward and to the side, attempting to get a lock on Ryker's eyes so I can gage how far gone he is.

With her neck exposed, Ryker leans down to nip at her throat and I tense, but his mouth works a path upwards with far more gentleness than I thought him capable of. He runs the tip of his nose across her jawline to her ear, inhaling her scent.

"I care about very few things in this life, Nymph, but make no mistake- you're one of them now. I can tell you already know; the scent of your arousal gives you away. For all of your bolstering, you want us and I intend to hear you say it." His eyes gleam wickedly with promise, but that's all.

I breathe a sigh of relief just before Ryker devours her. He pours everything into the kiss, his restrained passion and anger, his fear and acceptance. She returns it with vigor, their previous animosity culminating in a clash of teeth and tongues.

He lifts her easily and carries her towards the back bedroom the three of us are forced to share, his mouth never leaving hers as he lays her down on one of the small beds. I kick the door shut behind us, doubling back to make sure I flip the lock. Unable to restrain myself any longer, I trade places with him and cover her body with my own, kissing a trail from her collar to the edge of her jeans. I unbutton them slowly, maintaining eye contact all the while should she choose she wants to stop. When she gives me no indication otherwise, I slip them down her legs and toss them to the floor. I drop to my knees before her as she slips her legs over my shoulders. Leaning in, the scruff on my jaw rubs against her thigh as I gently bite and trail soft kisses up higher, closer to where I desperately want to be.

Dark blue silk covers her and I shove it to the side, exposing her to me. She squirms beneath me, needy and aching to be touched. From the corner of my eye I see Seros remove her shirt and capture her mouth with his own, no longer content to remain on the sidelines. Ryker makes quick work of releasing her bra and slides onto the mattress with her. He moves in behind her, supporting her as she leans back to give us better access. His fingers come up to toy with her nipples, pinching and rolling.

She moans softly in her throat, the sound captured by Seros as the sound vibrates through me. I plunge in, licking at her folds. The tip of my tongue flicks against the sensitive bundle of nerves and she jerks. Seros places a firm hand against her stomach to keep her pinned in place.

I continue my ministrations, licking and gently nipping. As I take her clit into my mouth and suck hard she bucks, crying out in desperate agony.

"Please, I just...I need..." she writhes against me, breathless.

"Say it, Nymph. Tell us what we want to hear," Ryker purrs.

She refuses to answer and I slow my motions, my brothers following my lead. She lets out a frustrated groan and twists, trying to get pressure back to where she most needs it.

"Now, now, why would we come where we aren't wanted? Or should I say, you?" Ry taunts.

In response, Raina brings one hand up to her mouth, dipping two fingers inside to lick. She reaches her hand between her legs in front of my face and begins to circle her clit before plunging two fingers inside with a gasp. She begins to work herself back into a frenzy, driving me mad.

Unable to restrain myself, I slip a finger inside to join her, brushing against her inside. She starts to pant as Seros dips his head to capture one of her hardened nipples in his mouth, paying attention to her other breast with his hand. Ryker gently bites down on her shoulder, claiming and marking her.

With a sharp gasp Raina finally puts Ryker out of his misery, "I want you. All of you."

I swat her hand away, eager to make her come undone. Mouth clamped around her clit and sucking while I thrust my fingers in and out, adding a third to stretch her as I quicken the pace. Clenching tight around me, she flies apart beneath us, her desire coating my tongue as she rides out her pleasure. Seros claims her mouth and swallows her gasps and moans as we ring out every last drop of her orgasm until she becomes boneless between us.

I start to lean back, but she presses her heel into my shoulder blade, halting my escape before I can get far. She sits up and slides off of the bed onto my lap on the floor. Wrapping her arms around my neck she kisses me, slow and deep. Her naked body presses against me, the only barrier my own clothing. With one arm across her back pressing her close and the other firmly cupping her ass, I guide her movements so that she's grinding against me.

Risking a glance at my brothers, I catch Ryker's eye as he briefly shakes his head. Sighing, I know he's right. Wishing we could bask in the moment awhile longer, or better yet continue it until we are sated, I lift her up and set her on her feet. A brief flash of hurt darts across her features before she quickly hides it and it kills me that I put that doubt there.

"Trust me, there is nothing more that I want than to continue this." I cup her cheek, forcing her to look at me instead of away in ill-placed shame. "But it's too soon. We've already made matters harder on ourselves by saturating the air with your scent. The poor men will be whipped into a frenzy, if they aren't already."

She sighs, but she looks more frustrated than hurt now so I will call it a win. I retreat to fetch her bag so that she can change into fresh clothes; ones that aren't covered in pheromones and call to every stray cock in a five mile radius.

The overwhelming desire to throw her down and claim her is nearly too much to bear. With the taste of her still on my tongue, I can hardly think straight, but the last thing I want to do is push her too far too soon. After all, she was raised human with human ideals and what we just did might be pushing her limits already.

Adjusting myself to try and make my arousal less evident, I head back to clearing away the wreckage of the front room.

The rest of the day wraps up quickly and all of us settle in for the night. Raina crawled in to sleep beside her daughter so the three of us are left crammed in the other bedroom, the beds practically on top of one another. I struggle to fall asleep, not from proximity, but from worry. There are so many 'what ifs' hanging over our heads that it makes peace hard to come by. Eventually though we all manage, letting the allure of oblivion draw us away from our worries for a short while.

I wake before the dawn, alert and ready to tackle whatever life throws at us. After a quick check in on the still slumbering females, I move to scan the perimeter. I step outside and nearly trip on a wrapped parcel left on the doorstep. Not just one, but several. Apparently word got out of where Raina is staying and several suitors left gifts on her doorstep, as if they could buy her affection. I scoff and bring them inside, pausing as I find a large one that smells of the foxes from the day before.

It must have taken me longer than I thought to bring everything in because Raina has awoken and come up behind me, placing a gentle hand on my arm and looking at me with confusion.

"Gifts. From your...suitors," I grit out.

After yesterday's display, a part of me expected Raina to announce her claim on us, assuming she will have realized between the soul-binding and the orgasms that she couldn't live without us. Unfortunately, that didn't happen and I blame Ryker's arrogant display as the reason. Raina is far too proud to back down if he turns it into a challenge or a demand.

She takes the ones from my hands, opening it in curiosity and belting out a hearty laugh.

Jealousy raging beneath the surface, I turn to find her holding a stack of t-shirts with hastily scribbled writing across their fronts. *Sorry I'm Late, I Didn't Want to Come. Ok I'm Here, What Are Your Other Two Wishes? Not Fragile Like A Flower,*

Fragile Like A Bomb. Sorry for the Awful, Accurate Things I'm About to Say.

The shirts obviously came from the market, all of them cut in a halter top fashion made for females with wings. I may be incredibly jealous, but Raina looks truly happy in this moment. Without any modicum of modesty, she tears off her shirt in front of me, ditches the bra, and slips into one. The rest she loads into her bag and ignores the rest of the gifts.

Grinning up at me, she gestures to her new shirt while awaiting my praise. The fabric clings to her body, her hardened nipples visible through the thin material. She certainly has more than just my praise right now.

Ryker enters the room and she switches her focus onto him. I can tell the moment he realizes what she's wearing and who it came from as he stills, but Ry is better at hiding his reactions than I am.

"Hey Ry, I meant to ask. For all your talk of the 'foolish mortals and their inferior world', how come you guys don't even have electricity? Let alone the internet."

"Our whole realm isn't like this, just the settlement under Callum's care. He has an old fashioned set of ideals that he enforces strictly. It's left this place falling behind the times, but no one here is willing to risk defying him to bring about change. You'll see what I mean when we get to our home in the mountains."

"He's that bad?"

"Worse. No matter, it's nothing you need to concern yourself with. We won't be staying here long, then you won't even need to waste time thinking about the mutt. So, I see your suitors have wasted no time in trying to garner your favor," he sneers, distaste evident in his tone, as if yesterday never happened.

Ryker always seems to bring about challenges when it comes to our mate, but she rolls with it and turns it back on him as if she was born to play the role. "They have! See what the boys made me?" She runs her hands over the top of her shirt, brushing over her breasts and drawing attention to how it clings to her, no doubt to torment him for being a dick, but torturing me just the same. If I stay here any longer I won't be able to stop myself.

"I'll be back shortly. Let no one in while I'm away."

The fresh air helps to clear my senses as I make my way to find the foxes. It takes me nearly half of an hour to locate them near a small drop-off by the river, the five acting like fools and leaping into the water beneath. They fail to notice my approach and I take advantage of it.

As one of them makes to leap off of the ledge, I snatch him by the leg mid-jump. He sputters and flails in shock, the look on his face so comical I can't help but to belt out a laugh.

"Are you Cam?"

Sputtering and eyes bulging, he shakes his head in denial, red hair flicking water onto my clothes and points to a dark haired male in the water beneath. With a smirk, I release him and he falls into the water beneath with a yelp. Tossing off my shirt and allowing just my wings to break free, I gracefully descend to the water beneath, hovering just above the water.

"Cam?"

"Who's asking?" The dark haired boy asks, puffing out his chest in an attempt to be intimidating. Ah, to be so young.

"I hear you crossed paths with Callum earlier while you were with Raina. Tell me what happened," I demand with crossed arms.

"Why should I tell you shit? If she wanted you to know, she would have told you," he sneers.

A growl tears from my throat as I lunge forward, grabbing him by the throat and lifting him up. Feet flailing and arms scrambling, he supports himself on my forearm to keep from choking.

"You may care little of what Callum will do to her if he gets his hands on her, but I certainly do. Tell me what you know!" I relinquish my grasp and he falls into the water beneath.

He stands, sputtering and red faced. "What makes you think I don't care, huh?! I happen to like the girl."

Of all the things he could've said, that was by far the stupidest. Before he knows what hit him, my fist connects with his jaw, sending him flying. In an instant, his brothers surround him, ready to fight. I drop to the shallow water before them, ready to give them one.

"She is mine, you hear me?"

"Funny, she didn't mention that earlier. In fact, I think she said '*I find this entire thing ridiculous*,' so if you think I'm just going to stand by and let you and Callum decide her life for her then you can fuck off," he seethes.

The scent of storms and citrus precedes her as Raina makes her way towards us and she jogs over upon spotting us. With a sharp jab to my kidney first, Raina places herself in front of the foxes. She squares off her shoulders and faces me with sheer determination. Her actions make me rage internally, but her dominance fills me with pride, leaving me conflicted and confused.

"Cain, what the hell? You think just because you're older than them, you can smack people around?"

"Bold talk from the one who just hit me, Little Muse." I can't keep the half smile from my lips.

"Well that's different, I'm smaller than you and you deserved it. If you're going to act like an ass, expect to get kicked. Now, what's your problem?"

"The little fox refused to answer my question and I need the answer."

Turning away from me, Raina strides over to Cam and extends a hand to help him up. I let a soft growl slip as their hands connect and she simply flips me the middle finger of her other hand without turning around.

"You alright?" she asks the mouthy fox.

"Don't worry about me, I can take this guy. Want the boys to take you home, or better yet, get you set up in a different one?" His attention focused solely on her as he pretends I'm no longer standing mere feet away from him, as if *I'm* the problem here.

"Nah, he's not going to hurt me unless he has a death wish; apparently we have some soul-bondage thing going on. Besides, he's not usually a dick so it must just be you, Cam." She shoots him a wink and he replies with a huge grin.

"Well I do bring out the worst in people," he laughs. "I see you found our gift in your massive pile! It looks good on you."

"I love them, honestly. It was incredibly thoughtful and you captured my personality perfectly," she grins, spinning so they can get an eyeful of her outfit. As they look her over my hackles raise, wanting to claw out their eyes.

"Raina, I thought I told you not to leave the house while I was away."

"No, you said *'let no one in while I'm away'* and I didn't. Besides, who died and made you king?" She sticks out her tongue and skips away from my reach before I can throttle her. The foxes certainly bring out a side of Raina more energetic and playful than I'm used to seeing and while it's infuriating, it pleases me to see her so carefree, even if it's temporary.

"Would someone like to fill me in on what I'm missing here?" I ask the crowd.

Raina responds, less hostile. "These are friends of mine, so you better quit being a Ryker if you want any hope of a repeat of yesterday. Callum was being a prick so I told him off, he got mad, shit's probably going to hit the fan later, blah blah blah."

"Ah, so the usual." I roll my eyes.

"Yep!" She beams.

"The fox said he likes you, Little Muse. I will share you with my brothers, but outside of our family is off limits." Narrowing my eyes, I await her response.

Her wings burst free from her exposed back as she flies directly in front of me. I think she is about to tell me off, but instead she places a quick kiss on my lips.

"Trust me Cain, the three of you are plenty. The foxes are my friends and I won't give that up just because you're insecure. You're going to have to learn how to have a little faith in me if there's any hope for exploring this soul-bondage further."

"Soul-*binding*. Bondage is a very different thing, Little Muse."

"They *could* be one in the same," she flirts with a wink.

Turning away from me, she rejoins the boys.

"Soul-binding, huh? That's a bit extreme for a girl that didn't want to take on any mates, don't you think?" Leo asks.

"Eh, I'm a go big or go home kind of gal apparently."

The foxes laugh with her and I move to join them, withdrawing my wings.

"Callum is a problem we will need to deal with. Raina, would you prefer us to leave?"

Sighing, she answers. "He has a point, though. If I don't declare my mates then people are just going to come after us and pick fights. If the door this morning is any indication, there will be quite a few."

The one with glasses chimes in, "Technically, you just need to announce your intendeds, not actually claim anyone. You could always change your mind later."

"So it's like...an engagement? Not a marriage?"

"Pretty much. While an intended announcement is similar to a human engagement, an actual claiming is much more than marriage. It's for life Raina. Unless all of your men die, you'll be bound to them forever."

She visibly shudders and I deflate a little. While the rational part of my mind knows that she has had much to take in during a very short time, the irrational part wants her to crave me just as much as I desire her.

"Oh is that all?" She rolls her eyes and carries on, "Either way, I don't want to leave just yet; I can't just run off and leave you guys at Callum's mercy- or lack thereof," she decides.

The blonde pipes up, "Raina don't make yourself a bigger target than you already are, especially not for us. We've handled ourselves just fine so far."

"I've never really had friends before, but I'm pretty sure you aren't just supposed to abandon them to get their asses kicked," she points out.

"So what, you're going to kill him?" One of the red haired boys asks.

"If I have to, sure," she shrugs. "What's one more body to add to the ever growing pile at this point? You may change into a skulk of foxes, but apparently I turn into a flying murder cat, so if there were ever a man for the job, you're looking at her."

I stiffen at the thought of her challenging him. Women may be revered, but an Alpha challenge means no holds barred. Callum won't pull his punches if he's defending his title.

"Little Muse, Callum has the pack behind him and your powers are still new to you. Allow me to slay him for you. Please."

She reaches out to lace her fingers in mine, leaning into me as her wings withdraw. "You're too good to me Cain. But if I let you fight my battles for me, what kind of person does that make me? I've spent enough of my life at other people's mercy. If I suddenly have all of this new power, shouldn't I use it for something worthwhile instead of sitting on my ass and letting other people fight for me? Callum is treating people like shit and they aren't all strong enough to defend themselves, so why shouldn't I step up if I'm able?"

I sigh, deflating a little. When she has her mind set on something, I doubt anything I say could change it. "As much as I hate it, you make a valid point. That's how I've always tried to live my life, so who am I to keep you from doing the same? But I *will* intervene if it goes too far," I promise. "Consequences and rules aside."

"As if you could stop me," she teases.

"You're going to give me an inferiority complex over here woman if you keep talking about how weak and helpless we all are," Cam interjects.

She fires him a radiant smile and offers no apology. The foxes all laugh and the sound is a balm to my ears. Too much time in this settlement has been spent ignoring the damning glares and condemning whispers, never letting the past become forgotten. The friendly air is a welcome change in my life, one I have Raina to thank for.

"Oh I almost forgot! Cain, Skye sent me to find you. Apparently we need to all be inside before sunset? She wouldn't say why- and trust me, I tried- just that it was important."

A glance at the sun's position and I estimate we have about fifteen minutes. "Well then, we best hurry if we are going to make it. Think you can keep up?"

"Try and catch me," she grins and flings out her wings as she launches off like a rocket as she heads for our temporary home.

"With pleasure."

Chapter 35
Skye

Pacing back and forth across the room, I wait for Mommy to come back with Kitty nervously. If the Whisperers are telling the truth, than we can't go outside, it's not safe. A sharp pain in my tummy makes me cry out, the pain unbearable.

"IT'S BURNING!"

Ser and Ry rush in, looking for the danger they can't see. But it's there, I feel it.

"Skye what's wrong?!" Seros shouts. I hate that they always yell like I can't hear them. I'm little, not deaf.

"It's burning!" I cry, trying to make them understand.

"What's burning kid?" Ry asks. At least he isn't yelling this time.

"Run. Young one, you must run. Death knocks on your door with torch in hand."

"...Everything. They're going to burn everything. We have to leave."

Chapter 36
Ryker

I've never had a child before, but even I know this Sphinx child is unusual beyond just her breed. For her age, she seems to speak with a maturity and understanding that I don't even hear from many adults. Sometimes it sounds like she's speaking nonsense, but nothing is ever as it appears with these girls. It's easy to forget sometimes just how young she is and if what she says is true, she has probably suffered more than anyone her age should be able to bear in a short amount of time.

Whoever speaks inside her head- or whatever- seems to impart wisdom and warnings aplenty, mentally aging her beyond her years. If only they could be a little more helpful and actually tell us what the fuck is going on or what to do.

"Alright then, let's go."

"Ry, we have to wait for Cain and Raina to get back, we can't just take off with her kid," Seros looks at me, dumbfounded.

"The child says we must leave, so we leave. Come on Ser, you know as well as I do that this kid knows a hell of a lot more about what's going on than we do. We'll leave a note for them that we're headed for the mountains and they can catch up."

I move to grab what we need, condensing as much as possible into two bags. Skye has her treasure bag already on, rarely removing it. We load up and head out, Skye's hand in Seros'.

We drop down from the trees, proceeding through the clearing and ignoring the looks shot Skye's way. I can't blame them for being curious about the newest girl child in their midst, but that doesn't mean I have to like it. I refuse to let my guard down since I know just how awful people can be. After all, I'm one of them.

We don't even make it halfway across the clearing before all hell breaks loose. Screams fill the air and the smell of smoke invades my senses. A quick glance around shows several trees quickly becoming enveloped in flames. People stampede every which way as they try to escape the chaos that descends on the once peaceful land.

Grunts meet my ears and I spy off in the distance several groups of men in the middle of battle already. They form a tight circle around their woman and children, meeting their opponents blow for blow. Men shift all around me, bears and tigers, hawks and wolves.

The scent of blood reaches me and I have to forcibly restrain myself from shifting. My Griffin bangs against my skull, demanding release. The coppery smell invades my senses and suffocates my rational mind. My fingers morph into talons of their own volition and I strain to make them recede.

A small hand clutches the hem of my shirt, grounding me. I place my palm over the back of her hand, seeking a tether to this world. I'm no good to her crazed, I need to be stronger than that. The thought helps to curb the worst of the instincts, settling my racing heart.

The reality of the situation settles over me…Raiders. They've come and set the settlement ablaze to cause enough confusion and chaos to make off with our females. I agree with Seros, I'm not letting either of them go.

We begin to run, seeking cover in the hopes they've yet to spot Skye out in the open. The tree line is just a stone's throw away and we nearly make it before hope for an easy retreat is stolen from us. With a shout to their comrades, they descend upon us. Surrounded on all sides, Seros lets his Quetzalcoatl free, hissing and wrapping his body around us.

"Skye I want you to fly. Fly hard and fast to the second tallest mountain and find our house. Wait there for Cain and your mom. Don't trust anyone. Listen to the Whisperers if you need to, they'll keep you on the right path. Go, Skye. GO!"

When she hesitates, I pick her up and toss her, praying her instincts will kick in. She shifts midair with a squeak and is off faster than lightning, thank the Gods. A couple of Raiders shift into birds of prey and dart after her, but I'm faster. With Skye now clear of becoming collateral damage, I give the reins to my beast.

With a cry, I catch up to the lesser shifters in a flash and tear them to pieces, their bodies shredding with ease. My talons sink into their oh-so-delicate flesh and rip, the slick wetness of blood making the motions smooth and easy. Their deaths only spur me on, adding adrenaline into my already flooded system.

I return to Seros, who has already felled several enemies. I tuck my wings against my body and plummet, catching a man by the shoulders and whipping him against the man nearest to him. I add extra force to my landing, letting my talons embed deep into his chest. With a jerk, he is ripped in two, blood splattering up to coat my feathers and fur.

From my peripherals, I see Ser sink his fangs into one man while his tail coils around the throat of another. The latter brings up a blade to attempt to free himself, but it simply skids off, deflected by the scaled armor covering Seros' serpent body. With a sharp crack, I hear the man's spine break and crumple into a heap on the ground.

Searing pain flows through me along with the smell of burnt hair. Whipping around, I knock the Raider's hand away from my side, his palm blazing as he seared fire into my rib cage. Fucking salamanders. Descended from dragons, but diluted through the generations, they have lost their powerful form, yet still retain their fire abilities. Stumbling across a true dragon is incredibly uncommon, but not unheard of, the vast majority slaughtered in the wars that followed the fall of my kingdom. I imagine if this man was one though, he wouldn't restrain himself to fighting in human form.

My sharp beak pecks into his eye as my claw comes up to slash at his face, blinding him. Just as I'm about to put him out of his misery, a hand to my shoulder causes me to spin and lash out at the new foe. Seros grips my neck with both of his hands, keeping me at bay.

"Easy! Fuck, Ry! Keep the last one alive so we can question him, will ya?" My brother asks.

I try to shift back, I really do, but with the taste of blood still fresh on my tongue and the feel of it coating my body, I just can't. I let out a sharp cry, trying to alert Seros and failing without my human tongue. The walls seem to close in around me, trapping and imprisoning me in my own mind.

I thrash my head from side to side, trying to clear it and smacking Ser's hands away from me. I let out a Gods-awful shriek that rivals that of a Banshee's, releasing my frustrations into the world around me. I stomp at the ground, stirring up clouds of dust. I'm hoping that if the dust clogs my senses it can dampen the copper smell that fills the air, but it's of no use.

My throat is so dry and my tether to reality slips further away with every beat of her wings. Skye. She's alone, she needs me. I have to catch up to her, but I can't risk hurting her when I'm like this. Damn females getting in my head and fucking with my emotions, leaving me useless. I knew Raina would bring nothing but trouble, it's been years since I've struggled this much to rein in the beast. What will happen when we actually claim her?

Backing away from my brother, I bump into the rough bark of a tree. I smack my head against it, hoping the pain will offer me clarity or injure the beast enough that I can force him back down. Over and over I throw myself at the wood, blood pouring from my scraped flesh, an endless cycle of healing and renewed wounds marring my body. I swipe out, leaving deep grooves in the trunk as I head deeper into the forest, away from my brother and those fleeing the chaos before I do something I'll regret in my loss of control. I need to get away before I turn on them.

Rational thoughts are coming slower, insanity wrapping its dark tendrils around me. I can't see. I can't breathe. All I feel is a hollow void threatening to pull me into its depths. I ache, I need and for what I have no clue. The physical pain can only ground me for so long. In a matter of seconds, minutes, hours; I'm sinking, drowning, suffocating. Time loses all meaning.

At some point I must have sunk down to the ground; I can feel the pressure beneath me holding me up, the steadiness only causing me to become overwhelmingly dizzy. It's too much…I can't. I can't fight it. I'm not strong enough. It hurts too much.

With every small bit of myself that I let go of, the ache subsides a fraction more. Numb, so blissfully numb. No more pain, no more failure. No hating myself, just…nothing. I can finally draw air into my lungs again without my chest burning. A wave of exhaustion washes over me. I'm so tired...

I have no idea how long I lay there just breathing alone in the darkness, but at some point it changes, my peaceful respite shattering. One moment I lay wrapped in a silent cocoon and the next there is a small spark of light there with me. I don't turn, don't speak. I can't. But whatever it is seems to only need me to listen.

"We are not done with you yet, Griffin. They need you. Your time for rest will come, but first you must earn it."

"It's too much. This pain...it's too much for one person to bear." Apparently if you're just thinking inside your mind it doesn't matter your form. Perfect, I'm having a conversation in my head with an invisible person. My mind has officially snapped. It only took a few centuries.

"Then it is a good thing you are not alone. The soul bond allows us a connection to speak in rare moments, but I am afraid I am unsure of how long I can maintain it, so I must speak quickly.

"The fate of the Sphinx rests in the hands of your brothers and yourself, there is no time to fall apart now. Our daughters are in danger and you are no help in this condition. Your mate wields the power to mend your fractured mind, but only once she allows it. Raina will only come into her full abilities once she accepts the mate bond, sealing the soul binding completely at last. Until then, you will all remain broken.

"She is the key.....only she can...."

"Only she can do what? Key to what?"

"...much longer... retrieve the young one. Follow her..."

With that, I'm left once again alone in the recesses of my mind. The silence echoes around me, ringing in my ears. The desire to sleep has faded with the bodiless apparition's words, gradually replacing the numbness with purpose. Skye, Raina. They need me, but I'm trapped here in a cage of my own making instead of by their side.

The telltale sign of Raina reaches me in the darkness. Her heady scent is intoxicating, the scent cleansing my senses and clearing my head slowly, giving me something else to focus on besides the cloying scent of blood. A fitting aroma for the woman, the power and destruction of a storm coupled with the cleansing element suits her perfectly. While she may be able to wreak havoc in her wake, she offers a clean slate and new beginnings. The citrus-new life in the aftermath. She smells like nature, like home. I let it consume me, to drown me and emerge reborn.

Details begin to take on focus; a hand stroking from my head down my neck, soft words at my ear. I clench my fist-now a human hand with claws-and let the nails pierce my palm. The physical pain helps to ground me in reality. The blood trickles to the ground, but I hardly even notice it anymore.

"Come back to me Ry, you're alright. I'm right here with you. Remember what you said to me in the grotto? *Sometimes you need to just not be alone and it makes a world of difference in shouldering your burdens. And if the misery can be lessened, then it can be replaced with something else.* Well you're not alone now. Let me take some of the pain off of your shoulders. Come back to me... I need you."

With an immense amount of effort, I manage to wrestle control of my beast and stuff him deep down, throwing him into the pit I just crawled out of and stepping on his body to boost me out. I'm on my hands and knees, panting, blood and dirt caking my skin. Raina's hands still run through the back of my hair offering steady comfort. I focus on her touch as I acclimate.

"Skye. We need to go, have to catch up to her," I croak out, throat raw from screaming.

"Seros already went ahead and Cain is beating answers out of the last man standing." After a brief hesitation she continues, "...thank you, Ry. You really did a number on those guys and I see what that cost you. Thank you for risking losing yourself to give my daughter a chance to escape."

She places a gentle kiss on my lips and the tender moment morphs into an all-consuming, burning need. After being so lost, I crave something physical to cling to and hold me here, crave her.

With desperation, I pull her flush against me, tumbling to the ground with her falling on top of me. I devour her with renewed life, letting the fire burn away the shadows. I claim her mouth in a searing kiss and pour all that I am into her, giving her power over me that I've never relinquished before.

Frantic for skin to skin contact, I slide a hand beneath her shirt, pressing her into me and grinding myself against her. She purrs her approval low in her throat and I swallow the sound. I pull her shirt upwards, pausing to see if she'll stop me. Instead, she grips the hem and yanks it off on her own before she is back on me eagerly.

I fumble with the button on her pants between our closely pressed bodies, starting to slide her jeans down her hips before growing frustrated and rolling over, pinning her to the grass beneath me. I yank them off the rest of the way leaving her in only her underwear beneath me.

I behold her with reverence, nothing but adoration and desperate need in my eyes. Raina's dark hair fans out beneath her, a sharp contrast to her pale skin and the forest floor on which she lay. Her lips are wet and swollen, slightly parted as she stares back unabashedly without a hint of embarrassment. Her tongue flicks out to wet her bottom lip and my cock jerks in response.

I descend upon her, trailing kisses down the side of her neck and slipping a hand to her covered sex. Gently rubbing and circling over her panties, she writhes beneath me, just as desperate as I am for more. Putting her out of her misery, I slip my fingers under the scrap of silky material and pinch her clit between my fingers. She lets out a soft cry and I lessen the pressure, continuing to rub my fingers back and forth, teasing.

Slipping one finger inside, I am rewarded with a blissful heat. Tight and oh so wet, she mewls her pleasure and thrusts her hips up, seeking more. Another finger, yet another and I can feel her desperate need for release already as she quivers beneath me.

I rip away the thin scrap of material, aching to assuage the building pressure. Hooking one of her legs over my shoulder, I line myself up and with one solid thrust I sheath myself to the base. She cries out, but I barely give her time to adjust to my size before I'm slowly sliding out just to slam back in.

Over and over I thrust into her, barely in control of my actions. I take her hard and fast, the pent up frustrations and desires making themselves known. Her nails score my back and I relish the sharp, stinging pleasure even more. More touch, more pain...whatever she can give me.

Adjusting herself to wrap her legs behind me, she twists, rolling us while still connected. Without missing a beat, she rides me, hips undulating steadily. I grasp her hips, urging her faster.

Unable to stand the agony, I thrust up sharply, eliciting a surprised gasp from her.

She leans forwards, her palms braced against my chest as I use my grip on her hips to jerk her back down onto me, over and over again. Her breasts sway from the rough motions and I cannot resist leaning forward to taste.

Sitting up, I keep her firmly on my lap, rocking against each other as my tongue circles her hardened nipple, flicking across before drawing it into my mouth. Raina's gasps turn into quiet moans as she rocks faster against me. My other hand comes up to pay attention to her neglected breast as she writhes against me.

As much as I want to draw things out and act out any number of fantasies, I doubt I can last much longer. She tightens around me, so close already. Pulling myself from her heat, I spin her around, gently pressing my hand to the small of her back to guide her to her hands and knees. I bury myself inside her again, reaching around to circle her clit faster and faster.

With my other hand on her stomach, I pull her up as I take her hard from behind. Acting on instinct, I lean down to where her neck and shoulder meet and bite down, drawing blood.

The sharp sting of my teeth causes her to tumble over the edge and she clamps down around me as she cries out in pleasure. As if possessed, she slides my hand up from her stomach and bites down on my wrist to muffle her cries, my blood flowing into her mouth and cementing our bond, whether or not she understands the significance and meant to claim me. Some things are just burned into our very beings and whether or not she knew she was one of us, she still has shifter instincts, no matter if she understands what drives her.

With a roar of my own, I find my release inside of her, stilling as her spasms milk me for every last drop. Panting and covered in a sheen of sweat, I collapse on top of her, supporting enough of my weight on my forearms as not to crush her. With a flick of my tongue, I lap up the blood at her already sealed wound. Still nestled inside her, I bask in the moment, not wanting it to end. But alas, all good things and the like.

With a groan, I remove myself in search of clothes. There are pressing issues we can't put off, much as I would rather hide from the world with this woman. Now that I've sunk my claws into her, I have no intention of letting her go.

I toss Raina what remains of her clothes, though I guess she'll also be going commando now that I destroyed her panties. With nothing to wear, it looks as though I'll be naked until we make it back to our discarded luggage. I walk over and grab the sides of her face as I pull her in to place a firm kiss upon her lips, hoping it conveys all of the feelings I can't bring myself to name.

"Me too Ry, me too," she whispers.

I know it must be a side effect of the bond and I wonder how much it impacted her feelings towards us, but I'm a selfish enough bastard not to look too closely at it.

With a lightness I haven't felt in decades, I take my Nymph's hand and begin the journey back to where Cain awaits. We walk in peaceful silence for a handful of minutes, but reality has a way of crashing back down right when you become complacent in life.

"I didn't do enough. What if something happens to her out there? She's so small..."

"You did exactly what you should have. You killed every man that wished to hurt her and got her far enough away that she wouldn't be caught in the crossfire. Now, that's enough beating yourself up about it. Skye is no ordinary girl, she very well may be more powerful than me and she has those voices guiding her. If any of us are going to make it out of this mess alive, it's her."

I know she's saying it to convince herself just as much as she is me, but I'll accept it because I can't handle thinking otherwise right now. With a nod, we break through the tree line into the clearing to see Cain alone, knuckles smeared with blood that's not his own.

"We need to go. Now," Cain thunders out.

Exhaling a breath weighted with worry, I straighten up and brace myself for the coming challenges.

"Well then lead the way; let's go get our girl."

Chapter 37
Seros

I know Ryker is completely losing his shit and it kills me to be so torn. I need to race after Skye, have to get any information I can from the blinded Raider and keep an eye on my brother. I can't just abandon him while he's defenseless. Fuck, what am I going to do?

Before I have to decide on a course of action, Cain and Raina come running. Raina is panting and out of breath and Cain's eyes are wild with panic and rage.

"Where is she!?" They demand in unison.

"Bullet point version- Skye's headed towards the house in the mountain. We were ambushed by Raiders and Ry got her away before he completely lost himself. I kept one alive, but Ryker's a mess and I need to go after Skye."

Cain reaches out to snag the man by the shirt. "Go! I've got this here."

With a nod I take off, shifting to track Skye's scent. She left flying so walking is pointless. I pick up her telltale scent- similar to her mother's -fresh rain and thunderstorms; but unlike Raina's citrus undertones, Skye's hints of cherry blossoms.

My body cuts through the air as I beat my wings furiously to gain ground. I follow the most direct path for around thirty minutes before the trail goes cold. Panicking, I drop to the forest beneath to search for it again. I pick up a very faint trace, but not enough to follow. Frantic now, I race through the area and come up short.

Tilting my head back to the sky I release a roar of despair before dropping to the ground in human form. "SKYE! WHERE ARE YOU!?"

Okay, okay, think like a kid. I know she was here so that's a good start. You're scared, you're alone, and you want to go to the mountains. I scan the area and realize that under the canopy you can't see the horizon, so she wouldn't be able to see what direction to head from here. So either she started walking or went looking for water or shelter while she waited for us. I refuse to think she was captured.

I close my eyes and take a deep breath to center myself. A slight breeze, rustling of leaves, small animals, and...rushing water? Chances are she tired herself out flying and needed water, so it's as good of a place to start looking as any.

Picking my way through the forest, I follow the sound, seeking any sign the little girl came this way. My breath stills in my chest when I pick up the fresh scent of blood. Feet pounding the earth, I stop dead at the sight of two severed hands and a trail of blood leading deeper into the forest.

They're definitely too big to be a child's, thank the Gods. So that would mean...she did this? Either she bit off one's hands as they dragged her away and I should follow the trail of blood droplets or she would have run in the opposite direction. *Shit! Which should I choose?*

Taking a minute to survey the area for any other clues, footprints, *anything,* I spy the river that called me here. It lets out into a small waterfall off of a small drop-off, but instead of the river picking back up in a pool at the bottom, it drops into a seemingly endless pit. Even with my superior eyesight, I can't see past the darkness to where it leads or how deep it is.

What I *can* see has my heart plummeting into my stomach. At the ledge, cast off to the side in the grass, is a small yellow backpack that's become a daily fixture in my life. Tentatively I reach out, knowing what I'll find. It still smells like her, the cherry blossom scent slightly masked from the water nearby. Inside is still her pile of gems and gold she stole from Ryker- her treasure. A soft strangled sound escapes me as I gaze at the darkness beneath.

Securing her bag onto my shoulders, I gather up a handful of rocks to shape out an arrow should my brothers catch up before I return. I let my wings burst free, their cool pastels and silver glinting in the filtered light and jump.

Chapter 38
Raina

Not daring to attempt flying so soon after Ryker's struggle, we carry on for what feels like forever, every step without my daughter a stab to the heart. The slick feeling of blood coats my palm as it brushes against Ryker's, but I choose not to comment, understanding exactly what he's doing. When the internal pain is too much to bear, when there's no visible wound to heal, sometimes focusing on real physical pain can help focus your mind. If you can see the wound, give reason to the pain, you can heal that instead and pretend you feel better for it. He is scrambling for any tethers to reality, something to ground him and I offer him that. It's an odd thing to bond over, but I can relate.

I've been so concerned about how all of this affects *me* that I've completely ignored how it affects *them*. I'm not the only one with scars and reservations, something I'd do well to remember.

"So did you learn anything?" I ask Cain.

"Nothing more than what we assumed already. They heard tale of two Sphinx females taking up residence in this settlement and sought to make off with them."

"Seros probably already caught up with her and we'll meet them at the mountain..." I trail off, my false hope evident. I need my daughter in my arms again. "Do you think that Cam and the boys got out alright?" But I don't need Cain to answer because right after the words left my mouth I was tackled to the ground by a tangle of furry bodies.

Callum snarls and gnashes his teeth at me as several different shades of foxes bury their teeth into his legs and torso. White, gold, and orange fur blur past my vision as my friends attempt to subdue the dark beast. Cain is on him in a heartbeat, his large hand slamming into the wolf's throat and pinning him to the ground. Ryker grabs my arm and yanks me to my feet, placing his body between mine and the pissed off canine.

Cain's fist rears back and snaps forward, right into the side of Callum's snarling face. With a howl of pain, he shifts back into his human body. Hand still threatening to crush his windpipe, Cain growls low in his throat down at the man.

"You dare try to hurt a female? And you call yourself Alpha..."

"That BITCH of yours brought the Raiders here! Many of my men have fallen in this attack, half the settlement is burning to the ground. If the bitch won't stand by my side then I won't let her power fall into their hands. The Sphinx got what was coming to them if you ask me, they're better off staying dead." He spits at my feet.

"Wait a minute, you know what happened to them?" I'm almost desperate for another piece of the puzzle.

"Oh fuck off whor-" but he is cut off by a sharp kick to the temple from Leo and knocked unconscious. Leo's once innocent, orange eyes churn with hatred. The sight has my eyes burning with unshed tears. Why must the world take anything sweet and innocent and seek to ruin it? First my daughter, now the only friends I've managed to gain? I destroy everything I touch; it's only a matter of time until Ryker, Cain, and Seros are ruined too.

I sink to my knees, pebbles and debris stabbing into them as I wrestle back the onslaught of emotions. Everything that has spiraled out of control in a whirlwind frenzy and *this* is the thing to finally push me past my limits? I guess there is always a straw that breaks the camel's back, but I would have banked on finding out my entire life was a lie was it, not this.

The white fur of an arctic fox nuzzles against my leg, settling down to lie against me. I reach out to stroke his fur absentmindedly and Cain mumbles his disapproval, but Ryker pipes up in my defense.

"It's not like you're thinking brother, she needs a friend right now; not her mates."

"And how are you so sure of that?" Cain retorts.

"....I can feel it," Ry declares, sounding unsure of himself. So it's not just me the bond affected then, coming to life like a living entity. *Fuck, what have I done?*

Ethan, Finn, Leo, and Cam make their way over in their small forms, surrounding me on all sides as if they can keep the world at bay. They give me my few minutes to break down without judgment and I soak up their companionship that they offer me, not used to having a friend to count on, let alone five. In the brief time I've known them, they have already come to mean so much to me and I wish I could return the favor.

"How does a new alpha get chosen around here?"

Hiro shifts back, sprawled out on his stomach and head resting on his arms, to answer, "Combat. Whoever is strong enough to kill the current Alpha gets to replace him. Why?"

With a nod, I stand up and my friends scatter so I don't trip on them. "Cain, can you do me a favor?"

"Anything Little Muse, all you must do is ask and it shall be yours." A girl could get used to hearing those kinds of words.

With a smile tugging at the corner of my mouth, I make my way towards my gladiator. He is still crouched over Callum, keeping him pinned with one hand should he regain consciousness. Bending down, I run my fingers through his white-blonde hair and turn his confused face towards mine.

"Kiss me?"

A broad grin flashes across his face before he eagerly obliges. With his free arm he settles me onto his thigh and tilts my head back for deeper access. I'm breathless by the time we pull apart. Yeah, a girl could *really* get spoiled like this.

"Actually, it's really two favors then. Would you mind dragging Callum back into the middle of the main clearing?"

"What for? Shouldn't we get going after Skye?"

I bite my lip, debating, but knowing I need to follow my gut. "Seros will have caught up with her by now, they'll be alright for just a little while longer. As much as I desperately want to get moving, this is something that I think I have to do before we can leave."

It makes me feel terrible, but something inside of me is screaming that it has to happen or it will come back to haunt us. The last thing I need is to race towards my daughter with a murderous wolf hellbent on revenge on my heels, leading him straight to her so that he can think to use her to get revenge on me.

With a nod and no more probing, Cain hefts Callum over his shoulder and begins the walk back. It takes longer than I would like, but we make it in decent time. The Raiders that descended on this place are all dead now and men are fighting the fires that still burn, but every eye finds us the second we breach the tree line into the clearing. I gesture for Cain to drop Callum directly in the center of the open space and he lets him flop to the ground in an unceremonious jumble of limbs.

Clearing my throat, I project my voice as loud as I can. "Men! Women! Before you lies your Alpha, a wolf who meant to kill me. I know none of you have reason to like me, heck, you don't even know me, but if what my friends have told me is true then Callum has treated you poorly. And so…" I take a deep breath, "I hereby challenge him for the title of Alpha."

Cries of surprise surround me from my group and calls of outrage from the crowd. I let them get it out, not interrupting their rants. They can think what they like, but if Hiro's right then it doesn't matter what they think, all I have to do is kill Callum. Easy peasy, right?

"Nymph, what do you think you're doing?!" Ryker grabs hold of my shoulders and tries to shake some sense into me. A rough hand knocks his hands off of me, Cain glaring down at his brother.

"Careful brother, you may have claimed her, but that doesn't mean I'll allow you to manhandle her."

Face flaming red, "You know?" I squeak out.

"You emanate sex from every pore Raina. I could smell it on you before you ever stepped out of the woods with Ryker."

"Are you…mad?" He barks out a laugh, making me feel incredibly confused at the turn in conversation. He steps closer, invading my space until I can feel the heat radiating off of him.

"Far from it Little Muse, I'm eager to show you just how much it excites me. Ryker needed *you* in that moment, no one else. I know in the very fibers of my being that you belong with us. Seeing you begin to accept what I know as truth? Knowing you were there for my brother when he was at his worst and brought him back to us? You're already one of us Raina, whether you see it or not. No, I'm far from mad, I'm damn pleased."

He sweeps me into his massive arms, but I have no fear of being crushed. If one thing rings true in this crazy new world it's that Cain would never do anything to hurt me.

Chapter 39
Skye

My wings are getting really tired and I don't think I can fly much longer. Slowly dropping through the trees, I trip on my landing and tumble on the ground, what remains of my clothes getting covered in dirt. I'm hungry, thirsty and the muscles on my back are screaming. The Whisperers never said I was going to have to work so hard just to get us a home.

I follow the sound of water until I find a river. Taking big drinks, I plop down in the grass to think, pawing at the ground as I catch my breath. I try to call out in my head, but no one answers me. They love to tell me what to do, but aren't actually there when I want to talk. Typical.

I wandered a bit too far…I'm not sure exactly which way I came from anymore. Looking around, I can't see anything except trees; trees, trees everywhere. Which way is the mountain? Uh oh…

There's a rustle in the forest a little ways behind me and my favorite voice whispers in my head, a wonderful sound when you're terribly alone. She's the nicest one and doesn't try to confuse me.

"Run Skye, you need to move before they find you. Go child, RUN!"

I pop up to my feet and run as fast as I can, but trip over a tree root before long. A large hand grabs the scruff of my neck and my legs scramble through the air. They rip the bag off my back and throw it off to the side, making me mad. That's *my* treasure! I twist and struggle, but can't break free.

"Well, well, well...what do we have here?" a male voice purrs.

"Looks to me like the pretty kitty is lost. We should bring her to Gabriel; a little girl shouldn't be out here alone, after all," another chimes in.

Just because they said Mommy couldn't kill Grandpa Gabriel, doesn't mean I want to go anywhere near him. A wave of familiar power fills me up, the Whisperers giving me their strength and taking control of my body. A part of me is glad because I think I'm too scared to get out of this by myself, even if I don't like the feeling. When I open my mouth, they speak for me.

"*You aim to take what does not belong to you. The price of thievery is a hand.*"

"What the hell?" But any confusion they have is answered as the Whisperers twist my body, biting through the wrist of the man holding me with one strong bite.

His blood fills my mouth as I fall to the ground, landing on all fours as I spit it out, trying to get the taste out of my mouth. I pounce on the other, swiping claws down his face as I latch onto his left wrist, severing the hand just like I did to his friend. They howl in pain, screaming and clutching their bloody arms. *Gross.*

With a hiss, I turn away to run towards the small cliff. Once I'm almost at the edge, I have a moment of panic before remembering that I can fly, but they don't launch me into the sky. No, instead they start whispering and chanting in some language I don't understand and the ground starts to shake. Where the water falls back into the river below, a massive split in the earth starts to widen into a very, *very* black pit. I hate the dark. No one told me that now that I am a monster I have to be the thing that goes bump in the night, I want to stay up here.

I leap off the edge, straight into the dark hole below and shut my eyes, praying that when I open them it will all have been a bad dream.

Chapter 40
Raina

Callum begins to stir and the crowd's roar dies down to a hush. He lumbers to his feet, eyes darting left and right at the change in surroundings.

"What is the meaning of this?" he demands.

"Exactly what you want, wolf, a chance to be done with me fair and square. I challenge you for the title of Alpha." A wolfish grin overtakes his features as Ryker and Cain growl their disapproval from behind me.

"Challenge accepted, Kitten."

Before I even have time to blink he is on me, hand gripping my throat as he slams me against the ground, pain reverberating through my skull. Cain and Ryker make to leap into the fray, but I seek out eye contact with Cam, pleading with him to keep them at bay. With a stiff nod, he moves to intercept them and the boys rush to support him. I know none of them are happy with my decision to do this, but I know the boys understand why I need to do this for myself.

Closing myself off from distractions, I head-butt Callum straight in the nose. With a sharp crunch, blood pours free, spilling onto my face. He howls in pain and weakens his hold at the unexpected attack. I bring my leg up between us and place my foot on his chest, kicking him off with everything I have. Scrambling backwards, I try to distance myself from him, but he is gaining ground faster than I can.

He launches forwards with a closed fist aimed at my head, but I roll to the side in the nick of time. I pull myself up into a crouch, seeking my power. Aaaaaaaaaannnnndddd coming up with zilch. Nada. Nothing. *What the frick?*

I dive out of the way, at a loss of what to do without my new badass-people-exploding power. I have no choice but to fight like a human so lucky me, he hasn't changed yet. A sharp yank of my hair causes me to let out a small cry of pain. Fisting his hand in my hair, he drags me close to him, lifting me off the ground slightly to whisper in my ear.

"I'm going to make you suffer little bitch, nobody denies me. I'm going to drag this out as long as possible until you're begging me to take you as a mate just to make the pain stop. And when I'm done with you? I'm going to hunt down your little fox friends and rip out their throats while I make you watch. Let that be a lesson in defying me, Kitten."

The pain in my scalp dissipates as my control snaps. I feel an onslaught of power course through my veins as rage bubbles beneath the surface. A quick glance of my peripherals shows my hands and arms being covered in golden symbols and I have never been more relieved. My body begins to move of its own accord, bringing my hand up to trace a line down his cheek, deceptively calm and at ease.

My voice takes on the echo of a thousand angry women, haunting and promising retribution. "Mighty tough words for a little pup, nothing better to do than pick on a girl?"

He begins to grunt in pain as a burning scar forms in the wake of my finger's caress, the putrid stench of burning flesh filling the air. With a jerk of his hand, he tosses me away from him and I land gracefully on my feet. If that isn't enough of a sign someone else is handling things right now, then I don't know what is.

The man shifts into a hulking beast, spit dripping from his snarling muzzle. With a bark he lunges, but I lazily throw my hand up to once again freeze him mid-air.

"Didn't learn well enough the first time mutt? Well, I guess what they say is true, you can't teach an old dog new tricks."

I bring my hand up to blow him a kiss, but instead of affection, a swarm of bright blue scarabs fly towards him. Even frozen in place I can see his eyes go wild with panic and fear. The beetles cover his body, biting, burrowing and feasting on his flesh. He is helpless to even scream, paralyzed as he is.

The crowd watches on in petrified silence, unable to look away from the horror that they are helpless to prevent. The brutality feels natural to me, vengeance settling into my bones. Divine retribution doled out by one pissed off woman.

My wings burst free of their own volition, as though they have carried me into battle a thousand times and I soar closer to his frozen form. With a wave of my hand, I shoo away the plague, leaving a mutilated being suffering before me as I sing a nursery rhyme of taunting misery, toying with him.

"Fires rain and waters burn,

Poison fills the sky.

Death visits me, a dear old friend

Tell me Wolf, what am I?"

I release the paralysis on his body and he thuds to the ground. "No answer? Clock is ticking, mutt."

Tears spring to his eyes as he shakes his head.

"Hell." And with that I step forward and take his head in my hands, swiftly jerking and snapping his neck. I drop his body, disgusted, and turn to face the silent crowd. The masses have grown during the fight and over a thousand faces look at me with a mixture of horror and reverence, along with a healthy dose of fear.

I step forward and the front line of people take a step back. "By your rules, this makes me now Alpha, correct?" A smattering of people nod, hardly daring to blink, let alone breathe. "Then let my word be known. In my absence, you will bring your concerns to a small council who will manage affairs while I am away. Ethan, Finn, Hiro, Cam and Leo will be my voice. They are good men and will treat you justly. If someone so much as thinks of laying a hand on any of them, my wrath will make the wolf's death look like a stroll in the park. Any questions?" Not a soul makes a peep and I take that as confirmation enough.

Turning, I make my way back to where my men have gathered. Cam is sporting a black eye, Ethan is latched onto Cain's back, Finn and Ryker are tangled on the ground and Leo and Hiro are latched onto Cain's biceps. They all stare wide-eyed with mouths agape as I approach. I quirk my brow and wait for someone to regain the use of their tongue.

As I should have expected, Cam was the first to recover. "Holy fuckin' Hell, Raina! What the flying fuck *was* that?!"

What started as a chuckle turns into full blown, doubled over hysterical laughter. The sound is contagious and soon the whole group of boys are falling over laughing with me. It's easy to forget we still have witnesses when I'm around them.

Leo howls with humor, "How long do you have to skip brushing your teeth to get freakin' bug-breath!?" He falls to the ground laughing so hard tears are streaming down his cheeks as he pounds the dirt.

"Oh Gods, his *face!*" Ethan and Finn crack up.

"You froze him! That's not the kind of stiffy you're supposed to give a guy, Sphinx!" Hiro of all people chimes in. The quiet intellectual obviously fits in better than I initially thought.

The other settlers must think we are certifiably insane by this point, but I can't bring myself to care. I'm finally snapped out of my slap-happy, post-murder craze when two of my men surround me.

"For the love of the Gods woman! You nearly gave me a heart attack!"

"Never scare me like that again Little Muse, I can't stand the torment. Seeing his hand on your throat...."

Cain's hands come up to trace over the bruising at my throat, but he stops himself before making contact with the abused flesh. With a growl, he pulls me against him, careful not to brush against any of the bruises he no doubt knows all of the exact locations of.

"Sorry guys, my badass abilities took a bit to kick in. I'll heal. Come to think of it, it wasn't until he threatened the foxes..." Huh, now that I think about it, besides my wings, my abilities have only ever come to life when someone I care about was threatened.

Ethan comes over, bumping Ryker out of the way. "So what's up with making us do all of your dirty work, huh?" he teases.

"You've lived here, know what the hell is actually going on and what these people need. If there is anyone that can bring about the change you say is needed, it's the five of you. And if anyone gives you any trouble, I'll just kick their ass for you," I taunt right back.

"I knew you were trouble, Sphinx, I just didn't realize how much," Cam joins in.

"Now go get your girl and your other mate and leave the heavy lifting to us *men*." Leo smiles, tussling the hair on top of my head before I bat his arm away.

"With pleasure."

With that I head out, an immediate opening forming in the crowd as they scramble away from me like I have the plague. Though come to think of it, I guess that isn't that far off the mark.

Chapter 41
Cain

I stride with purpose, leading our way through the forest towards our home. I pray that Seros has already caught up with Skye, our massive delay making me on edge. If any of us are able to find Skye, it's Seros. Though if the little one has even a drop of power like her mother, something tells me she will be just fine.

We were able to grab the couple of bags that Seros and Ryker dropped, allowing my brother the opportunity to finally cover up. We pass by the primary river that cuts through the forest to refill our canteens and Raina rinses off the blood and sweat from her battle. I try not to stare, honest, but as the water causes her clothes to cling to her in all the right places, I'm helpless to look away. I may strive to be a decent man, but I'm far from perfect.

As Raina fought as a human, it took four of the foxes to keep me from charging in, regardless of Raina's desire to fight the battle on her own. But just as I broke free, her abilities soared to life and I was stunned speechless at the raw power she wields. She didn't even need to shift to do it either. And when she turned into a vengeful Valkyrie, toying with the man as she brought him to his knees? I nearly came right then and there.

So seeing this vision of my wet dreams dye the river red with the blood of her slain enemy as every wet curve is visible? You would need to gouge my eyes from their sockets to get me to look away. Ryker comes to stand beside me and I clap a hand to his shoulder.

"She sure is more than we ever could have hoped for, isn't she?"

"And then some."

She returns to us, not even attempting to cover herself up as her hardened nipples peak through her shirt. I groan, physically hurting from the sight before me.

"Can one of you toss me a change of clothes?"

I move to pull them free from the bag I'm carrying and she starts to strip. Her wet shirt is the first to go, leaving her naked breasts on full display. As she removes her jeans my heart nearly stops. She stands there, sans underwear, with her hand outstretched. I step towards her unconsciously before Ryker laughs and takes the clothing from me to place it in her outstretched palm. Right, she was waiting for the clothes. We continue the journey in tense silence, lost in our own thoughts.

"Ryker, I don't want to risk you completely changing again already, but do you think you can manage a partial? Just your wings?"

Heat creeps over Ry's cheeks as he looks away to hide his embarrassment, shame reaching his face at the implied weakness. "Yes, I can handle that."

We begin our journey through the air, making quick work of the path now.

"When did you guys come to Colorado?" Raina asks out of the blue.

"We were only in town for about a week before we met you, why?" Ryker answers with a question of his own.

"So that's it then...well shit. All it took was a few hot guys holding pieces of my soul hostage to show up and I could've been a badass years ago."

I bark out a laugh and she blushes so I assume that was one of those thoughts she didn't realize she spoke aloud.

"Little Muse, I have a feeling you've been a badass most of your life without even trying."

"It makes sense," Ryker continues, "your abilities must have been suppressed while the bond was strained. So when we became closer to you, coupled with the threat to Skye, your powers started to manifest. While I was...not myself...I think one of those Whisperers that Skye talks about spoke to me. She had mentioned that the stronger the bond became, so would your power."

"How the heck did they get into your head now too!? And you only are mentioning this now?" she shouts.

"We've been a little occupied, Nymph. Apparently the bond between us allowed access into my mind briefly and she said something about you being a key, but not to what." Ryker informs us.

"Well fat load of help that is," she retorts.

After a few more minutes, Raina pulls to an abrupt stop. "Here! We need to stop here!" She rapidly descends, botching the landing and wiping out. "Oww...."

I help her up, but she takes off running without a second thought. We follow, approaching the edge of a small cliff. A group of stones are laid out in the shape of an arrow, pointing at a dark chasm below the falls that she must have spotted from above.

Ryker and I exchange a worried glance, but she's already two steps ahead of us. Without a word, Raina jumps.

Chapter 42
Raina

The men shout from above, but the sound is quickly drowned out by the rushing water echoing off of the rock around me. I plummet into the pit, keeping my wings tucked in as close as I can while the water coats them.

The drop seems to last forever as the chill of the water seeps into my bones. I'm starting to wonder if I found the entrance to the Underworld with as far down as I must be, but I would gladly go to Hell and back to find my daughter.

After an eternity, I can finally see a light. My wing clips the edge of the wall and I lurch forward, breaking free of the rocky tunnel in the nick of time before landing in a pool of water beneath me in an undignified belly flop. The sharp pain covers my skin like a thousand needles as I resituate myself enough to tread water. Ryker and Cain halt their descent gracefully, wings outstretched and hovering above the pool of water that tried to kill me.

Sputtering, I try to fly up beside them only to find the resistance of the water too strong to launch upwards with my wings submerged. Cain sees my struggle and laughs, but sweeps over to help.

"Retract your wings, Raina."

I do as I'm told and he immediately lifts me into his arms. One hand behind my back and the other beneath my thighs, he scoops me up and holds me closely. The muscles of his arm flex, sending a thrill through me. He carries us over to solid ground, but doesn't make a move to release me. Instead, I use my new vantage point to assess our surroundings.

Similar to the grotto that the mountain cabin lives in, the huge cavern is illuminated by veins of crystal reflecting bioluminescent foliage. The floor is made of smooth grey stone that extends the length of the open space. Across from the opening, painted on the cave wall, is a massive scarab. The blue body is the same shade as the tips of my wing feathers and in the center of its massive body is a giant, golden ankh. Wings spread out wide on each side; shades of greens, purples, and gold.

Beneath the mural sits Skye, gazing up intently at the image. I fling myself out of Cain's arms and run to her, careful not to slip on the stone as I drip water onto it. I reach down to pick her up, but freeze. In my relief at seeing my daughter alive I had missed a key part of the scene. Stretched out in front of her, face up on the ground, lies Seros- unconscious.

Panicking, I snatch up Skye and hold her close to me while darting forward, seeking a pulse or injury. "Skye! What the hell happened?! Are you alright?"

She continues to stare at the image as she deadpans, "The door will only open for you Mommy, I tried. Ro-Ro tried to fly us out, but I told him we can't leave yet. He didn't want to listen, so I made him sleep while we waited for you."

Well fuck, my daughter's a psychopath. Looks like that's genetic too.

"Sweetheart...you know that's not ok, right? You can't just go around knocking out or killing anybody you disagree with."

"You do." *Well shit, well played kid.*

"Guys? Want to back me up here?" I toss over my shoulder.

"No thanks, we're good." Damn traitors.

"Alright, well can you at least explain what's going on? What door do you even mean?"

She gestures with both hands at the giant beetle like I'm stupid. Sure feels that way anymore. I have no clue what the fuck is happening most of the time and it's ridiculous my four year old, prophecy spouting daughter knows more about this new world than I do.

"How the heck am I supposed to open a wall?"

"Blood." Oh right, of course. What else should I expect from this whole fucked up place?

I let my nails extend into claws and swipe at my wrist, blood welling from the slashes as I don't even bother to second guess her anymore. Skye gestures emphatically at the scarab painting again so I stride forward, adding my own red paint to the artwork. At first nothing happens and I think maybe I'll need to tap into another vein, but then a low rumble carries through the cavern, causing rock and debris to fall around us.

Cain throws Seros over his shoulder and I scoop up Skye again, Ryker right beside me. A large crack rings through the air as the beetle is split down the middle, a huge fissure in the stone. The crevice widens, allowing enough room to pass through single file. The soft lighting in the room lets me only see a brief way down the newly formed path. Heat wafts from the opening, instantly raising the temperature of the room.

Skye struggles to break free of my grasp and shifts before her feet can hit the ground. On padded paws, she takes off for the path despite our shouts, leaving us no choice except to follow. My earlier assessment may not have been that far off...

It looks like we're heading through the gates and into Hell.

To be continued in Obscured (Rise of the Sphinx Book 2)....

Books by J. Kearston
The Rise of the Sphinx Completed Series
Oblivion
Obscured
Obsessed
Wings of War (Standalone novels set in same universe)
Forged from the Ashes

Printed in Great Britain
by Amazon

79995831R00161